The key to making a million dollars
is
convincing a million people
to give you a dollar.

PETTY

a novel

by Isaac Jourden

Published in the United States and Canada by Tiny Ankh Publishing.

This book is a work of fiction. Names, characters, businesses, organizations, places, events, and incidents are the product of the author's imagination or are used fictitiously. Any resemblance to actual persons, living or dead, events, or locales is entirely coincidental.

Cover art and design by Rebecca Weaver.

ISBN: 978-0-9939467-0-7

www.isaacjourden.com

To my uncle, Thomas Jourden,
who always encouraged me
to find creative sources of income.

1

I've been watching orientation videos all morning for my new job, along with a hundred or so other new employees of Wonderments Family Fun Park. So far we've seen videos covering proper use of employee break time, representing the park properly while in uniform, sexual harassment and dating in the workplace, employee theft, and preventing stock loss. It's all standard workplace new hire fare, the kind of warnings no one is going to pay attention to, and management knows no one is paying attention to, but they show us anyway so there's no ambiguity when people get fired for doing all this stuff.

The video we're watching now is unique, however. Wonderments, the video explains, makes a lot of money every day, and all that money needs to be brought from the individual stores and food carts and carnival games to the front office to be counted. To accomplish this, employees are to place the money in provided cash boxes. The video shows a picture of one of them, which is essentially a World War II ammunition box. They're even dark green and weathered looking, with serial numbers painted on the top.

"In the event of an attempted robbery," the disembodied narrator says, "these cash boxes can be used as a weapon to fend off an attacker." The video shows a short, innocent-looking girl walking through the park holding the cash box when she is accosted by a large hairy man who demands the box. The girl in the video windmills the box over her head, smashing the guy in the face. The crowd of people here let out a variety of gasps along with some laughter and scattered cheering. I guess that's one way to wake up a room full of college students.

A ten-year-old girl could crack a skull with one of those boxes. Mostly, management wants to send the message that when it comes to the money, they are Not Fucking Around. I know this already, and that's why I won't be stealing from the park this summer. I'll be stealing from everyone else.

The video drones on and I look at my employee welcome packet in the dark. It's hard to read, but I can see that at the bottom of my copy of the contract, my specific job assignment has been filled in: I'll be working at a place called The Jolly Tinker. I wish there was a way to find out if anyone around me was working there too, without having to talk to them. This part of the orientation is just for the retail workers – all the games operators, lifeguards, and cleaning crew are in separate rooms – but it's still pretty unlikely. There are dozens of stores throughout the main park, and another half dozen in the water park as well. I suspect it's their unofficial philosophy here to make sure customers are within two minutes' walk of a cash register at all times.

There's a short discussion period about the video where no one talks about anything we just saw, then a question and answer session where no one asks any questions. It's their fault for how they structured the orientation, though: everyone got an itinerary, so everyone knows that lunch comes right after the Q & A. The human resources representative who drew the short straw and has to train us – a tall, middle-aged woman with thick glasses and small, thin lips – gives up after a moment of awkward silence and announces lunch time. The rest of the room sighs with relief like having to get paid to sit and be bored for a day is the worst thing that has ever happened to them.

I walk across the park to the employee cafeteria along with the rest of the people in my orientation. No one notices me, and I don't talk to anyone. I like it that way. When we arrive, the cafeteria looks more like an old warehouse building – painted brown, one door leading in, one door leading out, no windows. It's painted to blend in with the perimeter fence and down a side path to try and prevent any non-employees from wandering in. After being out in the summer sun, the whole place feels dim and dingy due to its lack of windows.

The line takes forever to get through. They could have saved so much time by giving us a bag lunch in the orientation. It wouldn't be any worse than the stuff they're serving here. I assume employee eating areas aren't subject to state health inspections, since this place is still open. The other new hires all chat while they eat, leaving me alone. I prefer to watch and listen instead of talking.

The afternoon passes as we're subjected to more training videos. None of the rest of them feature anyone getting hit in the face, and from the hairstyles and wardrobe choices, I'm guessing all the videos are at least twenty years old. I never do get to find out if anyone at the orientation works in the same store as me.

At the end of the day they split us into groups based on where we'll be living for the summer. The local teenagers get to go home, but the rest of us get shown to the dorms they rent to out-of-state employees for fifteen bucks a week. My room is a total pit, a collection of splintered wood, chipped paint, and a window I can't see out of because even though housecleaning washed the inside of the window, the outside is still covered in dirt and grime.

It's not without its charm, though. It's a place to sleep, which is all that matters. It's dirt cheap, which is going to make it a lot easier to keep the money I make this summer, and I have no roommate. The room is small but not cramped, with two dressers and a bunk bed. I'm sure I'll get a roommate eventually, but for now I'm happy to enjoy the privacy. I make the bed with the provided lumpy pillow and stiff, scratchy brown blanket, and lie on the bottom bunk. Various previous employees have written their names and year worked on the plywood above me that supports the top bunk, along with crude drawings of dicks, instructions to "fuck this place," and "get out before it's too late." Good advice if there ever was any, but I'm sticking around. For now.

I make it a point to unpack. I enjoy the process. I know I won't

3

be here long, but it makes me feel like I own the place. Own the choice to be here. Visitors live out of suitcases. I'm moving in. I don't have that much anyway – a few shirts, a few pairs of jeans, an iPod. Just enough stuff to fill a drawer. If I need anything else while I'm here I'll shop for it, but I suspect I'll spend most of the summer in a work uniform.

The last thing I take out of my suitcase is a plain white mailing envelope. Inside I have all the cash I brought with me – about four hundred dollars. I use banks when I absolutely have to, but I've always liked the feel of money in my hands. When it's in a bank, it doesn't feel real. There's a bulge in the envelope that crinkles the paper – a small bishop from a glass chess set. My uncle taught me how to play chess when I was young. I never kept up with it and don't really play anymore, but I remember how much he encouraged me, how he taught me to think and think quickly, be smart about what I said and didn't say, and stay focused on my goals.

He gave me a beautiful glass chess set for my birthday when I was ten. None of my friends played chess, but I always left it set up in my room anyway, just to look at. When my family moved two years later, the box with the chess set in it got banged around. The board cracked and half the pieces cracked or shattered. The white bishop – not exactly white, but more cloudy, like it was meant to be clear but the glass was flawed – was one of the pieces that didn't break. I kept it with me and threw the rest away.

I tuck the envelope in my drawer under the clothes and go downstairs. The employee store next to the lobby supplies the toiletries and other junk employees need, because if the park is going to provide housing for a few bucks a week, they sure as hell aren't going to supply toothpaste, towels, toilet paper, or anything else for that matter. We even had to pay for the pillows and blankets, which we were assured could be sold back at the end of the summer provided they were still in acceptable condition. After an entire summer with no air conditioning, I imagine it takes a lot of Febreeze to make them reusable.

The store is manned by a single employee, an old man with two days' worth of unshaven gray facial hair and an empty, bored look in his eyes. He watches me like a hawk while I shop. I can't tell if it's because he thinks I'm going to steal something, or just because there's nothing else to do.

I pick up items mostly at random. Toilet paper, soap, toothpaste, stuff like that. They have food, the sort that appeals to teenagers who can't cook and adults who are too lazy: mini frozen pizzas, instant coffee, single wrapped hot dogs, but most of it requires a microwave, so I skip all that. I wouldn't bother putting a microwave in my room even if we were allowed to, and the microwave in the store is bound to be disgusting.

"Hey, do you have any pencils, or ink pens, or paper? Office supplies?" I ask.

"Hey man, we're a convenience store, not Office Max."

I look around a bit more and give up, putting my stuff on the counter so he can ring it up. "You guys carry flip flops, but no ink pens."

He manually punches the prices of things into a cash register too old to have any sort of bar code scanning device attached. "Pens won't save your feet from the stuff growing in the showers around here."

I grab a pair of flip flops and add them to my pile of essentials. "I'll just borrow a pen from the front desk, I guess." It's going to be a great summer.

* * *

The girl behind the register is large in every possible way. Six feet tall, wide mouth, big nose. Curly hair exploding in every direction like she's never imagined combing it. Huge hands and fat fingers, graceless and grabby. Fat enough that she wears one of her own white shirts because they don't make the blue and yellow Wonderments gift shop uniforms big enough to fit her.

I've been here a week, and I've worked with her a few times. I'm not sure how long she was working here before I started but the park has only been open for the season for about a month, so it can't have been that long. I don't remember her name, and now I'll never have to, because right now park security is politely informing her that she is an idiot. Also, that she's fired. She's been stealing

5

money from the register – eighty dollars on three separate occasions. She's likely stolen less before now, but since the bean counters in the cash office expect mistakes, they overlooked it when the register was five or ten dollars short. When you hire someone to work for minimum wage seventy hours a week with no overtime pay, you expect a certain margin of incompetence. Apparently, eighty dollars is the cutoff point where someone goes from "probably stupid" to "probably stealing."

I guess she missed the part of orientation when it was made clear employees were supposed to smash in people's faces to protect the park's money. Or maybe she did see it, but the idea of an extra few hundred bucks was just too tempting. Now she's busy screwing over any chance she has at deniability.

"We need you to come with us, please," says the first security guy.

"What!?" she says, instantly defensive, like someone who has been committing petty crimes since they were seven years old and never even once gotten away with it. "I didn't do anything, I don't have to come with you." She says it like she's expecting the security guy to nod sagely, see her reasoning, and leave.

Security Guy's partner says, "Don't make a scene. We just need you to come talk to us."

"I said I didn't take anything. I'm staying here!" Real smooth. She looks more guilty than a five-year-old with a face full of frosting denying eating a birthday cake that wasn't meant for her.

The security guys escort her out, each holding one arm, and I'm expecting her to fight them, but she doesn't. How disappointing. A temporary store manager (apparently the original manager quit unexpectedly and they haven't found a new one yet) comes over to the register. He shuts it down, pulls the drawer out and puts in a fresh one. Without anyone saying a word, the large girl in the white shirt is gone forever. Everyone else has that look like they can't wait to talk about it, but for now, the gift shop swells with more people, totally unaware of the scene that unfolded moments before their arrival.

2

Almost everyone who works at Wonderments comes from out of state to do it. There's a big push by the company to get students from all over – even overseas. The sheer number of long distance employees is why they have employee housing on site. Even more than I noticed on the first day, my dorm is a genuine shithole. The paint is peeling off the walls, the floorboards are warped and uneven, the handrails on the stairs jiggle when you grab them. Most of the room door handles are tarnished brass, but the one to my room is made of glass. I'm not sure if I should take it as a bad omen or a good one. Mostly, I just take it as a sign that shit breaks on a regular basis around here, and no one cares enough to keep things looking nice.

Last night, I forgot my toothpaste in the public bathroom before I went to sleep. When I woke up I discovered some jackass had taken the toothpaste tube, put it on the floor in the hallway, and stomped it, exploding the toothpaste all over the wall. That's the kind of respect people have for this place. It was filthy when I moved in; I can only imagine what it's going to look like at the end of the summer.

I've had two roommates come and go in the last week and a half. One stayed for two nights and proclaimed he was going to look for housing outside the park – I still see him around occasionally. The other one came in, unpacked all his stuff, stayed one night, woke up the next morning, packed all his stuff, and left. I haven't seen him since.

The Wonderments housing department must be determined to use all their space efficiently, though, because I'm lying in bed at 10 a.m. (the quietest time of day, because everyone is either at work already or sleeping off a hangover) when there's a knock on the door. It opens before I can get out of bed, and a kid steps into the room with a suitcase, a duffel bag, and a cowboy hat.

"Oh. Woah. Sorry dude. I didn't think anyone was in here. Do you want me to come back later or something?"

I'm wearing sweatpants and a t-shirt. He's wearing a look of surprise most people would reserve for catching someone naked with a leather ball gag and a farm animal.

"No, it's fine." I sit up.

"I'm Cory, from Texas," he says. He extends his hand and I shake it.

He's young – pretty much no way he's over twenty-one – and when he smiles I can see he still has braces. I look him up and down a little bit. It's not just the ridiculous hat. He's got a heavy pair of dark blue jeans and a black belt with a giant belt buckle featuring what I think is the Texas state flag. His brown cowboy boots still look new. Really new. I want to ask him if today is the first day he's ever worn them. Even if I only wore them for a day, I wouldn't be able to keep them that clean. I'm waiting for him to tell me he's a character actor for the summer and that he's actually from New York. He doesn't.

I can picture him with a piece of straw in his mouth, spurs on his boots, and a holster on his hip with a shiny old-timey gun in it. Maybe he's looking forward to getting that stuff soon, and he's just waiting for Christmas or his birthday.

"Okay Cory, welcome to the party. This place is where the magic happens."

"Really?"

"No."

He looks disappointed. "Well, good enough. We'll go make our own magic if we have to. Do you want the top bunk or the bottom bunk?"

The bottom bunk has my pillow, blanket, and book on it. He just saw me get out of it not two minutes ago. "You can have the top," I say.

"Cool. Works for me." Cory ignores the ladder and vaults himself up to the top bunk, sitting so his feet are hanging over the side of the bed. He kicks his shoes off where they fall to the center of the floor with a loud thump. His suitcase and bag are already there, not put anywhere in particular, just dropped at random when he felt like not carrying them anymore. "I'm so glad to be here," he says. "It's an awful long bus ride from Mansfield. I'm beat."

"Do you have orientation today? I had orientation the first day I was here. It started at 8 a.m. I didn't get shown my room until the end of the day."

"Maybe. I don't know. I don't think anyone said anything like that. I'll figure it out later I think." He then swings his feet up to the bed, crosses his legs at his ankles, lies back, pops his cowboy hat over his eyes, and puts his hands behind his head. If he had a piece of straw in his mouth he'd look like a cowboy right out of a cartoon.

I have the suspicion Cory is going to be with me for the rest of the summer. I resolve to spend even more time outside the room than I otherwise would have.

* * *

I've been taking a hundred bucks a night out of my register, and no one here suspects anything. It's because I don't steal from Wonderments. If I did, I'm sure I'd be caught already. You don't become a multimillion dollar enterprise letting money fall through the cracks.

"Here's your change, enjoy your day!"

$34.15.

The kid I'm helping scoops up her handful of overpriced chocolate and runs off, money and candy clutched in one hand. Next is a high school kid buying matching sweatshirts for himself and his girlfriend. He hands me $80 and I ring him up with a big smile on my face.

"Here's your change. You guys enjoy your day."

$34.40.

Next is an old man who buys a baseball cap and a few lottery tickets. I can tell right away that he's not to be fucked with. He hands me $30 and I make sure he gets all his change. Sure enough, he looks at the register total, looks at me, looks at the money in his hand, and looks at the register total again, counting every dime. Satisfied, he puts on the cap and shuffles out of the store.

The kid here now has to reach up just to put the sucker he picked out on the counter. Where his parents are is anyone's guess. It shocks me how many parents just let their kids run around here all day unsupervised. I've heard that helping lost kids find their parents is a full time position for some of the security guys. He puts a twenty dollar bill up next to it and I ring him up. I could short him ten bucks if I wanted to.

"Here you go kid. Enjoy your day."

$35.50.

An amusement park is the perfect place to short people change. It's one of the last places in America where people still use cash more often than they rely on debit and credit cards.

The line of customers thins out for a bit and the girl working the register in the other corner of the store comes over to me. "Enjoy your day, enjoy your day," she mocks, using an absurd, nasally voice. "How can you be so fucking chipper all day?" She uses the word "fucking" like it's a guilty pleasure.

She looks perfect, or at least the version of herself she believes is perfect. Long, dark hair, thick, straight, and shiny. I've never met anyone with hair that long that manages to have no split ends or straggling hairs. I wonder how she pulls it off. She wears too much makeup in every respect – eyeliner a bit too dark, lashes a bit too thick, lips a bit too red, skin just a bit too pale. I have the strong urge to turn a garden hose on her and fuck it all up.

"You don't want people to enjoy their day?" I ask her. She doesn't notice, but I'm using a pen to make a series of hash marks on a piece of paper near my register to remind me of the total, for later. $35.50. I've haven't forgotten a total yet, but it never hurts to be safe.

"I've worked retail more than once, and I don't think I've ever seen anyone as happy to be working customer service as you are. You're just so... chipper." It seems like she knew she was using the word twice, tried to come up with a synonym, and failed. It annoys me, but I ignore it. I do get sad, or angry, or depressed, but generally I don't show it because showing it isn't useful.

"Look. This job sucks." I'm lying. This job is awesome. "But we've got to get through it one way or another, and being miserable about it doesn't help."

A customer comes up – a twenty-something girl with a friend – and buys a small plastic battery-operated fan. It's guaranteed to break in an hour or less. I give the girl her correct change. My cute coworker is pretty unlikely to notice any shenanigans, but it's not worth getting caught over a dime.

"Enjoy your day," she says to them with a big, exaggerated smile. I can't tell if she's taking my advice or mocking me.

"What's your name, anyway?" I ask. As soon as I ask I feel dumb, since she's wearing a name tag – we all are. She holds up the name tag, clipped to her thick and baggy Wonderments work uniform.

"Nicole," she says.

"So... Nikki? Nic?"

"Nicole," she says again. "Not Nikki. I hate the name Nikki. I told you my name is Nicole because it's Nicole."

"Okay, okay," I hold my hands up defensively. "Nice to meet you, Nicole Not Nikki."

She rolls her eyes at me and sighs audibly. It's starting to get busy again, so she turns with a flourish and returns to her register. She looks just as amazing from the back, and it fogs my brain.

3

I'm lying in bed with my headphones in, trying in vain to block out the sound of European techno blasting from the next room over. Eventually someone will complain and security will come by and bang on the door and tell the guys next door to turn it down, and they won't, and they'll keep partying until dawn, making sure no one on the floor can sleep. I wonder if the store downstairs sells ear plugs.

For now, ear buds will have to do.

"The phrase for 'good afternoon' is 'boa tarde,' a calm male voice tells me. A female voice repeats the phrase. "Now you try it," the track prompts. It's silent for a second.

"Boa tarde. Boa tarde." I say. I can barely hear my own voice over the music.

"The phrase for 'How are you?' is 'como vai voce.' Now you try it."

"Como vai voce. Como vai voce." There's another moment of silence while I say the words.

I pull the ear buds out of my ears. There has to be a better way to learn Portuguese than this.

When I was in high school, I remember one night when there was a party going on across the street. I watched in fascination as people came in and out, and I wondered how long it would be before the cops showed up to shut down the party. At one point pretty late on, a guy stumbled out the front door and just fell down the front step. He was so drunk he could barely get up. When he finally did, he stumbled over to a blue pickup truck seemingly at random and punched the driver side window. Nothing happened, so he punched it again. The glass shattered. Then he stumbled over to his own car, got in, and drove away, backing over the curb on the way out. It stuck with me not because of the vandalism itself, but because I couldn't understand why he had done it. He didn't take anything from the truck, and there was no yelling or fighting or anything. As far as I could tell he just punched out a truck window for no reason.

When someone robs a bank, or kills a guy for cheating on his wife, or sets up a huge pyramid scheme, I get it. I'm not saying I'd do it myself, but I get it. There's an end to the means. I don't understand crime purely for crime's sake. My reason for doing all this is the same reason I'm trying to learn Portuguese: São Paulo, Brazil.

My parents have never been outside the Midwest. Every few years they go on "vacation," which means driving a few hours to whatever nearby town has the cheapest stuff to do that their hometown doesn't, and staying in a shitty hotel for a few days while they see the sights of whatever forgettable place they decided to stop. I have bigger plans.

By the end of the summer, I'm going to have enough money to fly to São Paulo. Not just for a weekend, either. São Paulo is one of the biggest cities in the world, and I want to really experience it. I might end up in a shitty hotel as well, but that's the only similarity I want to any of my parents' vacations. I'm going to learn the language and explore the city. If I leave in September, I can spend six months living in São Paulo and see the Carnival in February before I come back, or go somewhere else altogether.

It's going to be a long summer. The cost for plane tickets alone is almost fourteen hundred dollars, plus at least another thousand dollars a month to live there. I figure if I can have ten grand by the end of the summer, I should be in good shape. It's a lot of money, but the thought of being anchored to some boring Midwestern town for the rest of my life terrifies me. Money will come and go, but if I can get there, I'll always have those memories.

Calling my parents "blue collar" or "the working poor" is the nicest possible way to say that childhood sucked for me. My family was never so poor we worried about eating or making the rent, but there was no money for things like new clothes for school, and getting anything like a Nintendo 64 or a Playstation for Christmas was certainly out of the question.

My parents work to the bone for every dollar and will never be able to retire, to which I say: fuck that. It's why I squirrel money away every chance I get, and try to get and keep my hands on as much as I can. I wouldn't do anything crazy like rob a bank and it's unlikely I'll ever be "rich," but I don't want my kids growing up being the kid that gets picked on at school because all his clothes come from discount stores, and I certainly don't want the life my parents lead, wondering if cable TV is too expensive or if there's enough money in the bank account to afford a pizza.

* * *

I haven't had occasion before now to be in the Stardust used book store and it's unlikely I'll be back after today, but I still appreciate that it exists. I don't read a lot of books – does anyone, anymore? – but it's so much more interesting to look through a bookstore to find something than it is to just click around online. I'm not looking for something for myself today, though. So far I've found half a dozen copies of *To Kill a Mockingbird* by Harper Lee, a copy of *Scientific Progress Goes 'Boink'* and *The Revenge of the Baby-Sat*, two Calvin and Hobbes compilations by Bill Watterson, and two old copies of *Catcher in the Rye* by J.D. Salinger.

Lee, Watterson, and Salinger all have the same thing in common: their signatures are worth a shitload of money. Any of them could fetch fifteen thousand dollars apiece on a good day, which strikes me as a bit disgusting. Lee and Watterson are still alive, and they can't sign a check without the signature being worth more than they're writing the check for. I've got to find ways to con people out of their money; they could just write it into existence.

The world is full of people promoting themselves to get famous, but there's real value in being a recluse.

Buy the books, forge the signatures, sell the books. Unfortunately, it's not hard get arrested doing this. If I use eBay to buy or sell any valuable editions, someone will notice. If I get the signatures authenticated or try and forge the authentication, I'm looking at jail time if I get caught. The best I can do is forge the signatures, play dumb if anyone asks, and tell them I don't know if the signatures are authentic or not. Then (as with just about any scam) it's time to let human greed kick in. Someone out there will try and rip me off by shelling out three or four hundred dollars for what they hope will be worth thousands.

Some people might helpfully inform me the signatures are worth a lot more than I'm asking for them. The saying that you can't con an honest man isn't entirely true, but it's close. Fortunately, honesty is pretty difficult to come by.

I put the books on the counter. I was hoping to find more, but this will do. The old woman behind the counter seems impressed with my selections.

"Brushing up on the classics?"

"Going to a book club," I lie. "Hoping I can convince a girl I like to come along with me."

She smiles. "Well, she'd be lucky to come. You've got good taste in literature."

Well, that's one good thing at least. Whoever I do sell these to will get to read a good old fashioned American classic. An English teacher would probably argue that's worth a few hundred dollars on its own. I'm happy to do my part.

4

Opening The Jolly Tinker is a hassle because no one who closes the store ever cleans anything. Most of the work I've ever done in retail – at Wonderments or otherwise – is pretty much a game of hot potato. You and everyone you work with tries to do as little work as possible because you know in a few hours you get to go home whether the work is done or not, and then it officially becomes someone else's problem. If something truly messy or disgusting happens, like a little kid throwing up in the store, you have to deal with *that*, but for the day-to-day tidying, if you ignore it, it goes away.

This morning the first thing I notice is the sparkly glitter on the floor. Someone must have broken one of the snow globes last night. They swept up all the glass, but didn't bother mopping up or hosing down the concrete floor. I can't blame them. I won't be doing it either.

With me in the store are two girls, both high school kids. Their name tags are orange instead of the white one I have. It's to remind managers they're legally required to give them breaks every few hours and to remind the bouncer at Knickers, the employee-only bar, not to let them inside.

I'm setting up my register when a guy in a work uniform strolls

16

in. He has a feminine walk and a smug smile on his face like he's looking to cause trouble or waiting to say something clever. Most notably, his name tag is green. Green tags are reserved for store managers. I'm not impressed. "Store manager" in an amusement park isn't special. Anyone competent is in upper management and is never down here in the retail trenches. All it means is that someone decided that he was slightly less likely to fuck up and break things than the rest of us. Based on the look on his face, I suspect that was an incorrect decision.

"I'm the new boss," he says, extending his hand to me. His hands are well kept and it looks like he's had a manicure recently. I'm expecting a limp-wristed sort of handshake, but it's firm and satisfying. His name is under the green stripe in all capital letters. DAVE P.

"Same as the old boss?" I ask.

"What?"

"Nothing."

"I'm going to be running the show around here which, between you and me," he leans in close to whisper, even though no one is listening to us and wouldn't care even if they heard, "means we're going to do the absolute minimum amount of work to keep this place from burning down."

I appreciate his commitment to laziness, but I say nothing. After all, he is still the boss. The fact that he makes twenty cents an hour more than me says so.

"Who are they?" he asks, looking over at the girls, who are chatting in one corner and doing the world's worst job of pretending to look busy while they slack off.

"I honestly have no idea," I tell them. "I don't normally work mornings and neither does anyone else I know, but they can't let minors open the shop alone, and today I drew the short straw."

"Do you work in the morning tomorrow?"

"No, I have the day off."

"Excellent," he says. "Are you staying in the employee housing?"

"Yeah. It's cheap."

As we talk, the national anthem starts blaring from the speakers outside the shop and also scattered every fifty feet

17

throughout the park. People think the songs playing in the background throughout the day are random, but they aren't. The same track list plays every day, and it all starts precisely at 10 a.m. when the park opens with the national anthem. You could set a clock by the music if you wanted to. Personally I can't wait for Donna Lewis (I Love You Always Forever)-o'clock, which means it's time for me to go home.

"Great." He punches me on the arm. "Meet me out front at 9 p.m. We're going drinking. I'll pay this time, since we just met. Don't be late, or I'll leave without you and give you all the morning shifts for the next two weeks."

He leaves to go talk to the girls without waiting for confirmation.

* * *

I'm outside the men's employee housing at 8:55 p.m. Dave is already there. He's in a circle of guys who all strike me as incredibly well groomed for amusement park employees. Dyed hair, shaped eyebrows, nice shoes, matching outfits. They are almost certainly all gay. It might seem mean to think in stereotypes and generalizations, but in my line of work – my real line of work – generalizations are helpful, because sometimes you have to read people quickly, and a stereotype is only a stereotype because it's true more often than not.

Part of me wishes I was alone in my room, but socializing is part of blending in, and keeping my boss happy is key to avoiding unwanted scrutiny all summer. Plus, he offered to pay. I like hanging out and having fun and relaxing. I just prefer not to pay for it if I don't have to.

"Okay, that's everyone I think," he says. He doesn't introduce me to anyone, and we're on our way.

I assume we're going to Knickers. Calling it a bar is probably the wrong word for it. It's more like a restaurant with an attached rec center, but you're not allowed in if you're under 18 and they serve alcohol, so it gets called a bar. It's also literally the only place to hang out after work without going into town or into the park with paying customers.

I walk along next to the group so I don't look strange, but I'm not talking to anyone. I don't mind being social, but it doesn't make me happy, either. I generally don't strike up conversations with people I don't know. I don't even really want to be here, but I could stand to get out more, and I don't know if Dave meant it when he threatened to screw up my schedule.

Dave's friends seem pleasant enough. They're loud and probably quite obnoxious to anyone looking to get to sleep early or enjoy a good book, but not any worse than any other pack of soon-to-be-drunk college guys. Dave seems to be the center of their social group; I guess that most or all of them are gay, but none of them ask me if I am or try to hit on me, at least not yet anyway.

I keep wanting to ask Dave if anyone else I know is going to be there, but there's never a break in his conversation and I don't like the idea of barging in, so I walk silently. None of them talk to me.

We get to Knickers and there's a giant of a man standing next to the door. Big, black, and bald, he's easily over six feet and is covered in thicker muscles than most people could pull off even with a lifetime of work. It's entirely unnecessary. Knickers can get a bit loud and the customers can get a bit drunk and sloppy, but I doubt there has ever been a time in the history of Knickers that they needed a bouncer to do anything other than call park services to load a drunk into one of their golf carts and take them back to the employee housing. I take that back. There was probably one incident, and there wasn't anyone there to handle it, so now this guy has job security for life.

He checks each of our employee badges to make sure we aren't tagged orange, and a few of Dave's friends take the opportunity to cop a feel of the bouncer's arms or abs as they walk by. The bouncer ignores it. I want to ask him how many times a night he gets felt up, but I decide against it.

We're all sitting in a giant booth, and I mostly just listen to the conversation without getting involved. It's enough to just act like I'm paying attention. I sip my lime margarita and not for the first time appreciate hanging out with gay guys. Dave is drinking beers in between shots of tequila, but enough of his friends are drinking stuff that lets my margarita blend in. Most alcohol tastes like ass, but you can't order something sweet in a group of straight people without them telling you how girly or gay your drink is. I'm sure no one goes gay just to expand their personal menu of acceptable alcoholic drinks, but if they did, I would totally get it.

I don't drink much. No one notices that I'm drinking slowly and before long they're all drunk anyway.

I wait until the first person decides to leave, then wait a few more minutes. Now that I won't be first I'm guessing I can leave without catching too much shit from Dave.

"Hey," I lean over and talk into his ear. "I'm going to get going. It's been fun though."

"If it's fun, why are you leaving?" he says.

I have no idea. I'm a bit annoyed that he's ignoring my obvious social cue but embarrassed I don't have anything to say in response.

Then he says, "I'm just fucking with you, don't worry. Come on out any time." He goes to shake my hand, then turns it into a drunken back slapping hug at the last second.

"I will," I say. "We'll do it again sometime. I'm sure I'll be around."

I'm not really sure of that at all.

5

I'm glad to have the day off work today, which is rare when you work for a place that can legally work you as many hours a week as they want without paying overtime. I still wake up early. I've never been able to sleep in. I get out of bed and the first thing I notice is Cory from Texas, passed out in his work uniform, foot hanging over the side of the bed. He has tan lines from spending the entire day in sandals. I wonder what he was doing last night. I didn't see him at Knickers, but I'm sure if he had seen me he would have come over and said something. I can't imagine where he would have gone without changing out of his work uniform first. I imagine him spending the night trying to pick up girls and coming home alone. It makes me smile.

I grab my shampoo, soap, and toothbrush and walk out into the hallway hoping the single shower on my floor is open. It isn't – I'll have to either wait or go downstairs to the main showers. I decide to wait, because going to the main showers means putting on a shirt and pants. The guy showering left the door open in case someone needs to take a piss in the single toilet, but there's no indication of how long he'll be in the shower.

Out of curiosity I walk down the hall to the stairs to see if my toothpaste is still splattered against the wall. It is, and now collecting all manner of dust, dirt, and bugs. They probably won't even scrape it up at the end of the summer. They'll just paint right over it. I'm glad I decided to buy some flip flops instead of walking around here barefoot.

A girl comes out of one of the rooms down the hall wearing nothing but her underwear, holding a small washcloth in front of her in a halfhearted attempt to hide her stunning tits. She has dirty blonde hair and wide, unashamed blue eyes. Growing up in the Midwest I never knew it, but Eastern European girls all seem to have amazing bodies. It must be all the walking everywhere and growing up eating nothing but nuts and vegetables.

I know I shouldn't stare, but.... damn. Apart from making out awkwardly with a few chubby high school girlfriends, I have no experience seeing a girl undressed in person. This girl is something else entirely, almost inhuman in her hotness with the added easy charm of someone who looks likeable and easy to hang out with. I never will though, never know her name or have a conversation with her, and certainly never see her like this again. I can convince someone to buy a pile of worthless junk or talk my way out of a fight with ease, but girls (women?) are foreign to me. I've got nothing.

She walks by me casually, smiling at me politely for a moment, like she's completely unaware that she's naked except for her lime green thong. She walks into the bathroom, ignoring the fact that I'm clearly waiting for the shower as well. I let her, soaking in the view as she walks by. It's more amazement than perversion. I'm not an asshole.

Inside the bathroom, I hear her say something in what might be Russian. I want to look around the corner, but I don't. I'm not sure why, but it doesn't seem right to go out of my way to look. Her walking by was her choice – me following her around to keep enjoying the view would be mine.

I hear the guy inside say, "What? I don't speak whatever it is you're speaking."

She says, "I need shower. Come on, come on."

He says back to her, "What? I... okay, okay. Just a minute." The shower stops almost immediately. The guy comes out of the bathroom dripping wet, wrapped in a towel. He hasn't even dried off a little. When sees me he just gestures with a nod toward the bathroom and says, "Holy shit, dude," and walks back to his room.

* * *

I'm assigned to close the store tonight, along with two girls I just met, Grace and Margaret. I'm pretty sure they just met each other as well. Wonderments hires new employees constantly, because even with so many out-of-state employees and a three month contract on location at one of the most exciting amusement parks in the country, the turnover is enormous. There's no pleasing some people.

They're ignoring me and talking with each other, which I'm fine with. They're funneling all the customers that come in to my register even though they should be working registers as well, but that's fine too. It's letting me skim more money than usual.

"Where are you from?" Grace asks her. They aren't even hiding the fact that they're doing more socializing than working. Even the customers don't seem to mind; a day at an amusement park can convince anyone that waiting in long, slow lines is normal.

"Grand Island," she answers.

"Where?"

"Nebraska." I wonder how big Grand Island is. My geography is pretty passable, but I had no idea such a place even existed. If I had to guess where a town called "Grand Island" was, I'd guess it was somewhere in New York or Maine or Florida. Not Nebraska. I'm pretty sure there are no islands in Nebraska. I've never been there and with any luck I never will be. They're called "fly over" states for a reason.

"Oh," Grace says. I'm not watching her face because I'm too busy ringing up a customer for their fifty dollar Wonderments sweatshirt, but I imagine her wrinkling her nose in disgust. Grace is the sort of person who has a perpetually judgmental look on her face, even when she doesn't need to. She's shorter than the rest of us by at least a head, but she has a penetrating stare and doesn't break eye contact when she's talking to you. She has an under-layer

23

of dyed pink hair blended in with her natural color. This blatant disregard for the Wonderments company dress policy gives her the look and feel of a rebel without having to do anything that's genuinely rebellious. "I'm from Burbank," she volunteers. "California."

"I know where Burbank is," Margaret says. They've known each other for a few hours, or maybe for a day or so if they worked together on a day I had off. They know nothing about each other except one thing: they dislike each other. I can hear it in their voices.

"It must be boring to be from Nebraska. Is that why you're working here this summer?"

"Nebraska's fine," Margaret says. I can't tell if she believes it or if she's just defensive about it. Margaret looks like everyone else from the Midwest: light brown hair not well kept, pale skin without makeup, glasses just a little too thick and without any attempt at style, and a few extra pounds without looking unpleasant. Not unattractive, just... bland. She looks like every girl I went to school with, every girl I met at summer camp, every girl sitting in the pews at church when I was little. The American Midwest: sixty-five million people that all need to be on Extreme Makeover. Myself included.

"I'm just working for the summer to help pay for college. They give us a lot of hours here. Where is your family from?"

"My family is from Burbank," Grace says. The condescension in her voice is palpable.

"Sorry," Margaret says. "I just thought maybe you were from somewhere else because you're Asian." I guess it's not that racist of a guess, since Wonderments employs students from all over the world. Or it wouldn't be, anyway, if Grace hadn't just said she was from Burbank.

Grace has straight black hair and pale skin tinted with copper. She'd be average looking in Asia, I guess. Here at Wonderments, being Asian is sure to catch the attention of all manner of douchey, dick-driven suitors. Even though Margaret looms over her physically, it's clear both of them think they're above the other. I can tell Margaret is the jealous one, though: a Nebraska farm girl trying to get attention standing next to an exotic beauty. Neither of them appeals to me. Their squabbling ruins their personalities before I even know them.

"My grandparents are from South Korea," Grace says. "My parents were born here and so was I. I'm just as American as you are."

"Sorry," Margaret says, backing away. They don't think of it consciously, but the female pecking order at The Jolly Tinker has been established. In that regard I consider myself lucky – since the only other guy who works in the store is my boss and also gay, we don't have to do any macho dick measuring for position in the social order. Hopefully it lets me avoid any drama this summer. I just want to stay quiet, stay out of the way, make my money, and disappear.

6

I'm at Staples making about twenty copies of fliers for my flea market scam when this old Indian lady walks over to me from a few photocopiers over. I don't actually know if she's Indian or not. She's ancient and hunched over with an impossible number of wrinkles and most of her teeth missing. Even if I had the ability to tell a real Indian apart from whatever other nationalities look like Indians, the years have smashed this woman so hard I probably couldn't tell now, anyway. She's got a feisty look in her eye, and I wonder what she looked like when she was young enough to find attractive.

"These places, they want all ya fuckin' money, ya know?" Her accent is thick and absurd, like you'd expect to hear in an old racist cartoon.

I nod and smile. "Yeah."

"Every time tha machine fucks up, it takes ya money. Think I know how to use these things? I'm no fuckin' doctor."

I'm trying to guess why she thinks doctors specifically are trained to use photocopiers. I can't think of anything.

She turns from me and yells in the direction of the girl behind the service counter. "Machine's takin' ma fuckin' money, you gonna help me or just take ma fuckin' money?" The girl doesn't look over, and continues helping the guy in front of her. There is no doubt in

26

my mind she heard the old lady.

"That's the difference between you men and us women. We know when to ask for help. You men never do. I got three college degrees, but I know what I don't fuckin' know."

I look over at her still-running machine, making copy after copy of the same page of some book, too dark and half the text cut off. I wonder if she's bullshitting me about her college degrees, or if she got them so long ago and from such a shitty third world country that no one had any copy machines.

She goes back to her machine to push buttons at random and watch the service girl who is going to put up with her shit for minimum wage. Working skilless service jobs sucks. Both my parents still do it, well into middle age. I wonder if the girl working here at Staples – all young and full of dreams – will end up working here for twenty years. I think of my mother. Sore all the time, tired all the time, a little dead in the eyes. Beautiful in all the old pictures I see of her but now just wrinkled and sagging and dusty, a life of hard work breaking her down one shift at a time.

I want to go over to the girl and shake her, tell her to go do anything else. Open a bakery. Compose music and sell it to pop stars. Become a stripper. Just tell her to do anything to get out of this job as fast as she can and never look back.

She goes over to the old Indian-ish lady.

"Can I help you?" she says.

The Indian lady yells in her face and smacks her on the arm repeatedly. They're harmless, weak slaps, not effective in the slightest despite the woman's best efforts. The girl just lets it blow over. I wonder if there's no manager to call, or she just doesn't care enough to call him.

After a few minutes of the girl trying to decipher what the woman wants to do with the copier and doing it for her, I notice the young girl smirking. She's trying not to laugh. If there's one upside to working terrible, low paying service jobs, it's that sometimes they do provide some comedy. When she turns away from the woman and starts laughing, I can't help but smile too. I suddenly have the urge to ask her out on a date.

She's out of my league. She has big doe eyes and an easy smile, the kind of person who was popular in high school and nice to everyone, the sort of person who thinks in absolutes because nothing has ever gone bad enough for them that it blurred the platitudes they were told when they were growing up.

I pay her for my copies. She thanks me and tells me to have a nice day in that way I can tell she doesn't mean; the way she says it to every other person all day long, until it's programmed into her and she doesn't even hear the words anymore. For a moment I think about saying something to her that will shake her out of the routine of it – what I'd say, I have no idea – but instead, I take my change and leave.

* * *

I open the door to my room and Cory is inside. I was hoping he wouldn't be here. He doesn't ask about the flyers I'm holding or how I spent my morning. I guess it's nice to have such an oblivious roommate.

"Hey dude," he says. It's always "dude" or "champ" or "boss" when he talks to me. I wonder if he remembers my name. Probably not.

He's getting ready for work, which involves two minutes putting on the standard issue Wonderments Water Park uniform, and several more minutes slathering his body in tanning lotion. He's a lifeguard in the water park and mostly has the body to match. Muscular arms and six pack abs with a nice tan, completely wasted on a face that looks like a dopey little kid. Big grin, short hair, tons of freckles, and the only person over eighteen that I've ever seen with braces. He has that sparkle in his eye like this is going to be the Best Summer Ever, filled with parties and booze and getting laid. If I was betting, I'd guess he's a virgin.

"I saw you hanging out with some of the girls from the park." I wonder where. "So I bought some scrunchies for the door."

He points to the dresser, to which he's attached three brightly-colored poofy hair ties.

"You know, so if, you know."

"Okay."

He's still not sure if I understand. "It's like, if you have a girl

28

over and want some time alone, for sex, or hanging out with them, or whatever. You can put the scrunchie on the door so I know not to come in."

I wonder how often I could put one on the door just to keep him out before he caught on and got pissed about it. He's not a bad guy, but I find myself hoping I don't see much of him.

"Sure thing," I say.

He's looking at himself in the mirror that he brought with him – bulky and square, sitting on a black stand on his dresser. It's attached to the frame so you can angle it. I can't think of any single guy I know owning a dresser mirror, let alone anyone that would ship one all the way from Texas. He tries tucking the bright yellow and red shirt into the bright yellow shorts, then untucks it again. He tries to smooth out the wrinkles in the outfit with his hand. It doesn't work.

"You work with a lot of girls in your shop?"

"I guess so, yeah. It's me, my gay boss, and a few girls. Other people rotate in and out but they're the ones I've been around the most."

"Being a lifeguard kind of sucks for meeting girls. You basically have to spend your time by yourself at your post." Apparently a summer of getting sun and being a hot stud lifeguard is not living up to his expectations. "You should introduce me to the girls you work with."

"I don't even know them that well."

"So? Just introduce me and I can do the rest."

"I don't know. They have boyfriends, I think."

"I'll come by later," he says, walking out the door. "I'm sure one of them will want a piece of this."

"I really don't think –" He shuts the door and is gone. I worry for the safety of the water park customers if he's as oblivious on the job as he is when he's around me.

7

I'm doing nothing behind the register, staring off into space. The middle of the day is incredibly boring – no one is coming into shops to buy shirts or candy or toys. No one wants to carry that shit around all day. Then, fifteen minutes before closing, everyone in the park will cram into our little store to get a souvenir. For half an hour every day, we're the busiest place in the park: last chance to buy shit you don't want but that is really important that you have.

"Hey," Nicole comes up to my register, looking at the tray of mood rings for sale on the counter. They're all dark blue, because they're heat activated and that's the warmest setting. It's hot as hell out. "I'm bored. Let's go to Shitter's for lunch."

"Sure thing, Nicole Not Nikki." I tell her.

She holds up a hand and stops me immediately. "Look. It's Nicole. That's it. It's not Nic or Nikki or whatever dumb nickname you want to give me. If you want to hang out this summer, cut that shit out right now."

"Won't ever say it again," I promise her. I want to ask her if this means we'll be hanging out a lot this summer, but it sounds overeager, so I don't.

I do not want to go to Shitter's for lunch. The food is the generic, forgettable stuff you can find in any family restaurant chain in America, except with a forty percent markup in price because it's inside an amusement park.

It used to be called "Chitter's" back when the park mascot was a giant gray mouse, so the employees called the place "Shitter's" as a joke. Then they dropped the mascot (claiming they wanted to be distinct from "other parks with famous mice as mascots") and changed the name of the restaurant. The nickname stuck, even though almost none of the employees here even remember Chitter the mouse.

So we take the shuttle to the back of the park and walk the rest of the way along the boardwalk next to the lake. The lake itself isn't very big, but stores and restaurants have been put up all the way around it, along with sandy beaches. Supposedly the beach is manmade and they have to import more sand every year to replenish it in the offseason.

"I love this walk. The smell of the water reminds me of my hometown." It's hot and crowded, and Nicole has been away for a month, tops. Still, it's a pleasant walk.

"Do you miss it?" I ask her. "Home, I mean."

She thinks for a moment. "No, not really. I miss some parts of it, like the smell. My parents have a house on a lake. We don't live there year round, but I spent summers there as a kid. That's why I like coming out here. I'm not looking forward to going back at the end of the summer, though. There's nothing to do there."

I try to imagine Nicole as a teenager. I don't think she would have been one of the popular kids – she's got that sort of late bloomer look to her like she's still trying a bit too hard, like being beautiful isn't something that comes easily to her, and she's doing all she can to hold on to it. It makes me feel an affinity for her, although in my case I suppose I'm less "late bloomer" and more "never blossomed."

We get to the restaurant and the outdoor tables, at least, are packed. What was once called Chitter's is now called Spoon's, and I wish they had just called it Shitter's instead. The apostrophe in Spoon's looks so unnatural to me, even if the sign does feature a giant, anthropomorphic spoon with a chef's hat.

The hostess greets us right inside the door. She's young – maybe sixteen or seventeen – and cheery. "Would you like a table or a booth?" She has menus in hand to lead us to our seats.

"How long is the wait on one of the outdoor tables?" Nicole asks.

"Ummmm.... fifteen minutes maybe?"

I do the math in my head. We get an hour for lunch, and it took us twenty minutes to get here, and it'll take twenty to get back. There is no way we're going to make it back on time even if we sit down immediately.

"We'll wait," Nicole says. She takes a buzzer from the hostess, and we go back outside.

Nicole leans on the railing along the boardwalk, looking out onto the lake. "So I met a guy last week, and he seems nice." Of course he does. "But I think maybe he just wants sex."

"You met a guy in his twenties, right? Of course he wants sex."

"No, that's not what I mean," she says. "I don't know how to tell if he likes me, or if he just wants to fuck."

This stumps me. I don't want to go so far as to say all guys only want to fuck and couldn't care less about liking you or not, but it seems like a good rule of thumb until you have evidence otherwise.

"I'm not sure. Does he ever hang out with you without trying to get laid?"

"Of course he does!" Then she's quiet for about half a minute. "Damn it."

"So.... did you?"

"Did I what?" I can't tell if she's genuinely not following, or just playing coy.

"Fuck him."

She lets out a little offended shriek. I don't think she's actually offended; she's just conditioned to the polite response to the question.

"Would it be that bad if I did?"

I shrug. "There's nothing wrong with fucking who you want to fuck. But he's a guy. Once you start, that's what it's going to be all about for awhile."

"I just want to meet a guy who likes me for me," she says.

It seems impossible to me. If a guy wants to fuck, he wants to fuck. It's not like he can just turn that off until he discovers a girl has a nice personality, and then turn it on again.

Lucky for me, the buzzer goes off before I can figure out how to say this to her without sounding like an asshole. We walk to our table past the noise and clatter of families on vacation. Almost everyone in here has tans and kids and smells like sweat and sunscreen. Most of the teenagers and young couples are at the front of the park, riding giant roller coasters. Once people have kids, they start migrating toward the back of the park, toward the kids' play areas, water park, and the beach. Everyone looks happy. We look out of place.

We get back from lunch forty-five minutes late, and no one cares.

8

It's just after 8 p.m. and Grace is getting back from her dinner break holding the sketch pad she always has with her at work. I can't blame her for having it – if I wasn't counting change all night I'd be pretty bored at a job like this myself. Anything to pass the time is a good thing.

She's actually back a few minutes early. It's no surprise that sending people on break together is against official Wonderments policy – everyone manages to double their time on break when they can hang out with someone. Lucky for us Wonderments is like most big businesses in that they are a lot more interested in creating policy than enforcing it.

Grace tucks the sketch pad away under her register, and she and Nicole go back to socializing almost immediately. They don't even pretend to do any work, but it's not like there's much to do anyway. Just keep the place from falling apart until it's time to close.

That's when I see it – the bright red and yellow uniform of a water park employee. It's Cory from Texas, and he's headed straight for me. I look at the time on my phone and sure enough – just enough time for the water park to close and for Cory to walk all the way to the other end of the park to cram himself into my little corner of the world. I wonder if tenacity is still considered a virtue when someone only has it because they're too stupid to know when to give up.

"Hey man," he says to me, ignoring a line of customers and almost disrupting my change count. "How's it going tonight?"

"It's pretty busy in here. You should come back later." Or never.

"No worries bro."

He walks away cutting through the middle of the line and approaches Nicole and Grace.

"Hey ladies."

"Ummm.... hi?" Grace is clearly unimpressed.

"Don't worry, I'm with him," I hear him say. It amuses me that he thinks this fact will in any way get him into their pants.

"Do you know this guy?" Grace calls over to me.

"Nope," I call back. I keep fluidly helping customers. They don't seem to mind if you're having conversations with your coworkers about pointless crap, so long as you don't slow down the line.

"Oh, come on," Cory says. "We're roommates."

Nicole laughs. "Look at him when we pick on him. He looks like a sad puppy. It's kind of adorable."

"Bark bark," he says, trying to put his arm around Nicole. She shrugs off his arm expertly and takes a step away from him. I'm aware I'm no rock star when it comes to trying to pick up a girl, but this is embarrassing.

"Don't ever do that again," Nicole says. "I mean, in general. There's not a girl in the world that's going to find that cute."

"Which part?" Cory asks. "The barking or the arm?"

"Either one," Nicole says.

"Okay, no barking and no arms around the shoulders," he says.

Nicole laughs. "You can put your arm around a girl, but wait until she's on a date with you. Don't just walk up."

"Got it," he nods his head earnestly.

Grace looks him up and down, then turns him around and does the same. "Well look at that," she says. "He's like a puppy. Kind of cute, really stupid, but trainable." She looks at Nicole. "You could do worse."

Cory turns around. "That's me, Mr. Eager to Learn. So, do you girls want to –"

"No," Grace says. "This is going to be as good as it gets for you for today."

He stands there, just sort of gaping and smiling.

"That means you should leave," Grace tells him.

He nods enthusiastically and says, "I'll be seeing you ladies again."

He does a little bow and makes a gesture like he's tipping an invisible hat at them. Then he turns and walks out the opposite door, without so much as saying another word to me or even waving. It's less like a walk and more of a strut, like he's just achieved a great victory or heard some fantastic news.

* * *

You would think the internet would be the bane of a scam artist, with all the free information out there. Not so. It actually makes things easier. People are so narrow-minded about what they take in, it rarely occurs to them to check sources, or, if they do, they only check with people that share the same narrow views. You can't spend an hour on Facebook without someone suggesting that Barack Obama is a secret pig-eating Muslim terrorist. I mean, at the very least, Google should let you know that Muslims don't eat pig.

I'm at the Salvation Army buying the rest of the props for my yard sale. The old lady behind the counter kind of thinks I'm insane, and I can't blame her.

"So, if you don't mind me asking, what do you need all this stuff for?"

Our conversation comes in gaps as I drop an armload of stuff on the checkout counter, then go back for more. The Salvation Army is perfect for what I need – random junk, as cheap as possible. I could use Craigslist or Freecycle to get the stuff for free if I wanted to, but by the time you factor in all the time spent e-mailing, traveling, and picking stuff up, it's just so much more convenient to come here, where I can buy in bulk.

"Art project," I say, dropping a load of old National Geographics and Reader's Digests onto the table.

Claiming I'm working on an art project is, by far, my favorite excuse. You can justify almost any behavior with it.

"Huh," she says, looking over my pile. It's got it all: old books, kitchen appliances, kids' toys, men's suits, old computer games, you name it. She's trying to imagine what kind of bullshit piece of modern art I must be creating with all this junk.

It's all camouflage. The trick is that everyone has heard "bargain hunting" stories and urban legends – woman finds first edition Edgar Allan Poe in bookstore, child buys set of 1912 baseball cards at flea market, man spots lost Picasso at estate sale.

That's all it takes. Grab a bunch of junk so I can make a garage sale or flea market plot look convincing, plant a handful of fakes around, and then wait for people to rip me off by paying me $100 for something they think is worth thousands. They won't know until days later that it's not real, and since the whole thing involves me playing dumb the whole day anyway, it's not like they can come back and explain that they were trying to take advantage of me and it didn't pan out.

I put a few criminally ugly desk lamps, marked down to the "please God someone just take them" price of $1 each, on the counter.

"So," she asks, "what's this art project going to look like when it's done? This is a lot of weird stuff."

I hand her the forty dollars the pile of assorted junk cost me. "It's a postmodern think piece. I wanted to explore light and color from a new direction, and criticize how consumerism works in the Western world."

You can spout complete bullshit whenever you want, as long as the person you're bullshitting is ignorant on the subject. Nearly everyone will quietly nod and smile instead of looking stupid. Someone once said "It is better to keep silent and be thought a fool, than open your mouth and remove all doubt." Honestly, whoever said it was just looking for an all-access pass to bullshit for the rest of his life without being called on it. Even the quote is bullshit – it's been attributed to everyone from Abraham Lincoln and Mark Twain to Chinese proverbs and the Bible. Whoever did say it is still bullshitting us from beyond the grave, even centuries later.

I'm sitting alone in the employee cafeteria. I get why they camouflage the place and make it look bland from the outside. The last thing management wants is customers realizing that the crappy food they eat in the park is being sold fifty feet away for a quarter of the price. People know they're being taken advantage of by amusement park prices already, but they're willing to overlook it most of the time as long as you don't remind them.

The food they serve here is simple – pizza, burgers, hot dogs, potato chips – basically anything they can count on a fifteen-year-old to pull out of a freezer and stick in a microwave without causing bodily harm to themselves or others. It's a relatively in-demand position: it's indoors, and if you're willing to suffer through the lunch rush, you get to spend a lot of time sitting on your ass.

Nothing here tastes good. It's not bad either; it's just forgettable in every way. It's all set up the same way as everything else the park does for employees: to be as cheap as possible. In its own weird way it's also a champion of American imperialism: no one notices it's there, but by the end of the summer, all the perfect-bodied Eastern Europeans and slim, alluring Asians who came here to work will have a few extra sloppy pounds on them, the beginning of their own personal spare tire, a lot less energy, and no real idea of how it happened. Surprise – being able to live off cheeseburgers for two bucks a day has some downsides.

I'm eating my discount lethargy-inducing hamburger (like any good American, I make sure that recognizing the problem in no way leads to taking part in the solution) when Nicole sits down across from me. She has no food in front of her. I wonder what she'd look like without a shirt on, and decide she'd be attractive even if she did put on a few pounds from eating shitty cafeteria food all summer.

She laughs out loud, obviously fake, and reaches across the table to take my hand. Then she stops smiling and stares at me intensely. "Make small talk," she says, "and give me that." She drags my hand across to the center of the table.

"So uh...." I'm more than a bit lost. "How is your day going?"

"That guy over there wants a date, but Grace warned me about him." She points with her eyes to a tanned dude with bleach blonde hair who is greeting and fist-bumping his way across the room toward our table. "He took her out to eat at some cheap restaurant and a movie then got pissed when she wouldn't put out."

I can't help myself. "Is that different than the other guys you end up dating?"

She digs her nails into the palm of my hand, hard. "Don't be an asshole," she says.

The fist-bumping douchebag arrives at our table. True to douchebag form, he doesn't introduce himself, ignores the fact that I'm even at the table, and talks directly to Nicole. I can't tell if he's too stupid to notice we're holding hands, too cocky to care, or just knows she's faking it. Whatever the reason, I'm still impressed by his approach.

"So, are we going out this Saturday?" he asks. "I can still get us dinner reservations in town."

"Aren't you dating Grace?" she asks. No matter how much of a jerk this guy is, she still won't shoot him down directly.

"We're not exclusive," he says. "Anyway, I don't think we have that much in common."

"I'm going out with someone else this Saturday," she says. "Maybe later."

At this point I'm a bit annoyed. Used as a fake boyfriend? Okay, sure. Ignored by the moron who can't take a hint? Standard. But the fact that she can't just tell him "no" and move the fuck on – that bothers me.

"With who?" he says. Now he annoys me too. It shouldn't matter to him who it is; there's nothing he can do with the information. I wonder if he's ever had a directed thought in his life, or if it's all just verbal diarrhea, an empty brain excreting waste out the nearest hole.

I notice Nicole digging her nails into my palm again. This, apparently, is my cue to speak up.

"Hi," I say to him. I'm giving him my best "who the fuck are you?" face.

He's trying to decide if I'm a threat. I'm not worried; I can already tell he's the kind of guy who goes for quantity and not quality on his dates. If Nicole turns him down, he'll ask girls out nonstop until he finds a date for the weekend. Getting shot down twenty times is fine with him just as long as he convinces one poor girl to go out with him so he can try and trade dinner for a blowjob. The part that annoys me the most about this strategy is that it works.

"I'm taking her to a play this weekend," I say when he doesn't take the hint.

"A play?" he says, almost laughing. "Are you gay?" It's clear he thinks this is a top shelf insult, his trump card.

"Yep," I say. "Can't get to sleep at night without sucking a big ol' dick. Say, what are you doing this weekend?" I saw a sign once that the definition of homophobia is a man's fear that a gay man will treat him the same way he treats women. In this case, it works like a charm.

"Well," he says, refusing to make eye contact with me as I leer at him, "once you're done seeing Shakespeare or whatever with this fag, come see me if you want a guy that knows how to treat a woman right."

I wish Dave were here now. I saw him threaten to punch a guy in the face once for using the word "fag." I decide not to risk it.

"Thanks," Nicole says as soon as the douchebag is gone. She lets go of my hand. There are clear nail marks in the palm. "Shit, sorry."

"It's fine. So, did you really want to go see a play this weekend? I can probably find some tickets."

"I think I have to work this weekend," she says. I'm a bit baffled by this. Why lie to the douchebag about me if she already had a legitimate excuse? "But if I do maybe we can do something the next day I have off."

I forgive her.

2

After closing is easily the busiest time of night for us in the shop, and it's the reason so many park employees would rather work on rides than in the stores. Working the rides is monotonous and there's never any interruption unless something bizarre, disgusting, or embarrassing happens. Maybe a small child pukes all over the ride, making it your job to hose off the affected seats and give everyone with splatter on them a free t-shirt to wear. Perhaps a really fat guy ignores the warning signs and test seats, so when he shows up and can't fit into the seat, you have to explain to him that he's fat. Then there's all the times when you have to explain to a mother that she can't have a picture of her and her child on the ride because the sorority girl sitting two seats behind them was flashing the camera, and it's against company policy to sell the picture.

You know when you look at all the pictures taken during a ride and some of the spots where pictures should be show a blank screen instead? Nothing is broken, it just happened that whoever was in the frame was doing something inappropriate when the cameras flashed. Usually it's just some kid giving the camera the finger, but every once in a while it's a girl showing her tits or a guy playing "sneaky nuts" and sticking his balls out through the zipper. This fucks everyone around them, since they can't buy the picture of your hairy ball sack flopping around. So then you usher the mom and the kid back to the front of the line, piss off everyone else who has patiently been waiting their turn, and hope the kid doesn't puke after riding the same ride twice in a span of twenty minutes.

Working the rides sucks, but they do have one advantage over those of us in retail: when their schedule says the shift ends at midnight, it actually ends at midnight, and they get to go home. Tonight, the park closes at midnight, which means they stop letting people get in line for rides at around eleven, or even sooner for the popular stuff. By a little past midnight the rides are shut down, but that means people still have to walk all the way across the park to get to the exit so they can pile in their cars and go back to whichever boring town they're seeking temporary relief from. Since most Americans would consider it a genuine travesty to leave vacation with any money left whatsoever, at this point they all have one thing on their mind: finding a place to shop.

Wonderments management isn't stupid, so they leave all the stores open as people leave, and they all flock toward the lit up shops to buy up every shirt, hat, trinket, candy bar, and novelty that they can get their hands on. So even though my shift is listed as ending at midnight, it's just after one in the morning when the last customer leaves. We shut the doors and lock them just in case there are any more stragglers coming our way. Now we can get down to the business of cleaning up, restocking the shelves, and counting the registers so *then* we can go home. I wonder for a moment how security goes about making sure everyone has left the park – it seems like someone could easily find a place to hide and sleep outside in the park overnight. I imagine plenty of people have done it just to say they have.

The store looks like shit like it always does at the end of a shift. I grab a broom out of the supply closet. Dave is inside writing up a list of damaged merchandise that needs to be written off, including a bag of Skittles that he "damaged" and is munching on as he does the paperwork. I don't mention it and neither does he.

42

I'm sweeping up while Nicole and Grace restock apparel, stuffed animals, and other overpriced junk at the back of the store. There, kicked over into a corner, I see it: a small black men's wallet. I sweep it over to me with a pile of dirt and pick it up before anyone notices. I take a quick glance around the store and see no one looking at me, so I stand behind the counter and hide my hands behind it to open it in safety. There's about $80 in cash, which I slip into my pocket. There's also a driver's license and credit cards along with other less valuable stuff like pictures of his family and his dog, but I leave all that stuff alone. I avoid crime that can be traced back to me whenever possible. It's hard to spend money in prison.

"Hey guys," I yell. "Check it out!" Nicole and Grace come up to the front of the store. Dave leaves his stolen candy behind and comes over as well. I set the wallet on the counter.

"Nice," Dave says. "I'll get the form." He disappears into another closet momentarily, and comes out with a yellow sheet of paper.

"Damn, I never find anything interesting," Grace says.

"That's because you never clean anything," Dave says. She punches him.

"Is there anything inside?" Nicole asks.

They're all interested because the official lost and found policy at Wonderments is that they hold any given item for thirty days. If that time goes by and no one claims whatever you turned in to lost and found, you can claim it yourself. Of course, that never happens with wallets, because tomorrow whichever schmuck dropped his wallet will almost certainly call the park and find out where his wallet is. Failing that, security will just wait a few weeks and mail it off to whatever address is on the driver's license. If you're looking to win the lost and found lottery you're much better off finding some jewelry or a watch or a money clip.

I open the wallet and show them that's empty with a shrug.

"Oh well," Nicole seems genuinely disappointed. I guess everyone, no matter how innocent they are, still dreams of getting something for nothing. "Better luck next time, I guess," she says.

* * *

The employee cafeteria is mostly empty this time of the morning. It'll be swarming with people in about an hour for the lunch rush, but by coming in a bit early I can avoid most of that. That's why it's even more annoying than usual when Cory from Texas walks up and sits down across from me with a pizza. It's definitely too large for one person, but pizzas are cheap here and served on a "one size fits none" policy.

"Hey dude," he said. "You weren't in the room when I woke up. I thought maybe you were here."

He opens the box of pizza next to me and grabs a slice. He doesn't have plates or napkins or anything. "Have a piece if you want."

"No thanks, I've got lunch already," gesturing to what they call shepherd's pie but is really just ground beef and peas with a side of mashed potatoes.

"So, uh, did the girls you work with say anything about me after I left?"

"No." I take a bite of the beef. It's completely tasteless. I'm no cook, but I imagine someone with even a little bit of experience in a kitchen could make this place so much better. It's just that no one cares enough to do it. In a way it seems like everyone here is just like me – all trying to get in, make money for a few months, and get out. No one wants to make this place any better. No one wants to do a quality job. They just want to take what they can and then never come back.

"Damn. Well, I think I made a good first impression anyway. What do you think?"

"I couldn't really tell. I was working."

"That brunette was pretty hot," he says. "I bet she's a freak."

Nicole and Margaret both have brown hair. Grace does too, but I assume that if Cory was talking about her, he would have called her "that Asian girl."

"Which one?" I ask him. "All the girls you met at my work have brown hair."

"Oh. Hmmm." The first piece of pizza has disappeared already, and he goes for another. A mouthful of food isn't going to stop him from talking.

"Well, I guess they were all pretty cute," he says. "I was thinking of the white girl with all the makeup on. But I've never been with a Japanese girl."

It would surprise me if he has ever 'been with' any girl, but I don't ask.

"I'm pretty sure she's Korean. Well, Korean-American."

"Sure, sure. I'm thinking about asking one of them out. If they say no I can always try and get with the other ones later. You're lucky, man, working all day with those girls with no competition."

"I don't know. I think they have boyfriends. They didn't seem interested. Aren't there any lifeguards you could hook up with?" I take another bite of my food and give up on it. I take a slice of the pizza. It's nothing special. Dry crust, bland sauce. I'm trying to decide if they heat the whole thing from frozen, or if they get the ingredients frozen and in jars, and assemble it before they cook it. I can't decide. It doesn't matter. It's pizza, so it's still pretty good.

"I guess," he says. "Lifeguarding isn't as cool as I thought it would be. I don't get to talk to girls or anything. I spend most of my day standing at the top of a water slide making sure no one tries to go down face first."

It makes sense to me that they put Cory on slide duty. I know I wouldn't trust him to pay enough attention to save someone's life.

"Well, I think I'm taking Nicole out on a date. We're going to a play."

"Who's Nicole?" He asks. I want to tell him he might have a bit more success with girls if he learned their names, but two things come to mind: First, that I'm fairly terrible getting girls myself and therefore am in no place to give advice, and second, that I don't want Cory hooking up with anyone anyway. If he did take my advice and was able to use it to pick up a girl, I'd have to apologize to her.

"The brunette."

"The one with the glasses? She's okay I guess."

"No, that's Margaret. Nicole is the other white girl. We've been hanging out." I assume I have no shot whatsoever at anything romantic or sexual with Nicole, but I decide to do her a favor and scare off Cory. "Hey, wait. Margaret wasn't even working when you came in. Have you been hanging around there when I'm not at work?"

He ignores my question. "Nice, dude." He goes for a fist bump with the hand that's not holding a slice of pizza and I return it. I want to tell him that no one respectable ever fist bumps anyone, but it's easier just to go along with it. "Why are you taking her to a play though? That shit is so boring. You have to take her to do something exciting so she's all revved up and ready to get laid afterward."

"I doubt that's going to happen regardless."

"Well, that's on you dude. I say go for it. If you don't, let me know so I can."

I say nothing.

"Do you want any more of this?" Half the pizza is still there.

"No, I'm good," I tell him.

He shuts the box and stands up. "Well, I'm off to hit the gym for awhile."

To my knowledge, there is no gym anywhere in the park. Either he's going all the way into town just to lift some weights, or he just likes telling people he 'hits the gym.' On his way out the door he tries to cram the pizza box into one of the waste bins. It won't fit through the little hinged door, so he sets the box on top of the cabinet where you're supposed to put the trays, and walks out.

10

Every few weeks Wonderments has an employee social event. There are some that are incredibly popular – like keeping certain roller coasters open late, or the Fourth of July pool party in the water park, or the end of season barbecue. Tonight is not one of the popular events. Tonight is miniature golf night.

Dave convinced all of us to go. Because the five of us were all working, Nicole, Grace, Margaret, Dave and I are all stuck together very close to the end of the line. The miniature golf course is in the back of the park, and we're one of the last shops that gets to close, so we're pretty much screwed when it comes to employee events.

When we finally get to the beginning of the line, we each grab a club and a different colored ball. The girls all make a big show of choosing which color ball to take, like they're deciding based on what their choice of color says about them as a person. Nicole takes pink, Grace takes yellow, and Margaret takes a dark blue. We grab our scorecards and the needlessly tiny pencils that go with them.

"Four or less to a group, please," a bored kid tells us from behind the window of the booth by the entrance. There's always a few people that have to work employee events instead of going, just to keep things from getting out of hand. "No food or drink inside except water."

"Come on, can't we go five? We'll hurry up," Grace says.

The kid has a look on his face that says he regrets volunteering to babysit a bunch of entitled jerks who can't follow basic instructions. Lucky for him Dave is already texting away on his phone looking for his own solution.

"There's a bunch of guys I know up ahead a little ways, one of them has a group of three. I'll skip the first few holes and catch up to them. You girls have fun."

The kid behind the counter looks like he's going to protest, and then just kind of gives up on it. He's young, but he's starting to learn what everyone intelligent person figures out eventually – it's not worth it to stir shit up over stuff that doesn't matter.

"You sure?" asks Nicole.

"Yep, it's decided. Unless one of you is actually a hot guy in disguise?"

"No hot guys here," Grace says. Nicole and Margaret laugh along with her.

I don't know if it's just me or if it always happens when there's a group of girls with one guy in it, but it seems like there's no time when girls bond more than when they're making fun of a guy. Of course, saying anything in my defense would be social suicide. We golf for awhile and laugh when we all suck at it, and not much comes up.

"So Margaret, got your eyes on anyone for the summer?" Grace asks.

"Not really," Margaret says. "Guys are dicks." Her lip curls up into a half smile, half sneer. We haven't hung out much, but it's her tell: she does it when she's masking what she's really thinking. She's always dismissive and insulting, and it always comes along with that sneer. When she's honest about something (and still dismissive and insulting), she frowns.

"Not everyone," Grace says. "This guy probably isn't so bad." She pokes me with the grip end of her putter.

"I guess," Margaret says. "Not my type though."

"Come on then, what's your type?" Nicole says. "I mean, you're both from the Midwest, so you've got to have a lot in common. Eating cheese or tipping cows over or whatever. I think you'd be cute together. You could live on a farm or something, and have one of those pictures painted where he holds a pitchfork."

I ignore the string of insults. If you're from the Midwest and you've traveled to anywhere that isn't the Midwest, you've heard them all already. Mostly I'm just mystified by her belief that because we are the closest geographically (and not even that close, really) that we should be dating. I imagine a guy approaching her in a bar, saying "me too!" when Nicole tells them where she's from, then using his smart phone to Google the name of a neighboring town so he can keep the conversation going and get laid.

Margaret doesn't answer for a minute as she concentrates on putting her ball up a ramp and over a little moat around a hole themed with a plastic castle. She misses and her ball plunks into the water, which she takes out and shakes off before responding.

"I dunno. I like 'em cute I guess. If they're going to be dumb they might as well be nice to look at."

The girls laugh. I have the urge to hit my ball at her as hard as I can. I'm pretty sure I could play it off as an accident. Instead I take a deep breath, and hit my ball up the ramp and over the moat, where it lands on the other side, rolls through the castle doors, and close to the hole on the other side.

"I'm right here," I tell them. "And you don't know me well enough to know how smart or dumb I am."

"Trust me, slugger," Margaret punches me on the arm. "I've known enough guys that I have a pretty good guess. If I ever need a pro mini-golfer, though, I'll give you a call. That was a lucky shot."

"Maybe he's as good with his hands as he is with his putter," Grace volunteers. I can't tell if she's trying to set us up or just make everyone feel awkward.

"Lucky for me you'll never find out," I tell her.

Nicole takes her shot over the moat. It sails over the water fine, but clangs into the plastic castle without going through the door.

"You'd pay for the chance," Grace says.

"Are you selling?" I ask her.

Of course I'm not serious, but the girls all bristle as soon as I say it. I knew trying to defend myself would be a mistake.

"Don't be an asshole," Nicole says.

"Pervert," adds Margaret.

"You wish," says Grace. "Go home and fuck yourself."

What I want to say is, "Fuck all of you, you started it, if you're going to poke fun at me, I'm going to poke back." I'm smart enough not to say it out loud.

"Sorry. I didn't mean to be a dick."

"See, this is what I'm talking about," Margaret says. "All dicks and assholes, down to the last one."

"You into the girls, then?" asks Grace.

This gets me thinking. Supposedly it's more socially acceptable for two girls to hook up than two guys, but I don't know any lesbians who work at Wonderments. I wonder why that is. Maybe it's just because I stay in the guys' dorm and don't know that many girls, so they're all over the place and I just haven't noticed them. Maybe I see more gay guys than the average sample because I hang out with Dave. Maybe there's a big gay newsletter that let everyone gay and under thirty know to meet up at Wonderments this summer. I bet a story about the gay community working here could get into the local newspaper. Then there'd have to be an official statement about how Wonderments feels about it. There would be outrage no matter what they said. Half the country would threaten to boycott and then forget about it in a week. God bless the USA.

"No way," Margaret says. "Girls are bitchy too, especially when they get around each other."

I expect Nicole and Grace to take offense, but they agree. It seems like the perfect time to point out the current situation, but call me a fast learner: I keep my mouth shut.

"Dating is pretty simple," she says. "The cuter a guy is, the more he's allowed to talk. I'll listen to a hottie talk about sports or punching things or whatever for as long as he wants as long as he's a ten and he's good in bed. I'd date a pretty ugly dude if he just shut the fuck up all the time."

"Well, what about, you know?" Grace looks at me meaningfully. I now strongly suspect she's trying to hook us up.

"I'm still standing right here," I tell her.

Margaret looks at me. "Not that cute, but tends to stay pretty

50

quiet. He's okay I guess. Not for me though."

I try to think back to situations where it was a bunch of guys and one or two girls, and remember how we treated them. I can't think of anything. Growing up, my group of friends would have treated a girl like a queen. Well, that's not true. In reality, we spent a lot of time looking at girls outside our dejected little social group like they were queens, but if a girl had tried to be friends with us, we probably would have treated her like shit.

Not much else gets said for the rest of the night. I wish I could just stay silent, or better yet, just leave. But if I do either of those things it'll get weird for days or maybe for as long as I know these people, which I don't want. So I say just enough to be polite, which is what I should have been doing all along. I can't wait to get home. It's not that I don't like hanging out around other people, it's just that I like it even more when I get to leave.

11

I couldn't be happier to have the day off. By the end of the miniature golf party I was totally on edge, and even the morning after I can still feel it – my brain just trying to go to dark and angry places, trying to convince my more rational parts that everyone hates me, that nothing will turn out good ever again, that I'll be forgotten the moment I leave. On some level I understand that the playful back and forth and trading insults is just what people do. On the other hand, fuck them.

I'm sure I'll get over my seething for them. It always passes after a day or two. Today though, I'm giving my brain the day off. No friends, no work, no errands. At about 9:45 a.m. – the quietest time in the employee cafeteria, since everyone is done with breakfast but not eating lunch yet – I went and got myself a cheap pepperoni pizza, and that's going to keep me holed up in the room for the rest of the day without any interruptions. It's just me, a pizza, and a book called *Ultimate Portuguese*. I bought it because it had good reviews on Amazon, but I'm having difficulty holding in what it's trying to teach me. The grammar explanations are decent, but if I try to read more than a few pages at a time, I get lost. It's frustrating – normally remembering things comes easily to me.

I alternate between reading, eating and sleeping until sometime in the mid-afternoon from outside the door I hear, "Oh. Shit." It's Cory.

To make sure I got spend my day off in peace and quiet, I locked the door to our room and put one of Cory's scrunchies on the door handle. I put the book down and see his shadow moving under the crack in the door. I imagine him there, debating what to do in his mind and being torn. Knock and violate the Scrunchie Code by potentially interrupting some hot and steamy sex? Unlock the door and hope it was just a mistake? After a few minutes of waiting, I hear him walk down the hall and down the staircase to the main floor.

It worked. The feeling of triumph is fleeting and superficial, but I'll take it. I go back to the book and read for another half an hour or so before I unlock the door and take down the scrunchie. Maybe twenty minutes after that, Cory opens the door and comes into the room, obviously in a hurry.

"Oh thank God," he says. "I totally need to change for work tonight and I'm already running late. But when I came back earlier I saw you were busy so I decided to wait it out in the lobby. Nice, dude."

He high fives me, which I halfheartedly return because it's faster and easier than asking him why he's an insufferable douchebag. "Was she hot?" he asks me.

"Oh yeah, totally. She left just a few minutes ago."

It's always intrigued me that people change their vocabulary and their tone depending on who they're around. I notice that I definitely sound dumber when I'm interacting with Cory. I wonder how much you have to interact with someone before the damage is permanent, and if Cory is gaining any sort of intelligence by interacting with me. Probably not. Someone has to be the stupidest person in the group, after all.

He strips and starts digging around looking for his work uniform. I feel like this violates standard social etiquette between guys: If you absolutely must change your clothes in front of another dude, don't take your pants off until you have the other pair of pants ready to go. This cuts the amount of time you're exposing other people to man-ass to a minimum. I wonder if all Texans lack this basic social rule, or if it's just Cory.

53

"Details dude, come on."

"She was a total freak," I tell him. "Liked to be in charge and get rough. I thought she was going to break the bed. She left just a few minutes before you got here, it was crazy." I imagine two people trying to have rough sex on the bottom bunk of a bunk bed and can't picture it without someone knocking their head and turning it into a comedy sketch. The answer seems to satisfy him though.

"Shit, I'm so late. My manager is going to have my ass."

He runs out the door and shuts it behind him. I notice that he skipped his usual routine of suntan lotion before leaving and I wonder if he'll get sunburned, even though his shift is starting later in the day than usual. I hope he does.

* * *

The first floor showers in our dorm don't look disgusting. In fact, they're better than most public showers I've ever been in. There's a long row of sinks with a single mirror stretching along the wall to accommodate all of them. It looks nice but it strikes me as impractical. If any part of the glass gets cracked or broken, they'll have to replace the whole thing.

Each shower stall has its own walls the same way a toilet stall does, so even though they're public showers, you can get in, shower, and get out without anyone seeing you naked if you want to. That's more than you can say for most gym showers, at least.

The only thing that makes the showers disgusting is their reputation. I've overheard guys describing "midnight circle jerks" when supposedly all the gays in the dorm get together to jerk each other off, as well as girls coming into the showers to get gang banged. Since I've never heard these stories from anyone who has actually seen them happen and they sound like exaggerated pornos, I assume these stories are urban legends.

I've also heard stories of more mundane things – guys pissing in the showers, puking in the showers, passing out on the floor after a night of drinking, leaving their nasty boxers hanging in the stalls, stuff like that. Since I know guys who are in their twenties, I assume these stories are true.

Every time I open one of the stalls I imagine the horror stories of how disgusting the showers are here, but I have yet to actually see anything disgusting, of either the exotic porno or mundane frat guy variety. I still try to shower upstairs whenever I can.

12

Nicole agreed to go on a date with me, which came as a bit of a surprise. It's not a date in the respect that I expect anything romantic or sexual to happen, but it's a night out with a girl doing something enjoyable, which is better than however else I would have spent the night.

We're doing something that I love because it seems classy without getting expensive: a local theatre production of *Grease*. It has all the same basic appeal and inoffensiveness as going to see a movie, without being too much of a cliché. It also lets me rub elbows with the local rich white people. I doubt that will amount to anything, but it doesn't hurt. I'm always on the lookout for a good chance to take advantage of someone, and rich people have a lot to take advantage of.

I see Nicole stepping out of a taxi that just pulled up. She's wearing a short black dress and matching high heels and a pink shawl that matches her purse. Her hair is in a French braid that makes her neck look long and sensual. Going to a play instead of a movie is also an excuse for your date to dress hot, which is a good thing.

She looks more beautiful the closer she gets to me. Something strikes me as a bit off, and I realize that she's not wearing any jewelry. The outfit really needs a necklace to tie it together. I won't be buying her one. A different guy might notice and find her something simple but expensive, and win her heart in a grandiose display of affection. I have different plans for my money.

"I heard this play is really good," I tell her, handing her her ticket. The discussion of who is paying doesn't come up. "I think you'll like it."

"I haven't been to the theatre in at least a year. I miss it. My parents go all the time. They're big donors to one of the theatres back home, so they get invited to all the shows. They let me come along with them when I'm home."

I look around at the well-to-do people in the lobby, checking their jackets at the front desk, shaking hands with one another enthusiastically, or talking local politics. I imagine these people as Nicole's parents, and it makes me sick to my stomach.

"If your parents are so well off, why are you working at Wonderments?"

"The problem with taking your parents' money is that then you have to do what they say. I'll probably go back at the end of the summer, but for now it just feels good to get away and have a little bit of freedom. My dad's harmless, but he's a bit overprotective."

"How many guys have you gone out with this summer, again?" I ask.

"None that I plan on telling my dad about," she laughs. "I make sure the pictures I send home just have me and Grace and Dave and all his gay friends in them. He'd be calling every day to lecture me if he thought I was drinking and fornicating and fooling around." She puts her hands up and makes a scary face when she talks about all the things her dad is afraid she's doing. A few of the people nearby turn and look at us disapprovingly, and shuffle away to mutter about us from a safe distance.

"Won't they find out eventually?"

"Maybe," she says, "but I doubt it. They won't see me until the end of the summer and then I can tell them any story I want."

The lobby lights flash, signaling everyone to go and find their seats.

"See, my parents just assume I'm doing terrible things all the time, and lecture accordingly."

57

"You?" She pushes me a little, playfully. "You've gotten into less trouble than pretty much anyone here I know. We need to get you laid."

I want to ask her if she's offering, but I don't, partially because I don't want to sound like a creep and partially because I don't have the courage. We file into the theatre, which is still mostly empty despite the lobby lights flashing behind us a second time. We take good seats near the top and in the center. There's a large and heavy red curtain concealing the stage. I try to push any romantic feelings out of my mind, which would be useless even if they were reciprocated, and they almost certainly are not. The night can be enjoyable regardless. I want to make a joke or a witty comment to continue the intimate line of conversation but it's over; the moment has passed.

The house lights go down and our arms brush as we both try and use the armrest between us. I have the urge to try and hold her hand and see what happens, but I don't follow through on it.

* * *

Today is the big day. After all the planning I'm at spot G8 in the weekly flea market, which takes place in the giant abandoned parking lot of what was once a department store, then a movie theatre, and now sits dormant. I look at the work I've put in. Boxes of random stuff everywhere – the suits, lamps, video games and all the other crap I bought from the Salvation Army. Mixed in with all the junk are all my forgeries – signed books, valuable-looking but worthless coins, expensive trading cards and baseball card mock ups, the works.

The problem is, I'm not getting any sales. Hardly anyone is looking through my stuff. When I tried this the last time in a suburban white neighborhood it was a piece of cake. My spot drew in plenty of looky-loos and bargain hunters and the other people around me had similar setups (without the fake goods, I suppose), so I blended in pretty well.

That's not happening today. Most of the people here are poor. There's an immigrant farmer across from me selling vegetables and listening to a Spanish music station on his radio. There's an old woman next to me selling arts and crafts, and I'm hoping she sells enough to buy a comb to run through her hair. There's a deeply tanned white guy with overalls selling what looks to be nuts, bolts, nails and power tools. Another guy selling knock-off tennis shoes and attempting to repackage clearly used casual clothes as new.

Selling things at a flea market used to be a middle class activity. I wonder if that's over now, or if I'm just unlucky. I feel genuine pity for the people here. They fascinate me because they seem happy and relaxed about their place in life, unaware of how bad they have it. They remind me of my parents, fifteen years from retirement at best and not a penny to their name beyond what it takes to survive week to week.

I wonder if my dad will turn into this guy selling his fake Nike shoes and ten dollar suits. I wonder if my mom will be sitting at home, making bead necklaces or strawberry jam or knit hats in the hope of making a few dollars so she can buy cigarettes. They're middle aged and healthy now, but they won't stay that way forever. Nicole's parents will be fine, living the good life and donating to local theatre, owning a house they can grow old in and paying someone to come in once a week to clean up after them. Hell, my own mother would be lucky to have that job.

Suddenly I feel surrounded by my own future, like Ebenezer Scrooge in *A Christmas Carol*. It's time to leave. Almost no one has given a second glance to anything I have here, certainly not enough attention to discover any of the "valuable" things I've hidden among the boxes.

I go through all of my stuff and pick out the things I think I can still find a way to sell later – maybe I'll have to risk Craigslist or eBay after all. Once I have everything, I pack it all into one box and leave. No one took my name or information at the entrance and I won't be trying this again here, so I leave the junk behind. By the looks of it, the people here could use the donations anyway.

13

I'd love to find out what Nicole thought about going out with me. Tonight I'm working with Dave and Grace and some Russian guy I've never met. He's a substitute because Margaret is out sick. Dave and Grace are pissed at her and assume she's skipping work, but I doubt it. She's never done it before and she doesn't seem like the type to me. In high school there were kids that skipped class and kids that wanted to skip class but never did it because they were worried about getting in trouble. Margaret is definitely that second type of person.

I wonder if Nicole has talked to anyone about going to the play with me. If she did talk to anyone it would be Grace, but I can't ask her about it without it getting back to Nicole immediately and embarrassing me. I keep hoping her big mouth and desire for gossip will work in my favor and get her to come over and talk about it, but the hours pass and nothing happens. Either she doesn't know anything about it, or she's better at keeping her mouth shut than I thought and I've misjudged her. Either result sucks. Damn.

Dave's boyfriend comes in halfway through the night. He's tall and a bit chubby with dark skin and curly dark hair. I've seen him around a few times, but I can't remember his name. The more I think about it the more I think maybe I was just never told. He's never introduced himself to me, and Dave just calls him "my boyfriend." They haven't been dating that long.

"Hey sweetie," he says, walking up and touching him on the shoulder, "I was on this end of the park tonight and thought we should go have some dinner."

"I really do have you wrapped around my little finger, don't I?" Dave slaps him softly, smiling when he says it. He seems genuinely affectionate.

"Wrapped around something, anyway."

The night rush is going to be happening soon. A responsible manager would never go on break right now, especially since he just went on break an hour ago.

"Okay, back in a little bit," Dave says. "Won't be too long." Grace looks like she's going to object, but Dave is gone before she can say anything.

Generally speaking, retail employees are huge complainers when they see someone slacking off, and I've never understood it. They pay us by the hour. Having Dave here or not having Dave here changes almost nothing about the job. Maybe we have to spend a bit more time at our registers, which isn't any shittier and more meaningless than picking stuffed animals up off the floor, or sweeping up broken snow globes, or counting pogo stick keychains for inventory, or any other of the hundred meaningless tasks the job consists of. We show up, we do stuff for the time we're here, then we go home. Makes no difference to me if the place gets trashed or there's a line out the door. As long as I'm home relatively on time, I don't see the reason for getting upset.

I'm sure Grace is going to come over to complain, but the shop is starting to get busy, which glues her to her register. The Russian guy – his name is Sergei, but it doesn't matter as it's unlikely I'll ever see him again anyway – doesn't have a register of his own since he's just a substitute here for the night, so he's hanging up shirts when they get knocked off the rack, or answering questions for customers. I overhear a woman asking him why we don't have personalized license plates for her son (undoubtedly named "Kayson with a Y" or some other "original" name), but I can't hear his answer, which makes me sad. The correct answer of course is that her son has a dumb name that no one cares about but her, but he'll have to figure out something else to say.

I'm helping an old lady buy shirts for all her grandkids and keeping a count of my change theft when Sergei the forgettable Russian comes up next to me.

"I have a question," he says. His accent is thick and I can tell English is his second language, but that's pretty normal around here. His English a lot better than some of the employees', including some that have English as their first and only language.

"There's a lot of empties on the rack of shirts," he says.

"Okay."

"So what do I do with all the unused hookers?"

I stop and turn to look at him. A few people in line stop talking and look at him.

"What?" I asked.

"All the hookers that aren't being used. What do I do with them?" He says it louder. I see a few teenagers in line start to giggle, but Sergei doesn't see them and I deliberately ignore them.

"I don't understand," I tell him.

He's quiet for a few seconds, thinking. "You put the shirts on them, to hook them on the rack so people can buy them. Then they take them off. What do I do with the empty ones?"

Ah. "They're called 'hangers,'" I tell him. "Just put them in the closet when they're empty. We'll sort it out later."

"Hangers. Yes."

He goes back to his work.

Dave gets back from his break and jumps on a register in a bit of a panic. It's pretty unlikely a supervisor would notice the long lines, but if they did, and if they then noticed Dave was supposed to be there and wasn't, they would be pissed. I'm not sure what Dave was expecting to happen, though. You could set your clock by when the crowds get crazy around here. I guess I've just never gotten used to the fact that most people don't think ahead.

"Did I miss anything?" Dave asks me when it calms down a little.

"Not much. But you should probably let the temp know the difference between a hanger and a hooker, and be ready to explain it to management if anyone complains." A week goes by, and no one does. People might get offended more easily than they used to if my parents are to be believed, but they never stay offended for long.

* * *

When we show up to Knickers for drinks, the place looks different than usual. The house lights are down and there's a makeshift stage set up on one end. Candles line the stage and there's a painted black stool sitting alone. The whole thing looks like a weird sort of shrine.

"What's going on tonight?" I ask.

"Oh, shit," Dave says. "I forgot about this. Maybe I'll just go home. This is going to suck."

"Be nice," Grace says. "You don't know it's going to suck. It might be interesting."

We stumble through the crowd to a booth. There aren't any more people here than there normally would be for a Friday night, but it all feels more cramped than usual with the stage eating up so much floor space. Dave slides in first and Grace and Nicole sit down after him, with Margaret and me taking the other side. I doubt a waitress is even going to notice we came in. There's a sign at the front of the dining area that says "Please Seat Yourself," but I've never seen it turned to "Please Wait to Be Seated," even when it's busy.

"No, it really is going to suck, trust me," Dave says.

"How do you know?" Grace asks.

I'm happy to stay out of their argument.

"Because I was here last year, and it sucked then."

To her credit, the waitress finds us in the dark. Dave orders two pitchers of beer for the table, and Grace orders a margarita. Margaret orders a Coke.

"You worked here last year?" Nicole asks.

"How do you think I got this job?" Dave says. "It's not my stunning credentials. They just look at all the applicants and if you've worked here longer than everyone else, they put you in charge of a store. You don't have to work here that long, either.

Obviously most people don't come back to this shithole."

A skinny blonde girl with greasy hair and a thick flannel shirt takes the stage carrying an acoustic guitar. I wonder what kind of person brings a guitar across country to a summer job. Apparently, it's the same kind of person willing to wear long sleeved flannel in the middle of summer just to make a fashion statement.

"Is it just me, or did the female version of Kurt Cobain just take the stage?" Dave asks.

The girl adjusts the microphone for a minute, then plays a soft, pleading version of "Pumped Up Kicks" that sounds a lot better than the original. Dave might be in the mood to complain, but the song quiets the room, including our table. When she finishes she doesn't say anything else into the mic, she just walks offstage with her guitar. A round of cheers and applause comes from one table in the darkness – the table the girl returns to – and then the low hum of conversation returns to the room.

"You should let me paint you," Grace says to Margaret.

"What?"

"I'm serious," Grace says. "I'm trying out a new style. I'd love to do a portrait of you."

"Why me?" Margaret asks. Even in the low light, I can see her blushing a bit.

"I don't know," Grace says. "Sometimes I can just see it in my brain that someone would make a good subject. Just come over to my room and sit for a few hours and let me do some sketches."

"No thanks," Margaret says. "Not my thing." It's almost like being flattered annoys her, somehow.

"Why can't you do me?" Nicole asks. "I'll do it for you if you want."

Grace turns a critical eye on her. "I don't know. We'll see."

A tall, thin, young-looking guy takes the stage. I can barely see him because he's wearing all black, including pointed black glasses and a black beret.

"Oh for fuck's sake," Dave says. "He's like a walking cliché."

"Shhhhh," Nicole says.

The thin guy does some shitty beat poetry. The room keeps talking the entire time, and no one looks up at him. Grace is drawing idly in her sketch book, but I can't see what. She keeps looking over at Margaret.

No one applauds when the thin guy finishes and exits the stage. I almost want to clap just to reward him a little for his effort, but I'm afraid he'd think I was just making fun of him.

Only a few more people take the stage after him. Another girl comes up and performs an original song on her guitar, but it feels amateurish as a follow-up to the girl from earlier. Then a few drunk guys come up and do an a capella version of "Fight For Your Right" by the Beastie Boys that gets them booed off stage, and no one comes up after them. The open mic night doesn't officially end at any point, it just sort of... stops happening.

We keep drinking as the crowd thins out a bit, and eventually someone turns the regular lights back on, which Dave takes as our cue to leave. He pays the waitress, leaves a big tip, and we go outside. The ground is wet with dew and the air is damp. The sun will be up soon.

"Fuck," I say. "What time is it?"

"Almost six, I guess?" Margaret says with a giant, gaping yawn.

"I have to work tonight," I say. "I am so screwed."

"Us too," Grace says, speaking for all the girls.

"Not me, suckers," Dave says. "Suck it up. The memories are worth a few tired shifts, right?"

He didn't even want to be here in the first place. I'm too tired to point it out.

"Why didn't they kick us out sooner? Aren't they legally obligated to close at some point?"

Dave claps me on the back. "Knickers is an employee rec center, not a bar. Open twenty-four hours, baby."

"Okay, goodnight," Nicole says with a half-hearted wave.

Dave and I walk home as the sun rises.

14

Tonight I'm visiting a local print shop. It's about two hours before close, and I hope I have the timing right. It's tricky – I have to show up after anyone important or intelligent has left, but leave enough time that the retail worker drone can do what I ask him to do. As far as jobs that will let you get away with shit go, working in a print shop is a pretty good choice. At my last job I made hundreds of dollars off t-shirts based on sports teams, comic book characters, and TV shows before the manager guessed what I was up to and asked me to quit. He stopped believing the lie that all the shirts I was making were for personal use after I made a hundred shirts in a month.

I'd just get a job here and do it myself if Wonderments didn't work us seventy hours a week. Since I can't do it myself, I'm going to have to rely on the unkempt guy behind the counter.

"I don't think I can help you, sir." This worker drone is not being cooperative. It could be for any number of reasons: too stupid to use the machinery, too lazy to bother, too smart to fall for my scam, too behind on his work to make time for me, or just too stubborn to break protocol. But I'm not giving up yet.

"Look. My niece has an art project tomorrow that they need these shirts for. If they don't do it tomorrow they'll never get the shirts made and pictures taken for the contest they're trying to enter. If I don't bring the shirts my niece's teacher is going to kill me. Have you ever dealt with an angry elementary school teacher and a room full of sad third graders? You have to help me. Please."

"I don't know," he says. "I'm pretty sure we're not allowed to put copyrighted material on the shirts."

"It's for a contest," I say. "We have permission." I show him my phone, which has a grainy picture that says "Wonderments Sweatshirt Contest!" and some small text that's indecipherable. There is no such contest, but I think it convinces him.

"It takes three to five days anyway. I'm really sorry."

I anticipated this. Print shops take all their orders, and they say three to five days so they only have to fire up the hot press once – it saves them time and gives them some flexibility if things happen to get busy. Pretty much any time someone gives you a time estimate on anything – production time, shipping, printing – they're giving you an estimate that assumes 10% of the time will be spent doing the promised service, and 90% of the time will be spent screwing up, goofing off, or otherwise fucking around. If you tell someone the work will take a lot of time to do, they grit their teeth and deal with it. If you tell them it'll be done quickly and then you're a little bit late, they get pissed.

"I used to work at a place like this," I tell him. "I know you can do this job in a few hours. You're not busy. Please?" He still seems hesitant. "Look, can I give you something else for your trouble? This is really important. I don't want to disappoint those kids." I pull a $25 gift card to Olive Garden out of my wallet. It's empty, but he doesn't know that. "Please."

"I can't take that," he says. "But I'll see what I can do."

"Thank you so much. I owe you one."

He takes my name, my phone number, and my order. I walk across the street to the Subway to sit and wait for him to call me. The kid working here doesn't hassle me or make me order anything. Minimum wage is barely enough to convince him to make decent sandwiches. Getting rid of loiterers is definitely above his pay grade.

An hour and a half later, I get the call that my order is done.

"Hey, it took me a bit of extra work but I managed to get them all done for you," he says. It's not a complaint. I heard once that the key to getting someone to like you is to ask them to do things for you. Once they do you a few favors, the brain takes over and says "well, I must like them, why would I do favors for someone I didn't like?" I'm not sure if it's true, but it seems to have done the trick this time. I pay him, thank him again, and leave with my new unauthorized Wonderments sweatshirts.

* * *

The bouncer at Knickers is standing squarely in front of the entrance with his arms folded, practicing his best look of stoicism while half a dozen teenage girls stand in front of him alternating between yelling, pouting, and arguing.

"Come on, let us in," the pack leader says. She's maybe five and a half feet tall, wearing hooker boots with massive heels to try and look taller. She doesn't move around much. My guess is that when she walks, her legs wobble like a newborn fawn. "We have ID." There is no chance this girl is over eighteen. One or two of the girls in the group might be, but I doubt it.

"I can't let you in without your employee ID," the bouncer says. It's pretty obvious that the girls are trying to use fake ID to get in, which is why they aren't using their work IDs to begin with. I don't think it would be too hard to make a fake "regular" Wonderments ID to use instead of the ones that mark them as minors, but these girls don't seem too bright.

"Come on," the girl says. "Please?"

She has no good argument. Begging doesn't work either. One of the other girls in the group, a taller girl with a thin face and a long, angular nose, says, "I'll show you my tits if you let us in. And we won't drink anything."

The bouncer sighs. "Please just go home. And don't flash anyone. I'm serious. If you try it I'll have security haul you up to the front office and call your parents."

"Hey, fuck you man," the skinny girl says. She doesn't flash him.

"Give me back my ID then," the leader says. "We're leaving,"

"No," he says. "Go home."

"What do you mean, no?" she says. She tries to get up into his face and look menacing, but she's still too short even with help from the boots.

"I mean," he says, "no, you cannot have your fake-ass ID back. Stay in school, kid."

She snaps. She starts hitting him with flailing, ineffective slaps, mostly on the arms. The motion makes her wobble in the boots and she almost knocks herself over. Her friends stop her after a few seconds, and they leave.

I walk up and hand him my ID. "Fun night, huh?"

"Always exciting," he says.

"What's your name, anyway? It seems like you're the only doorman around here." I expect him to tell me some ridiculous tough guy name, like Bruno or Tank.

"It's Oliver," he says, shaking my hand. It hurts. Some guys will intentionally try to shake your hand too hard because they think it's some bullshit display of dominance, but I get the sense that Oliver genuinely just doesn't know his own strength.

"Well, good to meet you. Thanks for caring enough to not let the kids sneak in."

"I have a little sister and a little brother," he says. "I know the kind of shit they try and get into."

I take back my ID and walk into the restaurant area, ignoring the sign that says "Please Wait To Be Seated." Nicole is sitting in a booth near the door with Dave and a bunch of guys I don't know. I'm not sure if the guys are here for Nicole or Dave – it's a toss up.

"I mean, look, are you going to fuck him or not? You're totally going to fuck him." Dave jabs Nicole in the ribs when he says this.

"No! Shut up." Nicole laughs while looking genuinely offended.

"I'll fuck him then. It'll be the night of his life. I mean, not because of anything I do. Just because I bet his life is boring as an old folks' home."

I sit down and say "hey" to everyone at the table. Everyone greets me back; no one bothers to share names.

"What are you arguing about?" I don't care. The words just come out of my mouth.

"We're arguing over which one of us is going to fuck you," Dave says. Nicole punches him in arm, hard.

"What?" I'm not really surprised by Dave's comment. Growing up in a small conservative town in upstate New York and also being a complete asshole (like every other Dave I've ever met), he gets off on making people feel uncomfortable about the fact that he's gay. I can't say I blame him. People's unreasonable reactions to it are amusing. "Fuck you," I say.

"Exactly," Dave says.

The waitress shows up to take our order before things get awkward. She asks what we want to drink (I get a Coke, Nicole and Dave get a pitcher of beer, and I sort out who at the table is trying to fuck Nicole and who is trying to fuck Dave based on whether they order beer or fruity cocktails) and leaves. This annoys me – Knickers has a full menu during the day, but by the time we get out of work after closing, there are only drinks and appetizers on the menu. I'm sure everyone knows what they want; she could have taken our order.

"Are you coming to the Wave Blast or what? I'm going to give away your fucking ticket if you don't commit soon, I swear." Dave has been pestering everyone about it for a few weeks already, but this is the first time I remember him asking me directly. He does not seem to realize this.

"Fine, fine. I'm in."

The Wave Blast is the annual Fourth of July employee-only party that happens after the water park closes. One of the large wading pools has a walk-up bar in the middle of it, which they'll keep open. Basically, it's an excuse for everyone to put on bathing suits and get shitfaced. I dislike the idea of being in a bathing suit around my coworkers, but I plan to counteract this by getting drunk as quickly as possible.

"Great," Nicole says. "We can share a locker."

"Sure."

The waitress finally returns and takes our order, and the rest of the night passes. I don't do so well with large groups. They laugh and joke and get more loud and more drunk the longer I'm there, and I just try to make polite conversation and not make an ass out of myself. I leave before everyone finds someone to take home and fuck, and do my best not to think about it. I hate the way I feel about any sort of romantic hook-up. I want to be calm and cool and just okay with it all, but if I'm honest, I feel mostly jealousy with a healthy dose of judgment, based on what I was taught by a religion I no longer believe in. I'm careful to make sure it doesn't impact my relationships, but it still bangs around in my brain. Maybe it always will.

The bar is on one side of the park and the men's employee dorms are on the other, so you're allowed to cut through. It's quiet, peaceful. There's something that is very serene about walking around here at night. Looking at the shut down rides, roller coasters, shops, and games, seeing it all dark, resting, asleep. Tomorrow, it will be back to blaring lights and sirens and yelling, laughing tourists, but for now, it's calm.

15

I'm in the closet folding shirts. Since it's a job that is relatively quiet, away from all the customers, easy to slack off at, and generally takes a long time, it's one of the most coveted jobs at The Jolly Tinker. There's always a little squabble for it whenever new shirts come in, and as a result I don't usually do it, since it's just easier to let someone else have their way. I don't really care which job I have to end up doing on any given day.

I'm not surprised when the door opens up behind me. Margaret steps in, which requires her to shove me a little bit and stand a lot closer than I'm comfortable with. If the closet were organized, it might be able to fit two people. It never is, and the few times someone attempted to organize it, it was trashed a few days later anyway. When new merch comes in by the day and sells out just as fast, there's no reason to keep your stock rooms looking pretty. Margaret shuts the door behind her. Standing here, surrounded by dust and dirt and overpriced shirts, both of us smelling like sweat, it reminds me of a depressing version of those scenes in movies where two kids get put in a closet to play seven minutes in heaven. If this is seven minutes in hell, Margaret doesn't seem to notice.

"You have to switch jobs with me," she says. "Go run a register or sweep the floors or something. Just let me have this."

"Why?" I ask. "What happened?"

"It's Dave," she says. "He won't shut up about his new boyfriend and I just can't take it anymore."

"You have a problem with gay people?" I ask. It's never come up before, so it seems odd.

"No." She shoves her way in next to me so she can also get at the pile of unfolded shirts. There is most definitely not enough room in here for two people. I can smell her. It's the smell of cafeteria grease and something else I can't identify that was once sweet but is now stale. It's not unpleasant. "I have a problem with that much PDA. He just goes on and on. Such a sweetheart this, so romantic that... it's been like an hour and he won't shut up about it."

Out of curiosity, I check my watch. I don't remember Dave saying anything about his boyfriend before I was in the closet, and I've been in here for about twenty minutes. I know better than to correct her version of the story.

"So he's got a crush. Is that such a big deal? Everyone gets that way when they meet someone new that they like."

"I don't," she says. "Not everyone has a shiny new boyfriend and wants to hear about that stuff nonstop. I swear whenever he's not with the guy, which, fuck him for taking twice as many breaks a day as he's supposed to by the way, he's talking about him. I'd tell him to fuck and get it out of his system, but I'm sure if he took my advice we'd all have to hear about it later."

I suspect she's exaggerating, but it *is* Dave, so maybe she's right.

"Sure, you can do shirts for awhile. Just hide out here until he gets it out of his system. I'm sure it won't be too long."

"I might be in here for a month," she says. "Remember to slide me some food under the door or something."

I finish the shirt that I had started and add it to the stack. "Will do."

"Seriously though, thanks." She touches my shoulder when she says it. It's an awkward gesture, since there's not really room for her to have full range of motion without elbowing me.

I don't say anything else and leave the closet. I'm always

surprised at how cool the rest of the store feels after I've been in the shirt closet, even though it's the middle of the summer.

Dave is indeed talking about his new boyfriend. He's trapped Grace into the conversation by the looks of it, but she doesn't seem to mind. Apparently he took his boyfriend to one of the fancy restaurants in town, some place I've never heard of. I'm not interested in the conversation, but it doesn't bother me either. I imagine Margaret alone in the closet and I wonder what happened to make her so cynical. I'll probably never know. I'm okay with that.

* * *

The Falcon is by far the most popular ride in the park. It's relatively new (debuted two years ago), it's fast, and it's huge. It's the only roller coaster in the park that consistently gets on anyone's list of "Top Ten Roller Coasters in the U.S.A." It's the reason people travel from states away to come to Wonderments, and the reason roller coaster enthusiast clubs show up en masse with their campers and synchronized outfits and hats with the club name on them. Average wait time on a Saturday: four hours.

I stroll up to the side gate to the park and see at least a hundred people in line. This is nothing – there will be at least as many at each of the other side entrances to the park and far more at the main entrance. The poor sucker who works the gate in the morning rush is walking down the line telling people over and over that they're not allowed to bring any food or drink into the park. People always get pissed at that. The park cites safety regulations, but everyone knows they only do it because all the food and drinks are ludicrously marked up inside. They don't even let you bring in water.

A fat woman is busy screaming at the kid about her water bottle and how it's bullshit and she's paying to get in and so she can take in whatever she wants and the customer is always right. The kid says, no, he has to comply with safety regulations, and points to a free water fountain just inside the gate and tells her that she can refill her water bottle for free as soon as she gets inside. He keeps emphasizing the "free" part since he knows everyone thinks the

74

park is there purely to rip them off. Not that that'll keep anyone from coming.

She screams at him for a minute longer and I try not to say anything as I walk up, but still smile a bit. I make sure I keep a fair distance. The kid is a stoic, unflinching statue as the woman unleashes a string of profanity in his face. He says, "Ma'am, I can get my manager for you if you like, but we can't let you in the park with any outside food or drink."

She finally opens her water bottle and holds it out at arm's length and dumps it, looking around as if saying, "Look at what this asshole is making me do, can you believe it?" When the bottle is mostly empty she starts shaking it, deliberately splashing some of it on him as he stands there.

"Thank you ma'am, enjoy your day."

"Fuck you, you little prick." The people in line around her bristle. Any sympathy the crowd may have had for the woman dissipates when the many nearby parents realize the new words they're going to have to explain to their kids because of her.

The gate worker starts to walk back to the gate and I catch up and walk with him. "So what's the worst thing anyone's ever thrown at you?" I ask.

"I got hit in the chest with a Starbucks coffee a few weeks ago. We keep a change of shirts in the booth in the morning just in case anyone hits us with anything that stains."

"Wow, that sucks."

"Yeah, I guess. I heard last year a girl got hit in the head with a full can of Coke and spent the day at the med center."

We walk past the long line up to the gate, and I show him my work badge. I'm wearing normal clothes, but since the guys' and girls' dorms, human resources, and the cafeteria are all in different places and only easily accessible to each other by cutting through the park, an employee badge will get you in any time, work clothes or not. He opens the gate for me.

"Thanks." He nods at me and shuts the gate again.

I look at my phone. 8:50 a.m. The park officially opens in ten minutes. I stroll down the main pathway, past employees opening windows on food carts and turning the lights on to various carnival games. Most of the employees look exhausted and hung over.

Lucky for them not too many people are going to want cotton candy and hot dogs at 9 a.m., but they're there just in case.

I round a corner and there it is: The Falcon. I walk up to the other half a dozen or so people already standing in line. They have the same idea I do. A few minutes pass and the National Anthem starts. The gates are open. We can hear screaming as the people who were near the front of the gates sprint in an attempt to get to The Falcon before anyone else – to skip that four hour wait, and maybe even be able to sit at the front. They round the corner and see us already standing there. If it upsets them, they're too out of breath to say anything. The first set of cars rolls up, and we get on.

16

Getting Nicole alone is no easy task. Our work schedules didn't put us on the same shift for a few days, and now that we're both here Grace is here too, which means the two of them are talking and pretty much ignoring me. They're both friendly and I get along with them, but I have no illusions – I know that when it comes to having someone to socialize with at work, they'll choose me over Margaret but other than that I'm last in line. They consider me a friend purely because of proximity. We'll have fun as long as we're all in the same space, but nothing lasting is being forged here.

I should know better and let my date with Nicole go and not bring it up again. It was pleasant. It's a good memory. If she was into me, she'd be putting forth the effort to get ahold of me more. As it is, I'll be resisting the urge to ask her if she had fun or if she was just too polite to say no when I asked her. I doubt she even thinks of it as a date, but it'll keep bothering me until I at least try to get a second date. It's better to get shot down and move on than pine for her the whole summer. At the bare minimum, it'll distract me until I ask her.

I keep waiting for them to separate, but Grace is an expert on wasting time at work. She fills the boxes of candy in front of Nicole's register, then washes the counter with a rag, then dusts a nearby shelf, each activity slowed to a crawl by conversation. She's talking about some hobby shop in town and Nicole is doing most of the listening. It seems pretty clear her intent is to spend the whole night attached to Nicole so she can talk about whatever self-important bullshit pops into her head. Fuck it. I'm going in. I go over to her register, leaning on the stool behind the counter.

"I am so bored tonight." I loathe people who complain about being bored, but I can't think of any other way to enter the conversation gracefully. There's no better universal conversation starter than how much work sucks.

"I know, right?" Grace says. "At least it's not too busy tonight. I hope we can get out of here fast. Do you think anyone would notice if we shut the doors early?"

"Probably," I say. Not to mention we'd probably be fired for trying it if we got caught, or at the very least put under a microscope for the rest of the summer. It's not even close to worth it. "We'll rush through the cleaning and take down a few of the registers early. See if we can finish up quickly without getting in trouble."

They both agree. "What did you think of the play the other night?" I ask Nicole.

"You went to a play together?" Grace asks. "How come I wasn't invited?" Well, that's not a good sign. I assume that if it felt at all romantic to Nicole, she would have told Grace about it.

"It was kind of a last minute thing. I could only get two tickets." It's a lie, and I realize almost immediately that it'll be transparent to Nicole if she thinks about it at all. The theater wasn't even full.

"It was fun," she says. "I don't think I've ever been to a play without my parents before." I can't tell if she's just letting my white lie go, or if she thinks it's the truth, or if it just doesn't occur to her to think about it.

"Maybe we can all go to something later this summer," I suggest. "I'll see if I can get more tickets and we can all go as a group."

That did not go at all the way I was hoping it would. We never even got to the point where I could try and ask her out on a second date – or is it a first date, if she didn't count the last one? Either way, it's pretty evident she has no interest. She would have told Grace. She would have spent time with me sooner. She'd be asking me if I wanted to do something again. At this point I'm just lucky that she's so non-confrontational about rejection. Either that or I'm so far off her radar that she doesn't even realize she's rejecting me. Either way I'm going to just take it for what it is and move on without thinking about her anymore. I hope.

17

Every night after sunset, about an hour before the park closes, there's the Wonderments Laser Light Show Spectacular. For someone looking to make a few not-so-legitimate dollars, it's the perfect opportunity. It draws people from all over the park into a huge crowd. It's dark and noisy. And no one at all is looking at me. It's a pickpocket's dream, but I'm no pickpocket. I don't like the idea of going to jail just for the contents of someone's nearly empty wallet. Also, just as a general rule you should never steal anything that you can convince someone to give to you willingly.

So here I am, pushing an official Wonderments merchandise cart, wearing a neon glow-necklace and a pair of glow in the dark sunglasses. Wonderments really does sell every novelty you can think of.

The hardest part was getting the cart. Normally you have to check out a cart when you get assigned to sell Wonderments merch, and then check it back in when you're done, along with all the money you made. Three weeks into the summer I discovered a loophole: there's a vehicle and cart graveyard near the maintenance shack. Wheels snap, doors jam, some kid pukes on the side or whatever. When something happens, you drop the cart off at the shack, report it damaged, and go on your merry way. That lets a guy like me sneak in, collect one of the "damaged" carts that just needs the hand brake fixed or a good spray wash, and use it without anyone noticing.

It wouldn't work at all if the maintenance guys were diligent in fixing the carts, but Wonderments assumes that a certain number of carts are going to be in need of repair at any given time. If the total number of damaged carts is at an acceptable number for management, maintenance is going to be off doing something else – fixing broken fryers, routine checks to make sure the roller coasters aren't about to break and start killing people, stuff like that. That's the beauty of working inside a big corporation: everyone gets assigned their one thing to do like a good little cog, but no one looks at the whole machine. Simply lying and sounding confident will let you get away with almost anything because no one is accountable; everyone is just trying to get you out of the way so they never have to deal with you again.

So that brings me to tonight. Light show, cart, and selling some middle-aged man a faux Wonderments sweatshirt at a massive markup.

"They're forty dollars each, sir," I say. He nods absently and hands me a hundred dollar bill almost without looking. He's too engrossed by the laser light show, which is currently flashing an animated steam locomotive while a few lines from "C'mon 'N Ride It" by the Quad City DJs blast on all the speakers.

"Thank you sir. What size would you like?"

"One extra large and uhh..." he looks down at his young daughter. "A medium I guess. She'll grow into it." He practically has to yell for me even to hear him. He's still barely looking at me.

I hand him the shirts and his $20 in change. "Thank you very much, have a great night!"

He finally looks over as he collects his things. "Thanks, uh... Cory."

A few weeks ago Cory lost his name tag and had to have a new one made. I found his old one under the bed a few days later and kept it. It's unlikely anyone would have reason to report me or anything, but it never hurts to be extra cautious, especially when it costs nothing.

I disappear back into the crowd. Another guy with a cart waves to me. He's selling obnoxious glow sticks, pinwheels and noisemakers certain to fill parents with buyer's remorse. The difference between him and me is that in his case, Wonderments is pocketing all the profits. Since it cost me $8 per shirt and I had forty shirts made, I'll have $1,280 by the end of the night. Not bad at all for an hour's work.

* * *

Sunny days are great if you want to spend a day at an amusement park riding rides, having fun with your friends and family, and forget that soon you'll be back to work at a job you hate. If you're working at an amusement park, however, sunny days are the worst. There's nothing to do because everyone is too busy out having fun to do any shopping. The work uniforms are thick and you end up covered in sweat but still hot. Some of the bigger stores have air conditioning, but not us. All we have is a ton of open doors. It's a shoplifter's dream, and probably explains why we don't sell anything worth shoplifting.

I walk by our boxes of trinkets and keychains and notice a few of the trays are close to empty. I don't know how it happens. I can't remember selling any of it. I have no idea who, at any age, says, "what I need is a keychain with a tiny pink plastic pogo stick on it," but there it is, the tray half empty. Nearby similar merchandise – keychains with tiny naked babies on them on the left side and keychains with "ROCKIN'!" in black font on a rainbow-colored plaque on the right – are both still full.

I head toward the supply closet. It reminds me of my dad's shed growing up, only a lot narrower. Cheap boards serve as shelving that goes from floor to ceiling and gets stuffed with merchandise thrown into brown paper bags and labeled in black permanent marker. I can feel the dust in my nose immediately. No one tries to clean in here. Margaret got told to organize it earlier in the summer, did a fine job, and said nothing as it returned to total chaos within a week.

I open the door. All the way in the back is Grace, perched on a stool, legs crossed. She has her elbow resting on her knee, holding a book up in front of her at an angle like she's posing for a photographer. I wouldn't be surprised if she asked me to take a picture of her to put up on her Facebook page or her Twitter or wherever else she undoubtedly plasters selfies on the internet. The book has a splash of red and white on the cover and the title *Power of Art*.

It takes a few seconds before she looks up at me. "Yeah? What's up?" She checks the time on her phone. "I've still got ten minutes for break."

I look at the various bags for the keychains and seem to find just about anything else. Bags labeled "Mini Mirrors," "Stamp Set," and "Wrist Bands." I'm pretty sure there's stuff in here that we don't even have out on the floor.

"You're taking a break and spending it in here of all places? It's hot as hell in here, and it smells like someone killed a mold monster and this is where they hid the corpse."

"I guess. But this is the quietest place in the store and I didn't feel like wasting half my break walking to one of the employee break areas." It's against company policy for employees to take breaks, smoke, engage in "displays of affection," or generally do anything other than look like a soulless worker drone in public areas. I almost point out to her that she and Nicole routinely take way longer than the allotted time on breaks, but I think better of it.

"Well, however you want to spend your breaks is up to you, I guess. I didn't peg you for much of a reader, to be honest."

"What's that supposed to mean?"

I avoid her glare by continuing to look for the keychains, and find them next to a bag labeled "Stress BallZ." "BallZ" is underlined and there's a drawing of oversized hairy testicles under the "Z."

"Nothing," I say.

"Well, I like reading, and I like painting even more," she says. She holds up the book. "So, book on famous painters," which she opens again. "That I really want to read some more of before my break is over." She sticks her nose back in the book, and I take the bag of keychains with me back out onto the floor.

* * *

83

By the time we've shoved out the last customer and locked the doors behind them, I'm just tired. This job is a great cover for all the other stuff I have going on, but sometimes I wonder if it's worth it. My feet hurt after twelve hours standing on them. I thought that after a few days I would get used to it and it would start to feel normal. It blows my mind that people either choose to or are forced to do this kind of work for their entire lives. Tossed bull riders don't need an aspirin as bad as I do right now.

"Hey," Margaret says, walking by with a handful of stuffed animals to restock some empty spaces on the back wall. "Are you guys going to the employee ride night tonight?"

I forgot there even was one.

"Fuck no," Dave says. "It's just all the shitty carnival rides. There's not even any booze."

Getting on any sort of carnival ride is certainly one of the worst activities you can pair with drinking alcohol. It's never happened to me, but you always hear about that guy that throws up on the Gravitron and manages to get puke on twenty people at once.

"I'm going if either of you want to come," Margaret offers. "I think it'll be fun. I always loved those traveling carnivals when I was a kid. We had one that would come to town every summer and set up in the mall parking lot. Teacups, Tilt-a-Whirl, all those old rides, plus overpriced junk food and ripoff carnival games."

Don't get me wrong, I love a good carnival game. Basketball shootouts with smaller than regulation hoops, weighted baseballs, ping pong ball tosses with mirrors and trick geometry, you name it. If there's a carnival game where the prize is worth more than the entry fee, you can be certain there's some trick that keeps people from winning as often as it seems like they should. The whole thing makes me smile. Businesses conning people and justifying it as selling people entertainment. People shelling out cash and knowing they're getting conned and justifying it because they're having fun. It's supposedly a ripoff, but everyone involved is walking away with what they wanted, so no one puts a stop to it. It's perfect.

"I'm going home after we close," I say. "All those rides made me throw up when I was a kid. I'm pretty sure my dad used to feed me cotton candy and put me on those rides just to see what color I'd puke up."

"Gross," Margaret says.

"That's pretty fucked up," says Dave.

"It was kind of awesome," I admit. "It's not like he forced me. I wanted junk food, I wanted to go on the rides, and I was okay with how that turned out. Anyway, it's not for me anymore."

Dave opens his register and starts counting it down. He's supposed to do it in the closet, but the doors are locked at this point, so it doesn't matter much I guess. "I'm going down to Knickers, drinking beer until I have a solid buzz, and seeing if I can find myself an employee ride of my own."

"Don't you have a boyfriend now?" Margaret asks. "Or is there some gay rule I don't know about?"

"I guess I do," says Dave. "But he's dodging the whole conversation about being exclusive. I don't know what's going on. He seems like a sweetheart, but he's doing the whole 'afraid of commitment' thing. I'm thinking that maybe a little jealousy is just what the doctor ordered."

I can tell Margaret is about to go off. It won't accomplish anything, but I know she just can't help it. She'll have to say her piece, and then there will be an argument, and then it'll be longer before I get to go home. The fact that she doesn't know when to shut up makes me think less of her. It's like she has no control over her own mouth.

"Why don't you count down your drawer too?" I ask her. Dave has his head down as he counts up the bills, so I give her a look that says "Don't fucking start anything" and hope she gets it. "I really want to get out of here. Let's leave the sweeping for the morning crew. Nothing happens in here before noon anyway."

"Okay, sure," Margaret says. I'm not sure if she took the hint to leave it alone, or if it's just that finishing work is a stronger desire than being a bitch about something that is none of her business. She grabs her drawer and heads to the closet. As soon as the door shuts I turn to Dave.

"So, do you just like pissing her off, or what?"

"Yeah, I guess," Dave says, "Sometimes when I see a pot of

shit, I just have to stir it, you know?"

"You're not even going out tonight, are you."

He laughs. "Yeah, I'm going out. Going to get buzzed and listen to some music and hang out for awhile. No fucking around though. I like this guy. If it gets messed up, it's going to be on him, not me. It'd be nice to be in a relationship that works for once. He lives not too far from my hometown, too, so if we hit it off maybe it can last longer than the summer."

"Good luck," I tell him. "I don't mind being single for the summer. So much drama. Chances are so small any of it lasts, anyway."

"Yeah, right," he says. "You can play it cool if you want, but I bet you'd totally jump on it if a cute enough girl came by."

I laugh it off, but he's probably right. It annoys me.

18

I can hear a soft groan coming from inside my room before I even get the door open. It's been a long night and I am not in the mood for this shit. I open the door expecting the worst, but it's just Cory by himself. He's balled up on his top bunk, spooning with a plastic trash can from god knows where.

"Uhhhh.... hi."

Cory holds his hand up in a sort of reverse wave acknowledgment. I kick my shoes off. I'm not sure why he had the light on since he's lying in bed, but I am very ready to get some sleep.

"I don't feel so good, dude." Well, that explains the trash can, I guess.

"Do you want the bottom bunk?" I ask. It would feel weird to me to switch beds with someone else if it was actually my pillows, sheets, and blankets, but since it's all identical shitty Wonderments-issue stuff, it bothers me a lot less. I read somewhere that you should change your sheets twice a month. I try and remember seeing anyone here ever changing their sheets or carrying them to get washed. I can't.

"No, I'm good," he says. He rolls over and most decidedly does not look good. He looks sweaty, exhausted, and like he hasn't kept anything down in ages.

"You look like shit," I tell him. "What's wrong? Too much to drink?"

"Nah, I haven't been drinking all week. Just some kind of flu or food poisoning or something."

"Well, hopefully it's not contagious."

I sit down on my bed and hope I can get to sleep without any more conversation.

"I'm starving, though. I haven't been out of bed all day." I think back to the morning, when I woke up, took a shower, got dressed for work, and left. Cory wasn't here when I woke up and I didn't see him at any point.

"Can you go to the cafeteria and grab me a pizza? We can split it if you want. There's money in my wallet on the desk." I'm only a few years older than Cory but now I feel decades older. Only a teenager would think that a cheap and greasy pizza was a quality remedy for an upset stomach. Hell, even thinking that is unfairly giving teenagers a bad name.

"Eating that shitty pizza is probably the reason you're sick in the first place," I point out.

"Yeah, but it's probably not any worse than any of the other stuff they have down there."

"Look, I'll run downstairs to the employee store and microwave you some soup and get you some juice and some NyQuil and stuff." Mostly I just don't want to walk all the way through the park to the employee cafeteria. I check my phone. "I'm pretty sure the cafeteria is closed by now anyway."

"What? What time is it?"

"It's after 1 a.m."

"Fuck my life," he says. "I have to be at work in like eight hours."

"Good luck with that," I tell him. "I'll be back with some food in a few minutes. Don't puke on my bed."

At the store downstairs, there's a handwritten sign that says "Bathroom – Back in five minutes" and the door is locked. I stand outside and wait at least ten minutes. No one comes back. I consider walking down the hall to check the men's room but first I bang on the door a few times, loudly. Sure enough, after a minute I can hear the door unlocking for the inside and the overnight cashier opens the door and snatches down the sign.

"Sorry man, I forgot the sign was up."

Of course his excuse is complete bullshit. There's only one way in and out of the place and definitely no reason to ever keep the door shut while you're inside. Unless he was taking a dump on the floor in here somewhere, he was totally using the sign as an excuse to do... what, I have no idea. He probably sees three or four people a night at the most, and never sees anyone who cares even a little about what he's doing in here. On some level I'm impressed that this guy has taken the job with the least amount of responsibility possible and still found a way to slack off even more.

I find the cup of soup first and start it going in the microwave.

"Hey, you've got to pay for that," the slacker reminds me.

I hold my hands up in mock defense. "Don't worry, I will." While the soup is heating up I gather up the rest of the stuff: orange juice, aspirin, cough syrup, a box of some kind of off-brand fruity cereal bars. I pay for it all and head out.

On the way out, I ask, "did you want me to shut the door and put the sign back up?"

The clerk appears to genuinely think about it and doesn't realize I'm subtly calling him a jackass. "No, I'm good," he says.

Back in the room, the light is still on, but Cory has passed out and the trash can has fallen to the floor. I stack all his food on the dresser and take just enough money out of his wallet to cover it. Then I put the trash can back up in his bed next to him, turn out the lights, and fall asleep almost immediately.

* * *

"Pode repetir, por favor?" I rewind the audio file a bit and listen to it again. "Pode repetir, por favor?" I say again. I just can't make it sound like the guy in the audiobook. I hope it's close enough. It's Portuguese for "Can you repeat that, please?" A phrase that I suspect I'll be using often in Brazil. The tape continues. "Repeat after me. *Desculpe eu nao entendo.* It means, 'Sorry, I don't understand.'"

I pull the headphones out of my ears and lie back in bed. Apparently this entire chapter is about teaching me how to effectively tell people in Portuguese that I don't speak Portuguese. Something tells me they'll be able to figure that out when I have to interact with everyone using charades.

I'm bored enough that I'd almost consider actually doing something with Cory, and that scares me. I have no idea how he spends his time, other than that he spends it away from here.

My phone buzzes to let me know I have a new text message and I pick it up hoping that it's something interesting. It's the phone company reminding me I have a bill due. I consider texting Dave to find out if he wants to do anything, but he's probably hanging out with his boyfriend. He never seems to want to do anything when I ask anyway – if he wants to hang out, he texts me.

I'd like to send a message to Nicole. I like spending time with her, and it feels good to flirt a little. It's comforting to have someone around and at least be able to pretend that they like you. I can tell she's not interested in me. If she was, she'd have sent me a text of her own by now.

I'm getting out of my room. I throw on a shirt and my shoes and head down toward the park, not sure where I'm going. I always feel restless after a month or two anywhere, even somewhere that should be exciting, like an amusement park. I walk past '52, a fifties-style ice cream parlor and restaurant where the employees get to wear long skirts and paper hats and dance to jukebox music. I'm pretty sure it's a chain that exists outside Wonderments as well, but I'm not sure. There definitely aren't any where I'm from.

I walk down the path and stop at the duck pond. It's a relic from another time. The rest of the park wants to feed you twenty dollar cheeseburgers and send you zipping around on heart-pounding rides. The pond doesn't even have a name on the official park maps. It's just kind of... there. Rows of benches surround the water, and there are a few machines where you can buy breadcrumbs to feed to the birds or fish. A deck overlooks the water so you can feed the fish without standing at the edge of the pond. There's a fountain out in the middle of the water. After it gets dark it will get lit up with different-colored lights. I wonder if

Wonderments management fights every year to turn the spot into a cement slab and put a restaurant on it, or if they just forgot this place is here. It makes me happy that there's at least one tiny piece of this place that hasn't been monetized.

There's a lot of people around, just sitting, relaxing, watching the water. One little boy catches my eye. He's maybe four or five, still at that young enough age that his running is clumsy and haphazard, like he could fall over at any moment and it's a small miracle that he doesn't. He keeps running over to the water and looking for fish, then back to the fish feeder to check and see if there's any food there that he can use. I look at the people on the benches and try to figure out which one of them is this kid's parent, and I can't. Parents abandoning their kids all day inside amusement parks is actually a big problem. A significant amount of Wonderments security staff is devoted exclusively to entertaining lost kids and keeping them calm and hydrated while they wait for parents to show up and claim them. I heard there were plans to start a complementary daycare at one point, but management was worried it'd be too popular and get overwhelmed. They're probably right.

I wait until the kid is distracted by the pond and go over to the feeder. I put a quarter in and give it a good crank, leaving the food behind. Eventually the kid runs over and checks the machine again. It catches him by surprise and his hands are too small, and a lot of the food spills onto the ground. The birds will clean it up.

The boy walks back over to the pond with his tiny fistfuls of newly acquired food, and throws the pieces, in that absurd, totally ineffective way that small children throw things, into the water. He claps his hands in glee and I can hear him saying, "Turtle! Turtle!" to no one in particular. Then he reaches down, picks up one of the fish pellets that didn't make it to the water, and eats it.

19

Tonight it's just me, Grace, and Margaret at work. The night has gone smoothly. They never seem to get along when we're in a group, but it's the most basic rule of the workplace: If there's no one else around to slack off with, whoever is closest is now your friend. I imagine it works the same way for people who get trapped in coal mines or stranded on desert islands. Apparently two things in life can forge a bond between literally any two people: coping with an isolated and imminent death, and working retail.

It's almost 1:30 a.m. and all three of us are exhausted. It wasn't a busy night or anything, it's just fucking late. The last customer left forty-five minutes ago and the park closed at midnight. The place is spotless. We even mopped. The problem is that Dave has the night off and only managers have keys. On nights when Dave is here, he can do the "final inspection" for the store and officially tell us we can go home. On nights that Dave has off, we have to wait for one of the managers from the office to come by and make sure the place doesn't look like shit before locking up for us and sending us home.

"Should we call them again?" Nicole asks.

"I already called them three times," I tell her. "They just say they're busy locking up other stores and someone is on the way and they'll get here when they get here."

"I bet it's those assholes over at Tropic Apparel," Margaret says. Tropic Apparel is the biggest store at the front end of the park and easily the one that makes the most money. As a result, it gets the most scrutiny from management. There's no way some lazy-ass manager is going to walk any more than they have to, so if they find something that needs cleaning or fixing in one store they just wait until it's done before moving on. Since our store is close to the very front of the park, it means we're standing around late – the more people in other stores fuck up, the longer we have to wait.

"This sucks," Grace says. "They should just give employees keys or leave a key here or something."

I can only imagine what that would be like. People taking keys home and forgetting them, sneaking in to fuck just so they can tell their friends they did, or just plain stealing shit. That's just the garden variety ruckus to expect. It'd be remarkably easy to coordinate theft of electronics or other stuff that's actually valuable. Giving low wage seasonal employees keys would rank close to the worst managerial decision possible.

"Yeah, this sucks," I agree.

"I wonder what would happen if we just left," Margaret says. "They wouldn't fire us."

"If anything happened to the shop they would most certainly fire us," I tell her. "We're pretty much the most replaceable employees of all time."

Pointing this out seems to aggravate her, but she doesn't argue. I'm spared more of their bitching because the manager from the office finally shows up. She's a thin, middle-aged woman with a dark tan and wrinkles that make her look even older. Most likely a combination of going to the beach, tanning beds in the off season, and smoking a few packs a day. I can smell the cigarette smoke on her. Given how strong it is, I'd be willing to bet she stopped for a cigarette break on the way here.

"How are you guys tonight?" she asks.

"Fine," I say.

"Just want to get home and get some sleep," Grace says.

"Don't we all," she says. "Hopefully you did a good job and this won't take long."

She walks around the shop inspecting things with an air of disdain. She looks at a few gaps on the shelves that are supposed to be filled with merch (and would be if Dave wasn't so lazy about reorders) and raises an eyebrow but says nothing. She moves some Wonderments snow globes on shelves aside and runs a finger along the back of the shelf. She finds at least a week's worth of dust, but says nothing.

"Is that glitter on the floor?" she says, scuffing at it with a faded black Velcro shoe.

"Yeah," I say. "Someone dropped a snow globe on the floor a few days ago and it broke. It takes awhile for all the glitter to disappear, no matter how many times we mop."

"Huh. I hope the stock loss got reported?" she says. Behind her I see Margaret roll her eyes and look at her wrist. She's not wearing a watch.

"Of course," I assure her.

"Okay, you can go home," she says. "But seriously, get this place cleaned up tomorrow night."

The three of us walk out and don't wait for her while she locks up.

20

The Jolly Tinker is located just past the Wonderments front gate, but behind us is the main fairway, a wide, colorful brick road with bright flowers in the center dividing it down the middle and pathways off to the various rides and restaurants. It runs through the first third or so of the park before branching off in three different directions. At the point where the main path branches off, there's a giant fountain, and above that, a giant screen. During the day the screen runs advertisements for various shows and attractions. Actually, it runs ads for Coca-Cola, overpriced Wonderments restaurants, and season passes, but they sprinkle in enough "Roller Coaster Facts" and "Wonderments Trivia" that it doesn't *quite* look like a giant nonstop commercial.

At night it serves as the backdrop for the laser light show and is officially the reason the screen was put up in the first place. It's a call back to an earlier time, when the stoners of the seventies and eighties thought laser lights were going to be the way of the future. Now it's just used as a cool gimmick to impress children.

A few times a summer, though, there's Employee Movie Night. They put up whatever action movie they could license for the least amount of money and it booms out from all the speakers along the main pathway. As park-sanctioned employee events go, it's really popular. Tonight they're showing *The Dark Knight*. I'd be willing to bet they showed it last year too and now they're just showing it again to avoid buying another license, but it's a pretty cool movie and I didn't see it in theaters the first time it was out, so I can't complain.

Right now we're looking for a spot for the five of us – me, Dave, Grace, Nicole, and Nicole's date. Nicole's date told us his name and I forgot it already. I almost never remember someone's name unless I know I'm going to see them again, and with Nicole and dating that's definitely not a sure thing. He's brought a blanket and an old-fashioned picnic basket with him, which I want to mock relentlessly, but it's actually a cute idea. The picnic basket is new. He bought it just for this date.

Eventually we find a spot on the grass. The angle to the screen is a little bit off and we're right under one of the speakers, so the volume is too loud and it echoes, since we hear the speaker above us before the others. It's still better than sitting on the brick lane I guess.

Nicole's date spreads out the blanket. There's not really room for all of us, so Nicole sits down on the blanket, pulling him over. Grace sits next to Nicole on the other side and Dave and I are left to fend for ourselves.

"So is Margaret coming or what?" Grace asks. "There are a lot of people here. She's never going to find us in this crowd." It surprises me Grace would have the decency to wait for anyone, let alone Margaret.

"She said she doesn't like action movies," I tell her.

Dave snorts. "Yeah, right. Who doesn't like action movies? She just hates being around us."

"Oh well, whatever," Grace says.

Nicole and her date are completely in their own little world. She's just kind of staring off in the direction of the movie, watching the Joker and his clown masked henchmen shoot each other in the comically implausible bank heist at the beginning of the movie. The guy next to her is just watching her. He seems like a bit of a sap.

I watch them as their date unfolds, completely out of place

against Christian Bale brooding his way through movie violence. The guy takes a pair of clear disposable plastic cups out of the picnic basket. They're the short, wide kind you see around punch bowls at Christmas parties. It's impossible to get just a pair of them – I wonder if he threw the rest away or if he just has a stack of them sitting back in his room. He pulls out a bottle of what I assume is very cheap red wine. He pours them each a glass. Nicole gives him a smile I'm sure he'll interpret as affection but looks to me more like pity.

Dave and Grace are both pointedly ignoring the whole scene. They want to be good friends, I suppose, and not blow the date for Nicole, but it's pretty hard not to laugh at some poor schmuck bringing his idea of an upscale picnic to a movie featuring a guy who gets half his face blown off. Wouldn't popcorn or candy or some other "movie" type snack be a lot more obvious?

Next he pulls out a fruit tray – the clear plastic sort that clearly came from a grocery store. It has strawberries, pineapple, grapes and what I think is chocolate dip in the center. Then some sort of sandwich, also in the clear "nothing says romance like the grocery store deli" plastic containers. There's even a few pieces of chocolate cake as well. Nothing in it is homemade or done with care other than a shopping trip. It's dark, they can barely see what they're eating. Nicole has a few polite bites of everything but kind of has an awkward look like she's wishing she could just leave. He didn't even bring any silverware, so he spills cake crumbs all over himself while trying to keep his eyes on Nicole, watch a movie, and eat cake with his bare hands and play it cool.

I bet he cleaned his room and told his roommate to be somewhere else tonight, too. I can't judge from anything he's done tonight whether he thinks this is romantic, or if he's just a douchebag who thinks a "fancy" picnic lunch is just the price of admission to a girl's pants.

The movie goes on for way too long – I've never understood why superhero movies try to cram too many villains into one film – and the date gets more and more awkward, with Nicole giving him the cold shoulder and him trying (and failing) over and over to get her attention. He says something, she says just enough to be polite and goes back to watching the movie. He touches her shoulder, or her hair, or her arm, but she doesn't touch him back. He's not aggressive or dickish, just sort of... adorably desperate.

After the movie Dave, Grace and I stand up and start walking and notice Nicole and her date hanging back, so we wait. We're far enough away that I can't hear them talking, but he leans in for a kiss at one point, which she dodges and gives him a pat on the shoulder. I wonder if he's too stupid to realize how badly things went, or if he just doesn't care and decided to go for it anyway. He goes in for a hug that Nicole returns, then turns and walks in the opposite direction of our group.

Since we're between him and the guys' dorms, I have no idea where he could be going this time of night. Just walking anywhere to get away from the awkwardness of being shot down. I almost feel bad for him.

21

Nicole isn't at work the next day, which is definitely a good thing for her, because Dave and Grace aren't above mocking her for her awkward date. Instead, the two of them are at the front of the store, Dave doing all the talking, Grace listening because the alternative is actual work. This leaves me in the back of the store to do the cleaning and keep things stocked. Wonderments could save a lot of money if they had someone in each store to make its employees act like employees. Then again, getting someone to give a fuck costs real money, so they probably figure it's cheaper to pay half a dozen people sub-minimum wages to slack off than it would be to pay three people plus a supervisor to keep them on task.

Grace looks bored, like she'd rather be doing anything (besides working, of course) other than talking to Dave. The worst thing about working retail is that your friends get chosen for you by management. It's the scariest thing about working in the service industry: your coworkers reflect your own failure.

I'm adding more stuffed animals onto the shelf to make it look full. The stuffed animal wall is always a huge mess and everyone hates dealing with it. No one ever buys the big ones, which means most of the shelf is filled with little anthropomorphic rabbits and bears and alligators and whatever other animals a corporate suit decides would look cute wearing Wonderments t-shirts and no pants.

I'm alternating the animals based on their style of shirt. There are two different designs with the Wonderments logo on it and one with the logo of The Falcon roller coaster. I don't know why, but stuffed animals never wear pants. Naked stuffed animals are fine, but once you've committed one to a shirt, it seems like pants should be mandatory. There is no reason for me to arrange them like this, not really. By the end of the day tomorrow it'll be impossible to tell I ever did it. Mostly, it keeps my hands full so I don't have to go and do something else.

Out of the corner of my eye I see Dave and Grace heading in my direction. It leaves the registers and the front of the store empty, which is both not allowed and completely standard here at The Jolly Tinker.

"Tell Dave he's an idiot," Grace says.

"Dave," I put my hand on his shoulder. "You're an idiot."

"Not so, my friend. I bought my new boyfriend this, and it's totally going to get him to commit."

He opens a small black case that reveals a simple diamond bracelet. It sparkles and the diamonds aren't very big, but I assume they're real.

"Wow," I say. "That's ummm... how long have you been dating this guy?" I consider finding a way to steal the bracelet. To keep Dave from doing something stupid, of course.

"That's what I said!" Grace says. "You can't just drop a gift on someone like that when you've been dating them less than a month. It's creepy and needy and you don't even know the guy."

"Yeah, yeah, yeah." Dave snaps the case shut and returns it to his pocket. "It's not about how long you've been dating someone, it's about how much you like them."

"It's a bad idea," Grace says.

Of course it's a bad idea. "Seems pretty hasty, but sometimes you gotta go for it I guess. I've done stuff just as crazy to try and get laid." That's not true at all, and I'm not sure why I said it.

Dave turns to Grace. "You just don't get it," he says. "You get to be all cute and Asian and have a vagina. I bet you never chase anyone, do you? You just let guys chase after you because it's fun being chased."

"Fuck off," Grace says. My guess is that hit a little too close to home.

Up at the front counter, a young guy is holding a pair of cheap plastic sunglasses that we sell for eighteen bucks apiece and looking back at us. "Hey, thanks a lot for the sunglasses guys. Really. World class service." He holds up a twenty dollar bill that he puts on the counter, and walks out.

Dave starts to say something, then just lets him go. "Shit. How long was he standing there? It couldn't have been more than thirty seconds."

"I guess so."

"You guys just don't get it because you've been single all summer and you'll probably stay that way. I like this guy, and there's nothing wrong with giving a guy you like a present." Dave walks to the register, rings up the sunglasses, and stuffs the twenty dollar bill in. He doesn't bother to make correct change.

"He's going to get his heart broken," Grace says.

"Everyone does," I remind her.

* * *

Another day, another shift. Another sunny weekday promising to be nice and slow. It doesn't take very long before all the days start blurring together. It's scary if you step back and look at it – how much happens to us that we just tune out and forget forever, because it's all the same shit we've done before. It's part of why I want to travel. It's easier for life to feel fresh and new when you can change the scenery.

I plan on using the day to try and think of another "creative revenue source" to work on on my next day off, and just generally space out and not think too much. I walk in the door of the shop and immediately I can tell I'm walking into an argument. Dave fucked up the scheduling.

Dave, Nicole, Grace, and Margaret are all standing in a circle.

"If they're going to send someone home it should be me," Margaret says. "I haven't been able to go home early once this

101

entire summer." I haven't been sent home this summer either, but I keep quiet. The last thing I want to do is walk up and start arguing.

"You just had a day off a few days ago," Grace points out. "This is my eighth day working in a row."

"Yeah, you disagree with me because you want something for yourself. We're all surprised."

Normally there are three or four of us here on weekdays. There might be more on our busiest Saturdays, but management will have a fit if they find out they paid all five of us to stand here in an empty shop and enjoy the weather. Dave's job is to call the office and ask them to "advise him on the situation." Nine times out of ten they tell him to send someone home, which is what they're all arguing about.

Nicole says, "We all want to go home, right? We should just pick someone at random. That's the only fair way."

Grace and Margaret turn on her in what I imagine will be the only time that they agree on anything this summer.

"Sure, that's what you want," Margaret says. "You were the one that got to go home the last time this happened. No matter who gets chosen, it sure as hell shouldn't be you."

"You just had a day off," Grace says. "Don't be greedy. You know it shouldn't be you. Stop trying to weasel your way out of work." All anyone does around here is try and weasel out of work, so I'm not sure why Grace is mad at Nicole for giving it her best shot.

Dave is surprisingly mature about it. He knows it won't be him that gets sent home, because he's the manager. He doesn't have a personal stake in it, although I can imagine him trying to angle to get Margaret to go home just so he doesn't have to put up with her.

"Look, we don't even know if they're going to send anyone home," he says. "Once we know that for sure I'll be the one to decide who goes home, and I'll try and be as fair about it as I can. I swear, sometimes you guys forget I'm the fucking boss around here."

No one seems to like that solution but everyone quiets down while Dave picks up the store phone – a beige, blocky thing that looks stolen from the police chief's desk in an eighties police movie

– and punches a few numbers to call the front office. He explains the situation and listens without saying anything for about half a minute, then hangs up the phone and comes back over to us.

"Well, no one is going home," he says.

Nicole, Grace, and Margaret all groan in a brief moment of solidarity.

"This is your fucking fault," Margaret says. "This is so dumb. There's no reason for all of us to be here. What a waste of goddamn time."

She gets paid to be here. She gets paid the same amount if we're busy or if the store is empty. She knew all week long she was going to have to work today and that was totally normal, but now she's upset about it. The possibility of having the day off didn't even exist until a few minutes ago, and now she's pissed that it's not happening.

"Oh, it gets better," Dave says. "They need someone to run the guessing game over by where the main pathway forks. The one over by The Wizard Arcade? Apparently whatever dumbass got scheduled to work it called in sick, so they want one of us – well, one of you – to go down and fill in."

"That won't be me," Nicole says. "I applied to work indoors for a reason. I will not be standing outside in the sun the whole day. I work in this shop, and I am not going anywhere."

"Margaret –"

Dave doesn't get out another word before Margaret interrupts him. "Oh, sure. I'm your least favorite person here so you're going to send me. I don't want to stand there by myself and run that dumb game all night either. You're not going to choose me to fuck over just because I'm the one you like the least. If Nicole gets to put her foot down and automatically get her way, then so do I. I'm not going."

Dave sighs.

"I'll go," I say. If I don't, I'm going to have to sit here and listen to them all complain all night long about how they're bored or how the job sucks. Standing alone in the sun seems like a much more pleasant option.

I open the door to the closet next to the register and rummage through the box of damaged stuff to be returned. Sure enough, there's a green visor with "Wonderments" on it in white letters. The visor itself is totally fine but the clear plastic packaging is torn. I come back out, tear the rest of the packaging and put on the visor.

"Nice hat," Margaret says. It looks like Dave wants to say something too, but he knows I'm doing him a favor so he keeps his mouth shut.

"Wish me luck," I say. I walk out before I have to listen to any more complaining.

* * *

The game I'm in charge of thanks to Dave's screwup is the nonsensically named "Guess Your Luck." It's one of the more popular games in the park, and I have a lot of respect for it. People like to feel clever. They like to win at things and feel strong and in control. Once you let someone feel smart and in control, they're easy to manipulate.

The premise of Guess Your Luck is simple. You pay me, the hapless, dim-witted Wonderments employee, five bucks. Then you get to choose one of three options: either I try to guess your age within two years, I try to guess your weight within four pounds, or I try to guess the month of your birth within one month. So someone walks up, and I guess they're twenty-five. If they're between twenty-three and twenty-seven, they get nothing. It works the same way for weight (the game comes complete with a giant scale for people to step on) and birth month (valid ID required).

Now, you can't rely on a kid making less than minimum wage to be smart enough or care enough to guess well all that often. The trick is that the dumb stuffed elephant or pony or caterpillar that you win costs Wonderments less than the five bucks it costs to play the game. Sell them for five bucks apiece, and you might move a few a day. Let someone pay five bucks for the chance to win that same animal, and people will line up to play. The fact that the employee running the game will occasionally guess close enough to make someone lose is just a bonus.

The first guy walks up to me with his wife and kid straggling behind him a little. They all have the same dirty blonde hair and blue eyes, and they look happy. The parents are in their forties with wrinkles from too many tans. Their kid has a snot bubble in his nose that's crusted over. They have secondhand clothes and her jewelry is cheap, but they look *happy*. I wonder how they do it.

"Okay, brother," the man says to me, handing me a five dollar bill. I wonder how much older he has to get before he stops calling guys my age "brother" and starts calling us "son." "I bet you can't guess my weight."

I look him up and down. He looks totally normal for forty – thin with a few extra pounds, khaki shorts, beat up sneakers with grass stains from mowing the lawn on his small three bedroom house they struggle to make payments on. A baggy, faded blue t-shirt with a company logo on it – the shitty kind you'd expect to get at the company picnic. He also most definitely has something stuffed under his shirt to make him look fatter, most likely a beach towel. He's not hiding it well. Only a total idiot would fall for this and I suspect many total idiots would still figure it out. I'd guess he weighs somewhere close to 190 pounds, depending on how much he's emptied or loaded up his pockets in a further attempt to manipulate the game.

"Uhhh....." I furrow my brow and put a hand up to my chin in an exaggerated show of concentration. "I'm going to guess two twenty. Two hundred and twenty pounds, sir."

He steps up on the scale. 188 pounds. He turns to his family and does a little fist pump of celebration, which his kid returns in earnest, his eyes glowing with the admiration that comes with knowing that his dad could totally beat up my dad.

I grab a big blue stuffed caterpillar with orange spots on it – the most vibrant stuffed animal I can find on the wall of sad discount stuff – and see the kid reaching toward me. I hand the animal to the dad. He should be the one to gift it to his kid.

22

One of the few legitimate perks of working at Wonderments is that beyond having access to the park whenever we want, we also get tickets to let in our friends. Everyone officially gets two, but you're allowed to apply for more if you want them. They want to make sure you're not selling tickets on the secondary market or inviting fifty of your closest friends to party, but otherwise they're pretty liberal about making sure employees can get their friends and family in.

I'm not as close to my family as I wish I was. I don't want to start hustling people in my hometown and end up in a spot where it'd be a bad idea to go back there. Life is just easier when I move around a lot. The fewer questions I get asked the better, and never staying somewhere too long ensures that if people do start asking questions, I'm not around to answer them.

I got the news a few weeks ago that my parents were coming to visit. They didn't ask me outright like I imagine normal people would; my mom just called and left a message on my phone.

"Your father and I are going on vacation and we'd like to come see you. Do you have tickets to the park? We would love to see where you work."

I can't imagine my parents ever being interested in coming to an amusement park. There aren't many shows or relaxing, sedentary things to do. It's mostly thrill rides and bad food. I suppose they'd like to go to the water park, maybe? I'm not sure how to entertain my own parents.

I'm waiting in line at the main office to talk to a middle-aged, overwhelmed-looking receptionist. She has flat, brown hair with gray starting at the temples, wrinkles around her eyes and mouth, and thick glasses. There's a women's magazine open on her desk, but she's too busy working to get back to it. I try to imagine her relating to anything in an issue of Cosmopolitan or doing anything it suggests, and I can't. Purely out of curiosity I check for a wedding ring. There isn't one. I want to ask her how many cats she owns.

I flash her a polite smile. "I won't take long. I just need two general admission tickets please. My parents are coming to visit, and I already gave my first two to some friends." I actually sold them in the parking lot to a couple of college kids. The ticket price at the gate is too high not to scalp a few.

"Sure thing," she says. "I just need your ID badge."

I fish it out of my pocket and hand it to her, and she punches the numbers into the computer. After a few clicks the printer next to her starts up and prints off two full-page certificates. Each one says "Admit One – Wonderments" and underneath "Not for Resale – No Cash Value." It strikes me as a little bit odd because the ones I had at the beginning of the summer looked like real tickets. I guess they figure it's easier just to use a cheap printout.

Immediately my mind flashes to making photocopies to sell. Not everyone is unscrupulous enough to buy a "ticket" that way, but it might still be worth it. After she hands them to me I look at them closer. It's got my name, my employee badge number, and the date on it. Damn. I could probably alter them, but it would be risky. Once they were hit with a flood of identical tickets, they'd be on the lookout for sure. I might get a few more later in the summer, but I don't think it's worth trying to pull something off on a wide scale.

"Thank you," I tell her.

On my way out I pass a handful of Eastern Europeans sitting in the waiting room chairs and looking bored. Every day plenty of people don't show up to work because they're sick, hungover, or just plain avoiding work, and someone has to fill those shifts. So every day, regular employees come and sit in front of the office, hoping someone calls in so they can take a shift. As if seventy hours a week wasn't enough. For them, though, the almighty dollar goes a long way, so I guess I understand. I wish I could move to a country where my spending power tripled overnight.

I send my mother a text message: "Got tickets. Let me know the date." She hates when I send texts instead of calling, but texting lets me dodge the conversation. I know I'll be happy to see my parents when they get here, but a little bit of family goes a long way. I imagine everyone feels that way about their parents, and parents feel the same way about their children.

* * *

Margaret is in the back of the shop, folding shirts and looking pissed off. She has half a dozen piles around her, separating them by color so it will look like a rainbow when she hangs them on the rack. No one else bothers to do this, but Margaret fills her time fixing it when the shop is slow. She does it so she has a reason to hide in the back instead of interacting with the rest of us. No one tries to disrupt this arrangement.

Nicole and Dave are at the front of the store gossiping and generally being useless. It doesn't matter – at four in the afternoon on a warm and sunny day exactly no one is doing any shopping.

I'm filling the sucker tree that is halfway between Margaret and everyone else. I'm killing time by putting the different suckers together by flavor – cherry, pineapple, chocolate, piña colada, whatever – another useless task. By the end of the day the tree will need to be refilled half a dozen times, but it gives me something to do.

"I can't stand any of them." Margaret says to me. She sees me as a bit of a kindred spirit, which bothers me a little bit. I wish it was only because we're both from the Midwest, but if I have to be honest it's more than that. Dave, Nicole and Grace are all obviously fashionable and popular, even in their dumpy work uniforms. Margaret is not. She isn't ugly, just... plain. Shoulder length disheveled hair, slightly crooked glasses, forgettable $20 bargain store shoes. No makeup. No jewelry. Some people dress like they don't care and are very careful to get the look just right. Margaret genuinely doesn't care. The two looks are not similar.

The fact that she sees me as kindred means she recognizes me as unfashionable, and she's probably right. I've tried, but it's just way more effort than I want to give to how I look.

"Are they really that bad?"

She shoots me a mocking glare that says *"Yes, they really are that bad."* Past her high cheeks and sharp nose, I notice that her neck and collarbone are graceful and soft and I have the fleeting thought that she could be pretty, if only she could learn to smile without sneering and talk without venom in her voice.

"They're just so fake. All they do is stand around and make small talk about useless shit all day." She says "useless shit" with that verbal inflection that typically comes along with spitting on the ground in disgust.

"I guess. I don't see it." It's the wrong thing to say and I know it immediately.

"Bitches like that are hot and put out easy so they get everything they want. They never get turned down because they can't keep their legs closed and guys think with their dicks. They've never had a real feeling or a sad day in their entire lives. They just do whatever they think turns guys on because they're empty, low self-esteem attention whores." She says the word "whore" like a projectile, like she wishes she could spit it out and smack it on Nicole's forehead. I'm not sure if she's including Dave in her assessment or not. It doesn't feel like it.

"You should come with us to the Wave Blast," I say. I have no idea how to respond to her vitriol, so I just ignore it. "It'll be fun."

"Right... no. I have better things to do than use my tits to get free drinks and hang out with people I don't even like. No offense. You're okay. But no."

"Come on," I say. "I'll buy you a drink myself, and I won't look at anything you don't want me to." The line is between friendly and flirting is thin, and I don't know which side I'm on. I don't even know which side I *want* to be on.

"Maybe," she says. "But if I do go, I'm not hanging out with *them.*"

On some level I appreciate her wanton disregard for my attempts at peacemaking. If her reason for hating her coworkers wasn't so superficial, it'd be admirable. I wonder how much she was picked on as a kid to hate people she perceives as "popular" so much. It's easier to think in stereotypes. On some level, everyone does.

Now I'm wondering why I even asked Margaret along, but it's too late. I don't want to spend the whole night keeping the peace between Margaret and everyone else. I hope she doesn't come.

Around 8 p.m., Grace comes into the shop. It always catches me off guard to see her out of work uniform – tonight in very short jean shorts and a yellow tank top. It's subtle in its simplicity but I'm sure it's let her catch the eye of plenty of guys on her walk over here. Grace approaches Nicole's register and steps behind the counter, talking to her while Nicole rings up customers at the same time. Grace is really animated. She's smiling and nodding a lot – not the pleasant, tight lipped smile that I'm used to seeing on her, but a real, tooth-baring grin. She has a face that normally ranges somewhere between "pleased" and "annoyed" but now, maybe for the first time since I've met her, she looks excited.

"Hey," I call Margaret over. "What do you think?" I nod toward Nicole and Grace.

"I don't get it. Why the hell would you ever come in here on your day off? I can't imagine anything they'd talk about that would make it worth coming in here when you don't need to."

"No, not that." Although honestly, I'm inclined to agree with her. "I mean, what do you think they're talking about?"

"Christ... this isn't grade school. If you want to talk to them just go talk to them." She rolls her eyes long and hard enough I can picture the origin of what makes parents say "If you keep doing that, your face will stick that way." I don't say it out loud.

"Don't be dense," I tell her, and regret it. It comes out of my mouth casually but I can tell it stings. She stuffs it away instead of calling me out on my bullshit, so I keep talking. "Look at Grace. She's actually excited about something. I haven't seen her that way all summer."

"Probably just some guy that she's going to fuck and forget about in two weeks. I really don't care." She walks away from me, back to whatever meaningless retail task she was working on. Not for the first time I wonder if people aren't as good at reading others as I am, or if they just don't care, or if they're just plain idiots. Since it's hardly advantageous to walk up to someone and start a conversation with "Hey, do you realize how stupid you are?" I'm unlikely to ever know the answer. She is right about one thing, though: if I want to know what's going on, the easiest way to find out is just to walk up and ask.

"What's the story?" I ask.

Grace doesn't hesitate. "My paintings are going to be displayed at a local art show," she says. "I've been doing a lot of painting since I've been here and now I get to show it off. Maybe even sell some of it."

"Wait," I say. "You've been painting? Here? What are you going to do with them at the end of the summer?"

"I just like doing it," she says. "I'll try and sell what I can and donate the rest to local restaurants and stuff I guess. The art show is being billed as showcasing 'local talent' but they let me in no problem."

Margaret comes up from the back of the store and joins the conversation. That didn't take long. For all her aloofness, I guess she was pretty curious after all.

"So what's the big deal?" she says. "They probably let anyone in."

Grace glares at her. "Well, I'm happy to show off my work, no matter why they let me in."

"Happy to sell out, you mean. Aren't you a little young to doing that already?" Margaret says.

I turn expecting Grace to get pissed, but she's laughing. It's high and shrill and mocking, and I realize it's the first time I've heard her laugh.

"You don't get it, but that's fine," Grace says. "I'll invite you along anyway as soon as everything is finalized. It'll be fun."

"Sure thing," Margaret says. "I have to ride sixteen hours on a Greyhound bus to get home from here. I work for less than minimum wage. My room is so shitty the wall would probably crumble if I try to hang anything on it. I'm not exactly in the market for a painting right now."

"Oh, sweetie," Grace says. The way she says it is oily and demeaning, like Grace mashed together saying "you're inferior" and "fuck you" and it came out as "Oh, sweetie." "You can just come and enjoy the art if you want. I understand if it's not your taste, but you can still have a nice time."

Margaret turns and walks away without saying another word. She goes into one of the side closets and slams the door.

"Well, that's going to make the rest of the shift awesome," I say.

"I don't get her at all," Grace says. "She comes over here and criticizes me, calls me a sellout, then gets pissed when I say one word back to her."

"You could, you know, not say anything," I tell her.

She scoffs. "Sorry, you may be fine with being a pushover but I'm not. If someone pushes me, I push back."

"I'll keep that in mind." I walk over behind my register and help a kid who just walked in to buy some candy. I short him a dollar. I wish more people would show up so it would be easier to get out of this conversation. No one shows up. Another beautiful summer night at the end of a beautiful summer day, keeping everyone out enjoying their vacations and far away from The Jolly Tinker until closing time. "I think it's cool that you're in an art show." I really don't care. "Something about it must rub her the wrong way, that's all."

Nicole uses a low, forced whisper when she says, "Guys, the doors here aren't exactly thick. She can probably hear you talking about her."

"Well fuck her then. If she doesn't want us talking about her, she can stop hiding like a baby." Grace does not whisper.

I duck down behind the counter and start pulling out bags, pens, scissors, and all the other junk we keep there under the guise of cleaning it out. It doesn't really need it, but I'm really hoping they take the hint and find work of their own and stop talking.

After half a minute or so of silence, a shadow comes over me.

I look up and see Nicole and Grace looking down at me from the other side of the counter.

"Well?" Nicole says.

I look at her for a moment blankly, but she doesn't add anything. "Well, what?"

"Are you going to go back there and patch things up, or what?" she asks.

I reach deep into one of the drawers behind the counter, hoping to find a loaded mousetrap or a feral chipmunk that will maul my hand and keep me from having to deal with Margaret. "Uh, I'm going to go with 'or what' on this one. Why would it be my job to sort this out? I had nothing to do with this. Send Grace back there to apologize and it'll be fine."

"Fuck that," Grace says. "I don't apologize. If she wants to dish it out she can learn to take it. Or she can stay in there for the rest of the summer if she wants, that's fine."

"Well, glad we solved that then. I'll call Dave after work and tell him to bring in some crackers or something to slide under the door tomorrow." I come out from behind the counter and try to walk away from them, but they follow right behind.

"Just do it," Nicole says. "Come on."

I turn and look at them and lower my voice. "Fine. But it's the last time I sort out your bullshit with her. Next time Grace says something snarky and pisses her off, which is *going* to happen, I'm not involved. I hate dealing with this stuff." I really do.

Grace and Nicole walk away from me to the other side of the store. I go up to the closet door and I see them creep a bit closer so they can listen. Even when it's their own fault and they practically begged me to fix it for them, they still can't resist snooping. I shoot them a glare that says "what the fuck are you doing?" They either don't get it or simply ignore it. I knock on the door.

"I can hear you guys talking about me," Margaret says. "Go the fuck away."

"Just let me in for a minute," I say. I hear nothing back, so I wait about half a minute and open the door. I tense up, expecting her to slam it back on me, but she doesn't.

Inside the closet she's sorting all the shirts by size. It's a useless venture. Shirts are some of our best-selling merchandise. By next week all this stuff will be gone and this room will be refilled by some morning crew employee who couldn't care less about keeping things organized.

I know I have to start off by generating some good will, so I whisper, "I'm sure they're outside trying to listen, so let's keep it quiet."

"Okay, whatever," Margaret says. "I don't care if those bitches –" she says the word "bitches" loudly and toward the door "– listen to our conversation."

"Look, what's the big deal?" I ask.

"The deal is, every single shift here she looks down on me and finds ways to mock me and just prances around like she thinks she's better than everyone else." In my experience, the only time people get offended by someone acting superior to them is when they think the other person might be right. I don't tell her this.

"Can't you just ignore her?" I ask. "I mean, why not just leave her alone instead of coming up and starting shit?"

She snorts. "So it's my fault now?"

It is. I do not say this either.

"Look, I'm sorry," I say. "They sent me in here to get you because they don't want you to be pissed at them. They aren't evil. They're just too dumb to think about what they say before they say it." As far as I'm concerned, most people – Margaret included – fall into this category. It amazes me how people just say whatever nonsense pops into their head. Language is a tool. Tools should be used with purpose.

"Their idiocy is not my problem." She still isn't whispering, and I hope I don't have to explain any part of this conversation to them.

"I know," I whisper. "Can you just do me this favor and come out and act normal? I know you're right here, but I just want to get everyone back to work so we can get through the night and go home. This place is going to get busy pretty soon, and it'll be better if you're out there."

"I guess," she says. "You're not a bad guy. I'm doing it for you, not for them. Just give me a few minutes."

"Thanks," I say. "I mean it." I open the door and walk out, shutting it behind me. It annoys me that she thinks she's doing me a favor. It doesn't even occur to her that she should come out and work because that's her fucking job. Grace and Nicole are both standing right outside the door, not even trying to look busy.

* * *

Cory is sitting on his bunk with his feet hanging off the edge. I can't help but notice how long and dirty his toenails are. You'd think a guy who spends his whole day in flip flops would take better care of them. He's got a deep tan at this point, the tan lines from his flip flops a shockingly pale white. I try to remember if he was that pale when we met. I can't.

He's playing with his phone, and doesn't look up when he says, "Hey dude, how's it going?"

"Fine," I say. I take my shoes off and change out of my work clothes, waiting for him to move his feet so I can get to my bunk. He doesn't.

"Heads up," I say, slapping him on the calf a little.

"Oh, sorry," he says. He swings his feet back up to his bunk. "Hey, sorry I haven't been into your store in awhile. You have to hook me up with one of the girls you work with."

No, I don't. Not only would none of them be interested, it would just be mean of me to do that to one of them. "I wouldn't recommend it. I swear it's like drama every day down there."

"I don't want to talk to them," he says. "If you know what I mean."

I don't think I've ever heard someone say that outside of a movie or a TV show.

"I'm not into the whole thing of setting people up. You can ask them out yourself if you want, but that's on you."

"I can help you out," he insists. "We can go on a double date or something. Or I could find out about the girl you like for you."

Cory and I have nothing in common. I'm certain that any girl I liked wouldn't like him, and I'm equally sure that I would find it unbearable to be around any sort of girl who would go on a date with Cory, if such a girl even exists. The concept of simply asking a

115

girl out doesn't seem to occur to him. I expect him to keep pushing or bothering me about it, but he doesn't. One good thing about an entire generation attached to their phones and internet connections every minute of every day is that everyone has the attention span of a toddler. Just leave them alone for a minute and they'll forget you're even there.

I lie there, listening to the sound of laughing cartoon pigs as he plays Angry Birds. Every minute or so his phone chirps letting him know he has a text. He pauses the game, answers the text, and goes back to it. I imagine some girl on the other end of the messages doing the same thing. He's hitting on her, asking her what she's wearing, asking her if she wants a dick pic, or whatever passes for flirting in his idiot brain, and then returning to his game between every text because he can't sit still and just wait for a few seconds between replies. He thinks he's going to score, thinks she's so into him, but on the other end of the line there's some girl, switching between their conversation and Words with Friends or Pet Rescue Saga or whatever, her nasty feet hanging over her bed, just as bored and zoned out as he is.

23

I hate standing in lines. I try to be a pretty patient person so I suppose you'd never notice that I hate it so much, but I do. So much of life is spent standing around waiting for things to happen. Not only am I stuck standing in a line, which annoys me, but also I'm standing in line in the human resources office for the second time in two days, which annoys me even further, because I have no one to blame but myself. If I had realized I'd need to be here twice, I could have combined the trips and saved myself the trouble.

I decided I want to hire someone to help me learn Portuguese. Learning from books and tapes is okay but none of it sticks, because I'm never using it for anything. Maybe some conversation in Portuguese will help. Wonderments hires students from all over the world, so there has to be *someone* here that speaks the language, right? Plus, since they're willing to work here, they probably wouldn't charge very much per hour to help me out.

I look down at the flyer I have with me. I just wrote "HELP ME LEARN PORTUGUESE – will pay!" and put my phone number at the bottom. I tried to hang it on the wall in the dorm a few times, but the girl working behind the desk threw a fit. First she informed me that anything I hung up had to be on the bulletin board, then when I moved the sign over to the bulletin board, she informed me I couldn't hang anything there unless it had a stamp of approval from Human Resources. Until I worked here, I always thought "stamp of approval" was just a turn of phrase, but sure enough, all the papers on the bulletin board have a stamp of a thumbs up with the word "APPROVED" curved around it at the top.

There's a middle-aged woman working behind the desk. I'm pretty sure it's the same woman I saw before about the tickets, but I'm not sure. I finally get to the front of the line. The receptionist is on the phone. I start explaining myself but she holds a hand up to me, focusing on the phone, and I try not to look impatient as she finishes the call. After she hangs up, she waves over a dark-haired Russian guy, who comes and stands in front of me like I'm not even there.

"Frontier photo booth," she says to him.

He doesn't say a word to her as he turns and walks out. He may be dickish, but at least he's efficient. I appreciate it.

"Hi," I say.

"What can I do for you?" the receptionist asks.

I hand her four copies of my flyer. "I'd like to hang these on the bulletin boards in the dorms, but I need a stamp for it."

"Four of them?" she asks.

"Yeah. One for the guys' side, one for the girls', one for the employee rec room, and one for the cafeteria."

She nods. "Employee badge please."

I hand it to her and she writes my badge number on the top corner of each flyer, then hands it back to me and drops them into a pile on her desk.

"Your request will be reviewed by management and should be ready for pickup in seven to ten business days."

"What?" I ask.

"Your request will be reviewed by –"

"No, no, I heard you," I say. "I mean, seven to ten days? That's two weeks. We're only here until the end of the summer. Isn't there a way to speed it up?"

"Not really," she says. "Sometimes someone will get around to reviewing them sooner, but you never know. If you want you can call the office and ask about it – just don't call too often."

"That's remarkably unhelpful."

"Sorry," the receptionist says. "There are a lot of requests, and looking over them isn't exactly a high priority."

"Sure." It makes sense, I guess. I'm glad I made a few extra copies now. I'll just sneak one up later and hope for the best. "Well, thanks for helping as much as you can," I tell her.

"No problem," she says. "Anything else I can do for you?"

"That's it," I tell her. "I'll call next week."

If I had to guess, I'd say I'll never hear from them.

* * *

There's a box in the lobby marked "free" where people put their stuff when they're done with it. For the most part it's junk – broken headphones, unused notebook paper, plastic beer cups. Once I even noticed a Discman in there. I was genuinely curious about who in this millennium still owned a Discman, but the next day it was gone, so apparently not only did one person own one, but another person was excited to get one secondhand. I wish I knew who these people were. Even my grandma owns an mp3 player. I'm reading a pulp law thriller I found in the box. It's not very good.

A lot of Wonderments employees bring laptops, against the advice of the Wonderments employee handbook. To prevent theft, Wonderments officially recommends that employees rent computers for the summer from Jake's Computers. It's a pretty solid deal they've got going – it's fifty dollars a month to rent a computer so old that it probably couldn't be sold for that much on Craigslist. But as long as they can get it running Facebook and World of Warcraft, they'll have people lining up around the block to rent them. An entire summer without a computer would likely cause most twenty-year-olds to go into fatal withdrawal, even with public use computers right downstairs and an amusement park next door.

I like not having one. When I have the internet I feel compelled to constantly check e-mail, or get sucked into checking webcomics, or Facebook, or Twitter, and all the other stuff that everyone my age is addicted to. I can't put it down when it's in front of me, but if it's not, I don't seek it out. It's comparatively satisfying to be doing pretty much anything else.

My phone goes off. It's Dave. His text reads, "bf is an asshole lets go drink" and I ignore it. I'll send him a text in a few hours apologizing for missing his text.

Ten minutes go by, then someone starts banging on my door, hard. "Come on, fucker." It's Dave. "It's time to get shitfaced. I know you're in there." I realize that there's no way he could know that I'm in here. Then again, I have no idea how he knew which door to come banging on, either.

I contemplate waiting to see if he goes away. He bangs on the door again and I can see it shaking as he does. Dave isn't particularly large or strong. I'm confident a reasonably strong person could bash into any room without too much effort. It encourages me not to say anything. I want to see if Dave can pull it off.

"Okay, okay," I say. "Hold on a minute."

I open the door. "You look like shit," I tell him. "If you looked any worse people would think you were straight."

He really does look like shit. Usually he makes sure to dress well and keep his hair combed and all that other stuff, but not so tonight – jeans, t-shirt, and a scowl.

"What's going on?" I ask him.

"My boyfriend is an asshole, and now I'm lonely, so we're going drinking," he says. "I don't want to talk about it."

There is no phrase in the English language I like less than "I don't want to talk about it." It's not that I don't like not talking. Not talking is fine. In fact, it's one of my favorite things. But when someone says they don't want to talk about something, they always do. They just want to spend the whole night hoping you'll pry it out of them.

"Okay, let's go then." Since I really don't want to get involved in Dave's personal life, I choose not mentioning it.

We walk in silence. At the bar, I see Oliver working the door like usual.

"Hey," I say to him.

"Hey guys," he says back. He doesn't check our IDs and we walk in.

"You know that guy?" Dave asks. "Is he single?"

"No idea," I tell him. Since I assume Dave still has a boyfriend, it's the perfect opportunity to ask him about that. I do not take the opportunity.

Knickers is still pretty empty at this hour since most people are still at work. In a few hours the place will be packed as usual, but for now it's quiet. The waitress brings over half a dozen shots and puts them down in front of us. She's gone again before I can give her an order for anything else. I wonder where she has to be in such a hurry when there's no one else here.

"Great," Dave says. "Didn't you want anything?" For a second I think Dave really does plan to do all six shots himself, but he slides two of them over to me and picks up the first one.

"To not having to deal with assholes," he says, clinking glasses with me. He knocks the shot back and picks up a second one before I've even done mine. He takes the second shot as I take my first. It's going to be a long night.

I don't try to keep up with Dave's drinking. The hours pass with us doing the usual bullshitting – complaining about work, about not getting paid enough, about shitty Knickers food. At first he gave me a hard time about not matching him shot for shot, but at this point he's just gulping them down without waiting for me. I'm still drinking occasionally to be polite but Dave is the one scoring most of the liver damage at this point.

"I thought, maybe he was a nice guy, you know?" Ah. Here it comes. "But no. We have a big conversation about being exclusive and then he's hitting on a guy down the hall the next day."

"Well, at least you found out sooner rather than later. Imagine if it took six months or a year."

"Guys are such assholes sometimes," he says.

"People are assholes," I tell him. "It's no better on this side. I took Nicole out on a date and she didn't say anything about it afterward at all."

"That's cold," he says. It feels like he wants to say more about her, but he doesn't. "Do you actually like her?"

"Yeah," I say. "I mean, she's okay. I don't know if I have any

121

feelings toward her or anything. I like spending time with her."

"Can't figure out if you're thinking with your heart or your dick, huh? I get it. Are you going to ask her out again?"

"I don't know," I say. "Probably not. I'm not willing to chase after a girl too much. It's not my thing. If she likes me she'll make a move."

"I guess," he says. "Honestly, if you're going to sit around waiting for her to make the first move you're going to have blue balls all summer."

I don't want to talk about the state of my balls with Dave. "Hey, did you ask Margaret if she wanted to come with us to the Wave Bash? It didn't seem like she was planning on going."

"Fuck no I didn't. That girl is such a downer. Every time I talk to her she's bitching or complaining about something. Whenever she hangs out with us it's a total buzz kill."

"Well, I invited her," I said.

He rolls his eyes at me.

"I couldn't help it. She was bitching about something and it just sort of came up. I thought it might make her happy for two minutes if she was included in something."

"Well, it's on you." Dave does another shot. "I'm not hanging out with her. I'm nice to her at work because I'm not a jerk and I don't think she's a bad person or anything, but I'm not going to stand around and listen to her complain all night."

"I'm sure it'll be fine," I tell him. It's a lie. "She's not that bad is she?"

"I guess you're going to find out. I gotta take a piss."

Dave tries to stand up and wobbles. I'm sure he's going to fall over entirely but he puts a hand on the back of one of the chairs which, to my surprise, does not tip over with him. "Shit," he says.

"I think we're done here," I say. I stand up and put his arm around my shoulder. "Can you make it back to your room or are you going to piss yourself?"

"I'm gonna piss myself," Dave says.

I take him to the bathroom and prop him up against a urinal while he pisses with his face mashed into the wall in front of him. I wonder if Knickers has a policy for cutting people off. I've never seen it happen. My guess is that the same rule applies to the waitresses here that applies to most of the jobs in the park: they get paid enough to do their jobs, but not enough to care about it.

Dave finishes pissing, zips up, doesn't wash his hands, and stumbles back over to me. He puts his arm back around my shoulder after he nearly falls over again, and I lead him out.

"You owe me one for this," I tell him.

"I sure do," he says. "But I'm not sorting out your girl shit. You're on your own with Nicole, and you're really on your own with Margaret. I don't do drama."

24

Wonderments gets millions – yes, millions – of visitors a year. There are a lot of locals that buy season tickets and come more than once, or use the place to walk around the same way old people use shopping malls, so that pads the numbers a bit. Even taking that into account, millions of ticket sales is no joke. That's a serious amount of tourist money, money wasted before it's even gone, carefully put into savings accounts, counted meticulously, and then earmarked to buy forgettable, overpriced junk. People come from all over the state. They come from all over the country. Roller coaster nuts will even fly from all over the world.

That's why it baffles me that there's so shockingly little to do in the surrounding area. There's some mildly interesting stuff to do in town – an IMAX movie theater, an aquarium, a shopping mall – and its fair share of summertime "fests" – Rib Fest, Jazz Fest, Beer Fest, an artsy Film Fest – but very little that would separate it from any other mid-sized town in America. The only thing that sets it apart is the number of cheap motels.

I know it doesn't matter. My parents will be perfectly happy to do whatever crappy things we decide to do, because anything slightly different from their boring lives is vacation enough. It still disappoints me. They don't go on vacation very often. It'd be nice to have something to show them when they get here other than pizza and a movie.

The brochures in the front office of Wonderments were no help, as they almost exclusively advertise things to do in the park. When I saw the brochures the first time I thought for sure that they were protecting their brand and trying to keep tourists and their money inside the park. It turns out, there's just nothing else to fucking do.

I'm using one of the computers in the common area, which has slower internet than I even knew existed anymore, but it's better than having to navigate everything on my phone. There's a girl in line behind me who presumably has the same idea. She has brown hair in dreadlocks, a long, flowing pink skirt, flip flops and a backpack. If sixties hippies were still teenagers today and decided to update their outfits, she is what they would look like. There are public computers in both the guys' dorms and the girls' dorms, so I wonder what she's doing here. She probably has a hippie boyfriend upstairs who is still passed out or is busy playing in a drum circle with some Europeans he just met. I wonder what their sex is like. Hairy and funky smelling, most likely. The girl fidgets impatiently and I go back to ignoring her. I click around in Internet Explorer on a site the city has set up for tourism. I'm only using Internet Explorer because the site doesn't format correctly in any browser from this century.

All the options for recreation seem to be geared toward college students whose only requirement for recreation is cheap beer or retirees looking for the quietest and least exciting activities possible while they wait to die. I wish there were an actual human being I could get a recommendation from. There are some locals that work here in the summer, but I don't know any of them. Most of them are teenagers working summer jobs, anyway.

"Hey, sorry." It's the girl behind me. There are two other computers (one in use, one broken) and I'm curious as to why she singled me out. "Do you know how much longer you're going to be on? I only need the computer for a few minutes, but I have to go back to my room and change before work."

"Nah, I'm done, you can have it."

"Thanks," she says. She walks over to me as I stand up, close enough that I can smell her. It's a mild and pleasant perfume, like vanilla and some sort of flower. It makes me want to stand in even closer to her. For a moment I'm jealous of her boyfriend.

* * *

The Wave Blast is the biggest employee event of the summer, but Wonderments isn't going to shut down stores early just so its employees can get drunk sooner. Since it's a weeknight we close at ten, but by the time we close up and walk all the way back there, it'll still be almost midnight. Dave scheduled me, Nicole, and Margaret to work, giving himself the night off so he could get to the party earlier. I assumed the girls would bring their swim suits to work like I did so we could go straight from work to the water park, but they didn't, leaving me to walk there alone while they went back to the girls' dorm to get ready. I try to imagine their conversation for the entire walk there, and I really have no idea what they could talk about. They have nothing in common as far as I can tell – not like night and day, not two sides of the same coin, but two things so separate you couldn't even cast them as opposites.

Lights and lanterns are all along the main path, alternating red, white, and blue to remind us we're not just getting drunk for fun: it's our patriotic duty.

The water park is decorated sparsely for the party. The paper lanterns continue along the path from the entrance to (I'm assuming) the giant wading pool. No doubt management is hoping that keeping the path lit will keep everyone on it and out of the dark corners, closed rides, and secluded utility closets that are going to seem very inviting once everyone is drunk and looking for a place to make out. It's a confusing mish-mash of ideas: the lanterns and low lighting make it feel like a romantic atmosphere, the packs of roving drunks make it feel like a frat party, and the backdrop of a shut down amusement park makes it feel like a horror movie.

The highlight of the party is a bar built to look like a hut you'd see at a Hawaiian luau, complete with fake torches flickering with light bulbs inside them. It's the same decorations that are there during the day. Replacing them with Fourth of July decorations or colors must have been deemed too much of a hassle. Floating around in the pool and getting drunk at the bar are the only things to do. I do not envy the guys who have to work the bar tonight, no matter how much they make in tips.

Dave and Grace are somewhere inside the park. They didn't set a time to meet up with me. It feels like their polite way of avoiding me tonight, but it could just be the general apathy and lack of planning so many people my age suffer from. I send Dave a text – "Where are you guys?" I might be the last holdout, but I refuse to use "R" or "U" as a word.

I'm waiting for a text back when I feel a tap on my shoulder. It's Margaret. How she managed to spot me in this crowd I have no idea. I'm stunned. I expected her to "change her mind" once she got back to her room and send me a text message about how she wouldn't be coming after all. I check my pocket, unsure if I even remembered to bring the ticket I told her I would pick up for her. I did. I'm not sure why the tickets matter – no one is checking them at the gate, and when I went to pick them up there was a stack of them in a tray on the office desk. Still, Margaret strikes me as the type to take offense if I had forgotten her ticket – and therefore, forgotten about her – so I'm glad I have it.

"I thought for a second that you were going to stand me up," I say, handing her the ticket from my pocket.

"Well, I'm here. I hope it's worth it. I bought this bathing suit just for the party. If it sucks in there, I blame you. This thing cost me eighty bucks." She must have bought it here in the park. They notoriously gouge the price of swimwear. Of course, they gouge the price of everything, but it's particularly bad on the bathing suits. People think they can get into the pools or on the water slides in cut off jeans or khaki shorts. People even try it in their boxers sometimes. When they find out they can't, they get sent to Surf's Up, the shop where they can get a Wonderments-approved bathing suit for only three times the manufacturer's suggested retail price. They're the best-selling item in the water park.

"Nice," I say. She's wearing a large-cupped red bikini top, cargo shorts, and flip flops. The outfit surprises me a little. With all the complaining she does about fashion, I would have expected her to pick a frumpy one-piece. Her tits are significantly larger than I had previously noticed. She must wear her work shirt up a size from what she needs to keep it extra baggy.

"Grace and Dave are inside, I think. I'm waiting to hear back from them."

She rolls her eyes. "You're going to make me hang out with them all night, aren't you?" It seems to be a favorite tactic of Margaret's to complain about doing things she actually wants to do. She wants to go to the party, but she wants me to beg her to go. A weird variant on fishing for compliments, I guess.

"It won't be so bad. Everyone is just going to get drunk and relax. They're not bad people."

My phone goes off. Dave has sent me a text back: "we r inside where r u." Even ignoring the horrible texting grammar, it tells me nothing about how to find or meet up with them.

"Okay, I take that back," I say. "They're fucking horrible."

It takes three more text messages to find out they're by the lockers. I hate texting so much. I'm ashamed to live in a world where people get offended if you call them without texting first.

"Where's Nicole?" I ask. It makes sense to me that Margaret would have volunteered this information, since they left the store together in the first place. I don't know why she's making me ask.

"Back at the dorm still," Margaret says. "She was still getting ready after I put on my suit, so she told me to just go on ahead. Come on, let's go."

I'd prefer to wait for Nicole, but it's easier to be led along, so I follow Margaret through the gate. As we walk by I look up at water park logo: a smiling, green, cartoon dolphin jumping over ocean waves. The smile is uncanny. Dolphins shouldn't have teeth.

We find Grace and Dave near the lockers. Grace is wearing a solid red bikini top and a towel wrapped around her waist. It looks like it could be the same exact suit Margaret has on, just in a smaller size. I wonder if it will bother them, like when two women on a TV show realize they're wearing the same outfit and rush home in a panic to change.

Dave already has a drink in his hand. He's has on a pair of long gray trunks, worn low. I'd bet money he chose them just because they do such a good job of showing off his abs. I'd probably show them off too if mine looked that good. Dave and Grace are surrounded by a small group of guys all hoping to get lucky, each made from the same mold of muscles, crew cuts, and tans.

"You keep telling me they aren't bad people," Margaret says. "But if that's true, how come they always attract a cloud of douchebags?" It's hard to argue with her logic. I wonder if Margaret would sleep with one of those attractive douchebags given the chance. Probably.

We walk up and the circle expands to let us in. None of the guys looks over at us. They talk about parties they've been to, a new club opening in town, or their workout regimen for the summer. Margaret and I might be standing in the circle with all of them, but we're not part of the conversation.

Eventually Nicole arrives and stands next to Margaret. "Hey," she says. Immediately the cloud of douchebags makes an effort to include her in all their social flexing and preening. It just makes their ignoring of Margaret even more blatant.

"Here's our locker key. You can put your clothes and stuff in there." She tosses it to me and I catch it clumsily. I assume immediately that Nicole wants to fuck one of these soulless suitors – she treats me like a date when she's around guys she wants to get rid of, and a buddy when she's not. It's pretty clear that I'm a buddy tonight.

As soon as Margaret and I have the locker open, Dave says, "My drink is empty. Let's hit the island bar." He tosses his cup in the general direction of an overflowing trash bin. This place is going to look like a landfill in a few hours.

I stuff everyone's towels in the tiny locker and try to shut it. It won't, so I lean against it, hard, and it slams shut. Dozens of these lockers jam a day, and staff has to help people pry them open. I wonder if we'll ever be able to get in that locker again, then realize our small cloud of people is already drifting toward the water.

At the bar, they serve all the booze in red plastic cups – no glass in the pool! – a choice that reinforces the frat party vibe. For a moment, I wonder what the proper cleaning procedure looks like for a pool this size. During the day there's a strict "no drinks leave the bar area" rule in effect, but red cups – either in the hands of partygoers or just floating in the water – are starting to slowly drift out from the bar area like a drop of red food coloring in a pitcher of water. The ratio of staff who give a fuck to twenty-somethings who do not significantly favors those with no fucks to give. No one seems to be bothered by the occasional drink spilled in the water. I wonder how many people have to puke in the pool before they shut the party down.

I agreed to come to the party with Dave and Nicole, but I'm standing in the waist-high water next to Margaret while she reclines in the floating version of a poolside deck chair. I'm not sure where Dave and Nicole and all the rest went – they were near us originally and just sort of drifted off. I wonder how they're going to get the locker key from me without being able to text me to figure out where I am.

"See, this is better," Margaret says. Her eyes are closed. She's drinking some fruity colored drink that looks ridiculous in the red cups.

"Yeah, it's cool," I say. I feel like we don't have much to talk about. Pretty much every time we end up in a conversation, she's talking about who she doesn't like or what she doesn't like. I realize I have no idea what she *does* like. I wish we could join up with the rest of the group.

"So, what do you like? I mean, what are you into?" I don't add, "you usually just bitch about stuff."

She takes a long drink, like the question is a hard one to answer. "Buddhism. Old music. Theatre."

"Bullshit. You might as well say you like long walks on the beach. What do you really like?"

She looks pissed, but she doesn't deny it. "Italian food. Period piece dramas with female characters that aren't stupid. And music from the fifties and sixties. I really do like old music. If you think that's dumb then fuck off."

"I don't."

"So what are you into then?"

I decide to give her the honest answer. "Money, fucking with people, and caffeine first thing in the morning."

She nods in approval and raises her cup toward me. "To fucking with people." I tap my cup against hers and we both drink

130

until they're empty.

The two of us stay near the island bar. Margaret's floating chair is sure to be taken if she ever gets out of it, so I'm stuck standing nearby in the water, making the trips back and forth to the bar for both of us. I'm on my way back from the seventh trip when I discover Margaret has gone from peacefully lounging to standing in the water surrounded by a crowd of drunks. I spot Dave and Grace immediately. I don't see Nicole. The cloud of people with them has some girls now. I can't tell if the guys in the group are the same douchebags as earlier, or new ones.

"I just want the fucking key so I can go the fuck home!" It's Dave. He's drunk. This is not going to go well.

"I don't have the key. It's not my locker." Margaret's voice is thin and quiet – her attempt at dangerous, I think.

One of the douchebags says, "Give him the goddamn key already." He steps close to Margaret, staring down at her with stupid dead eyes and hulking muscles. I can tell he's the kind of guy who is used to intimidating his way to success.

"So uh... what's going on here?" I'm hoping this will diffuse quickly. Dave starts to turn toward me and bumps into Margaret, who stumbles. The water is only waist deep, but she goes down anyway and comes up sputtering, hair soaked and coughing. I know it's mean, but I hope she pukes. It'd resolve the situation pretty quickly.

Unfortunately, she doesn't. "Watch it, fucktard!" She clenches a fist and for a moment I'm sure she's going to hit him, but common sense or cowardice gets the better of her and she stops herself.

"Shit. Sorry, sorry, sorry," he says. "Look, can I just go home?" I see his face for the first time, and he has a black eye. It's not the time to ask.

"I've got the key," I tell him. "Let's go." I hand my drink to Dave and the fruity drink to Margaret. "Hold these." Dave takes a big gulp of the rum and coke I handed him before I can fish the key out of my pocket. "Where's Nicole?"

"I'll take her stuff," Grace says, "Let's just get going."

"Some dudes showed up and she went off to fuck 'em," Dave volunteers.

"She did not, you asshole," Grace says. "You're going to

apologize to her later for saying that."

The four of us wade out of the pool area, bumping and shoving our way through the crowds of people as we pass. It intimidates me. Bodies close, beautiful girls everywhere. I try not to touch anyone as we pass but it's impossible. No one seems to notice or mind. Somehow, that makes me even more uncomfortable.

It looks like one of the guys is going to leave with Dave, but the rest of the people that showed up with him stay back at the bar. Margaret and Grace follow me and Dave until we manage to get back to the lockers. It's late enough at this point that people are pouring out of the gates to head home, although the crowd inside, somehow, doesn't feel like it's thinning out.

I put the key into the locker. Sure enough, it won't open.

"Oh, for fuck's sake." Dave hits the locker, hard. Nothing happens. He hits it again and it dents the locker a little bit. Nothing. He hits it a third time and it pops open. "Ow.... Fuck, fuck fuck," he says, rubbing his hand. I wonder if he broke it.

Margaret is laughing. Dave sees her and I'm expecting a fight, but he just says, "Okay, I deserved that. Let's go."

We take all our stuff out of the locker and say our goodbyes. Dave stumbles off toward the guys' dorms, and Grace walks toward the girls' dorms. Margaret stays with me near the gate. She still looks unsteady on her feet, drunk well beyond what I assume she's used to. I consider calling Grace back. I assume their petty dislike for each other would be temporarily put on hold if Margaret was really desperate for the help.

"I should catch up to Dave and walk him home," I say.

"You know," she says, words slurring just a bit, "I was having a nice time until all those fuckheads showed up." I don't know if she didn't hear me about walking Dave home, or doesn't care.

It was mostly alcohol and small talk. I'm not sure I'd qualify it as particularly nice. "Yeah, it was fun," I tell her.

"You could come back to my room, you know." She wobbles a bit, making me hold her upright.

"You're... really drunk. Let me walk you back to your room, but that's all, I think."

132

She latches on to my arm, leaning on me heavily as we walk. Either she's faking at least a little, or I should be impressed she's still conscious. We don't say much on the way to the girls' dorm. She presses herself into my arm and I can't help but like it. On some level, any attention is good attention.

We make it up to the front door and Margaret scans her key card. I'm a bit jealous; the guys' dorms are even shittier than these and don't bother with a lock on the outside doors.

"Okay, this is as far as I go," I say. "Be careful getting up to your room."

She leans in, practically falling into me, and kisses me. It's a sloppy, drunken kiss, with a lot of tongue and little subtlety. I let her kiss me for a few seconds, hoping the kiss will just break off. When she shows no signs of stopping, I pull away and stand her up straight.

"We're really drunk." A convenient excuse. "We need to sleep this off. I'll see you later." I lean in and kiss her quickly, mouth closed, on the lips. I'm not sure why. I don't want to. It just seems polite. She's still standing there as I turn and leave.

25

I'm passed out in bed sleeping off the alcohol when Cory from Texas slams open the door and flips on the light.

"Woah, are you asleep, dude?"

"Not anymore, man." I open my eyes slowly. The light hurts.

"How early did you get back from the Wave Blast? It's not that late." He's got a coffee in both hands, and he hands me one. I wonder if he planned to drink them both and is giving one up, or if he was planning on catching me in the room.

I sit up. I realize I fell asleep in my clothes. The bed is damp from the swim trunks. "What time is it?"

"Like two a.m. I guess. How did it go? I saw you there when you were coming in, but I was chatting up this hot European girl."

"Uhh... the girl I was hanging out with tried to make out with me a little awhile ago, but she was drunk."

"Nice, dude. The hot girl in the red bikini? She's smokin' hot."

"There were a hundred red bikinis there, but yeah."

"I mean, there was the hot Asian girl in the red bikini, and the other girl in the red bikini."

I consider throwing my coffee on one of us to end the conversation. "The other one."

"Still nice, dude. Did you hit it?"

"No man, we were both drunk. I don't really like her anyway."

He seems confused as to why this would keep me from sleeping with her. "You should introduce me to the hot girl."

"No luck for you tonight either?" There is no way in hell I am introducing this kid to Nicole.

"Nah. Why didn't you hook up with the drunk makeout girl?"

I briefly consider hitting him in the face. Because you shouldn't take advantage of a drunk person? Because meaningless hookups are stupid? Because you shouldn't have to fuck everything that moves to define your self worth?

"I work with her. If it goes bad it shits all over my whole summer. That's not worth getting laid."

He still looks confused. "I guess so."

I don't want to admit that hooking up with Margaret probably keeps me from dating Nicole. Nicole is way out of my league. She doesn't like me. I'm just convenient to her. Margaret is there. She likes me. She's cute and accessible. Her personality drives me insane. I'd rather chew sandpaper than hang out with her on a regular basis.

"I have my eye on someone else," I confess.

"Hot red bikini girl, right? Dude, any guy in his right mind would want to get with that. It'd be a straight up religious experience." He makes the sign of the cross in front of him. I'm not sure if he's serious or joking, but I'm fairly certain he's not Catholic. "Won't it be weird at work anyway? I mean, you work with her too."

I really hate having a roommate.

* * *

Anyone who thinks they should go out and get smashed and work the next day is an idiot, and that includes me. Things are even more miserable than usual because Dave called in sick, which is obviously bullshit, but no one important enough to do anything cares. As a result we have some other manager filling in for him, a short, stocky woman with curly hair and no interest in being social whatsoever. Everything by the book, which means me, Margaret, and Nicole in different corners, each working our registers and

135

cleaning our areas. No goofing off or conversation here. It occurs to me that even though Dave is a dick, we still lucked out having him as our manager. When you're working a meaningless job you hate for very little money, there are few blessings greater than a lazy boss.

Nicole keeps looking over at me, thinking she might be able to sneak in a little bit of a conversation. Margaret is doing exactly the opposite, avoiding looking at me at all costs. Maybe having the new boss here today is a good thing. I don't want to try and talk to Margaret about what happened between us last night, and I don't want to talk to Nicole about whatever happened between her and whoever last night, either.

From all her hand waving and body language, it looks like Nicole wants to get my opinion about last night. I can't hear what she's saying, but I can imagine the story in my mind already: "Hey, so everyone was drunk and I fucked this guy after I knew him for two hours, do you think he likes me for me?" It sets my teeth on edge.

The store is totally empty like it is every day in the middle of the day. Nicole comes over to me and says, "hey, do you want to go to lunch? I need to talk to you about some stuff from the Wave Blast last night."

For the first time during the shift Margaret looks at me, a death glare that would cook me alive if she could figure out a way to convert jealousy into heat. I ignore it.

Luckily, the temp manager chimes in to save me from the conversation. "Sorry, honey. Company policy says there has to be three people in this store at all times, so you'll have to go one at a time."

I resist the urge to ask her what the company policy is on calling employees 'honey.'

"Oh, come on," Nicole says. "The store is dead. It's going to stay dead for the next five hours. We could practically lock the doors and all go to lunch together and not lose a sale." As if to fuck with her, a small child wanders in, grabs a handful of candy that seems to have been chosen more by proximity than flavor, and puts it up on the counter in front of Nicole's register. The boss shoots her an "I told you so" sort of look, and goes back to inventory or Angry Birds or whatever she was doing in the closet.

Margaret leaves her register and walks to the front. "I'm going to lunch," she says, and walks out. I wonder why she's pissed. It doesn't feel like she has any reason to be. Oh well. I wonder if I should tell everyone else about her drunken kiss. If she keeps being such a bitch at work, I'll have to anyway at some point just to explain it.

Nicole is edging over to me. The closet door is only open a crack, so I know she hopes to sneak close enough to have a whispered conversation. She gets about halfway to me when I hear from behind the door, "Stay at your stations. One of you can go to lunch when the other girl gets back."

Nicole snaps back to behind her register. Despite the mild hangover, this day at work is shaping up to be a lot easier than I thought it would be.

26

I was lucky to be able to avoid everyone yesterday, but today is my day off, so it should be easier. I'm using a dusty ten-year-old computer in the employee rec room. I don't have a Facebook page of my own, but that doesn't mean I don't use it. Today, I'm working on a Facebook profile for Amber Jones. Amber Jones isn't a real person, but if you spend enough time playing Farmville and Candy Crush and any other game that rewards you for adding people to your friends list, anyone can have a convincing number of Facebook "friends," whether they actually exist or not.

I really hate Farmville. I hate it to the point where I hate everyone who plays it, because I can't respect someone who spends their time on something so asinine. The entire game is designed with every basic psychological trick in the book to keep you playing and clicking. It's not fun or interesting; it's designed purely to be addicting. I only subject myself to the tedium to accumulate people for my friends list, and as an added bonus, the people I accumulate will on average be pretty gullible and a bit dim-witted, which is exactly what I need from a Facebook "friend."

Once I'm finished gathering enough friends to make my page look real, it'll be time to inject a scene of social injustice. Poor Amber is a hardworking, underpaid waitress, so when tragedy strikes because of racism or sexism, it won't be hard to spark a little internet outrage.

I'm not the first one to try this. I read a story about a year ago about a girl that faked a racial slur left for her on a customer's receipt and posted it on Facebook. They eventually caught her and now she's getting sued into oblivion, but not before she'd generated almost twelve thousand dollars in "tips" from helpful internet folk looking to right a wrong in the world.

I suppose most people would hear about this and learn that you shouldn't trick people. I learned that if you're going to trick people, do it well enough that they don't notice. That's how Amber is helping me out. She doesn't even exist. She doesn't need to. The great thing about the 24 hour news cycle is that news outlets barely check their sources, if they check them at all. They just copy and paste from other news sources, and people on the internet don't notice or care where the news comes from. The British tabloid Daily Mail gets more page views than the New York Times.

That means, in theory at least, I can post my story of bigotry and woe, causing a few dozen people to share it on their own pages. Then everyone's gullible grandma or uncle or cousin will share it too. A few shares later I can tweet it over to Daily Mail, they post it without bothering to check any sources, and then reputable news sources copy it over to their own sites.

It's unlikely anyone will ever know what happened, since on the internet everyone is pissed all the time but only stay that way about any one thing for a few minutes. Before long I'll have thousands of dollars in donations and the ad revenue from millions of clicks to the donation site. In the unlikely event that someone does catch on and alerts the media, and if the news networks are having a slow enough week to report on it, I can just delete everything and disappear with the cash.

It's a potentially huge amount of easy money for comparatively little time invested. I'll make sure to donate a portion of the proceeds to Amber Jones' imaginary family.

27

If nothing eventful happens at work today, I'll consider it a good day. I estimate my chances of having a good day at close to zero. Two of the teenage morning crew didn't show up to work, so it's me, Margaret, Dave, and no one else. I remember the short, curly-haired boss from my last shift saying company policy was to always have three people in the store. The Jolly Tinker shouldn't even count as a store. It's a big closet stuffed with toys and candy. There is no toilet here. I wonder where company policy says we're supposed to take a shit since, officially, we're not allowed to go anywhere.

Dave is puttering around doing nothing with his black eye and a big shit-eating grin. The tension in the air is palpable and he loves it. I asked him about the eye but all he said was, "We were drunk, and I got punched." It didn't seem like he was being evasive or anything. Apparently, getting punched is just on his list of fun times when alcohol is involved.

Margaret has given up on her avoidance tactics (bored, maybe?) and is talking to both of us using short, abrupt sentences she's practically forcing out of her mouth. No matter what she says, you can tell it was originally "fuck you" and was changed at the last moment. The original malice is still there.

Fortunately Dave and Margaret are going at it, and with any luck, their drama will keep them both away from me for a long, long time.

"Look," Dave says. "I was drunk, and I was pissed off about getting hit, and I yelled at you. I shouldn't have. I really am sorry. I wasn't trying to be a jackass."

Margaret hasn't said anything about their fight at the Wave Blast. She's doing that thing girls do, when they're pissed off but they make you drag it out of them instead of just telling you. They *want* to tell you, but they want the attention more.

"You can't just be pissed the rest of the summer," Dave says. "Well, most people couldn't but you probably can. Still, it's a shitty thing to do."

"You almost drowned me," she says. "I can be mad if I want."

"I didn't almost —" he rolls his eyes and throws up his hands in a "what the fuck?" motion. "What do you want? Dinner? Movie tickets? Get your hair and nails done?"

Margaret makes an exaggerated face with her hand on her chin. "I don't know. Hmmm. No, I do know. Me and him are going to lunch. I don't know how long we'll be gone, but we're going. You stay here and deal with it. We'll be back later."

Dave is facing me and Margaret has her back to me, so I'm shaking my head at him in a pronounced, "No, no, fuck no," kind of motion.

"Okay, fine," he says. "You two can go on lunch, but then that's it. You accept that I'm sorry. No staying mad, no keying my car, no sneaking up and punching me in the balls, or whatever other weird revenge fantasy prank you come up with. We're even." I silently mouth the words "Fuck. You." at Dave and go back to normal before Margaret turns around.

"Deal," she says. "You. It's lunch time." It's 10:30 a.m. I don't want to have whatever conversation this is leading up to.

"Have fun, lovebirds," Dave calls after us. I wouldn't do it myself, but I hope someone punches him in the other eye.

The silence as we walk is palpable. She doesn't make small talk. She doesn't get mad at me. She doesn't get desperate and beg for a date. She doesn't even ask me where we want to go to eat. She's waiting for me to be the one to break the silence. I refuse to, so we don't talk. It feels juvenile, but I don't see any way out of it other than giving her what she wants.

Despite the fact that Dave basically gave us all the time in the world for break, we end up at the employee cafeteria anyway. I'm staring down at today's special, which is Fritos chips covered in chili that almost certainly came out of a can, and cheese that may or may not have been bought on discount because it was about to spoil. Margaret is nursing a plate of chicken nuggets and french fries, taking a bite roughly once every seventeen years. I wonder if I'll die before she finishes lunch, and if I do if it will be because she kills me or just due to old age.

"What did you do on your day off?" she asks.

"Not much. Slept in late, studied some Portuguese." She gives me a look like she's pretty sure I'm making a joke, but doesn't get the punchline.

We are most definitely not on lunch together because she wants to ask about my day off, but she's playing the game where she wants me to panic and fish it out of her. I'm not falling for it. If she wants to sit there and make small talk trying to make me nervous, that's fine.

It's one of the things I like about Nicole. She's a shitty, self-absorbed human being, but at least it's honest. I don't even mind a good liar – at least if I get tricked, or conned, or swindled, or whatever you want to call it, by something I don't see coming, I stand to learn something or get an interesting story. The whole song and dance where Margaret and I both know where the conversation is headed but she won't go there is the worst. It's the social equivalent of a staring contest with a four-year-old who is going to scream and pull your hair when they lose.

So I'm sitting, eating my lunch that has close to the maximum number of calories you can have in a meal while containing zero nutritional benefit. I wonder if they'd be able to switch the chili for dog food without anyone noticing, then realize they wouldn't, because the dog food would be more expensive.

Margaret is getting more and more agitated on the other side of the table. She's not nervous or anything, but she's taking it personally that I'm not trying to pry conversation out of her.

Silence falls over the table. It's only a few minutes, but it feels like forever. She cracks first.

"So, what the hell happened the other night?"

I don't answer.

"We were hanging out all night, having drinks, talking, then when it got to the end of the night you blew me off."

"We were both drunk out of our minds," I point out.

"So?" she says.

She's pulled me in now, but maybe I can do this like ripping off a band-aid. Quick and painless. "So, we don't even know each other that well. That night was the first real conversation we ever had and I don't even remember half of it. You're from out of town and so am I and we're both leaving at the end of the summer. On top of that we were so drunk there was no way it was going to be good sex, if we remembered it at all. That's not my idea of a good time."

"You would have done it with Nicole," she says.

Now we're at the heart of the issue. I'm not sure if she genuinely likes me at all or if this is her personal attempt at proving, in some way, that she's better than Nicole and Grace. It's hard to tell the difference between her bravado and her real thoughts.

"Maybe, maybe not. So what?" It's the honest answer.

"So that makes you an asshole hypocrite who's bullshitting me."

When someone is kind enough to reject you in such a way that you can withdraw with grace and dignity, take it.

"Sorry, but I don't see how that follows at all. I wouldn't sleep with you after one date, a date that wasn't even really a date, just an invite to a group function? *And* we were both drunk? Sorry, I think it makes me an asshole if I *had* slept with you." Okay, I think that was fair. But I never want to have this conversation again. "I liked spending time with you. I didn't think sleeping with you was a good idea, and I still don't. But hey, if taking you back to your room and fucking you from behind until I blow a load on your ass, and then leaving and telling all my friends about it while I ignore you for the rest of the summer is your idea of what it takes to not be an asshole, then let's go. I haven't been laid in awhile and I'm sure we

143

can get it over quickly." Well, that was over the line.

Margaret stands up slowly. "If you follow me out of here, you will regret it."

She stands up and storms out of the cafeteria, slamming the door loud enough to stop every conversation in the room for just a single second, before everyone goes back to never noticing she was there. She left her tray behind, and thanks to her slow eating, most of the chicken nuggets and fries were left behind as well. I pull them over to me as soon as I'm reasonably sure she's not going to come storming back in. They're much better than my chili cheese Fritos.

* * *

It's been a long fucking day. I waited another thirty minutes in the cafeteria before I left to go back to the shop, and I still beat Margaret back. She didn't come in for almost an hour after I returned, and spent the rest of the shift talking with Dave and ignoring me, which I'm fine with. I wonder how long she plans to keep it up for, or if there's anything I could do to make things right. I decide there probably isn't, and even if there was, I'm not sure I want to bother.

It's after midnight when I get back to my dorm room. The first thing I notice is that the Czech guys next door are booming techno music like their room is a dance club; this is normal. The second thing I notice is that my door is open, even though Cory from Texas isn't in the room. This is not normal.

I don't see anything wrong with the room, but the first thing I do is head to the drawer with my money in it. Everything inside is covered in some sort of red... juice, maybe? I ignore that and dig around for the envelope. The money is still there. I pull it out, and as far as I can tell, nothing has been stolen. I pull the bishop out of the envelope and hold it in my hand. It still feels smooth. Most of the other pieces were broken or chipped, but not this one. There used to be a piece of velvet on the bottom of it, but when it started to peel off I removed it and washed off the sticky residue that was left over. I know it's not worth anything, but I like having it.

I open the top drawer and find the same red liquid everywhere, along with the culprit: Two empty bottles of cherry-flavored Powerade. I don't know if red Powerade stains or not, but it looks like it does. Most of my stuff is ruined. I didn't have much to speak of in the way of clothes in the first place, but there's still the inconvenience of having to replace everything.

I wonder why they didn't take the money. Didn't see it, I guess? I shut the drawer and lie down in my bed. Immediately I notice something new scrawled over the old graffiti. It says, in red Sharpie: "DO NOT FUCK WITH ME. –M."

It has to have been Margaret. I imagine the effort it would have taken for her to pull this off. It wouldn't have been hard to get into the building. The front desk is supposed to check our ID when we come in, but they never do and everyone knows that. She'd still have to convince the front desk to tell her which room is mine. They're not supposed to give out information, but when your front desk help is a rotating cast of sixteen-year-olds, you expect a certain amount of basic incompetence.

Then she would have had to go to the convenience store and find something to dump in the dresser. Then, once she'd figured out which room is mine and found something to vandalize the room with – at this point I'm just thankful the convenience store doesn't sell eggs – she had to convince Cory from Texas to hang out with her, wait for him to leave to take a piss or go to work or whatever, and convince him to let her stay in the room. I wonder what she would have settled for doing if any part of this had fallen through. Bag of shit on the doorstep? Leaving a gossipy hate message about me in a bathroom stall? Who knows.

A montage of angry sitcom women slapping men in bars or throwing drinks in their faces comes to mind. We were right there having lunch. She could have slapped me. She could have thrown a drink in my face or dumped chili fries all over me or yelled at me in front of the whole place. Instead, she chose to wreck all my stuff. I almost admire her level of commitment.

28

I wake up to the sound of my phone ringing. I have the sneaking suspicion it's my mother – anyone else would just send a text. It's either her or someone trying to sell me something. I let it go to voicemail, then shortly after starts ringing again. Now I know it's her. I don't know why, but whenever my mom tries to call someone and they don't answer, she hangs up on the voicemail message the first time, then calls back to leave one. I roll over and go back to sleep.

It's almost noon when I wake up again. I don't have work today, so I skip the shower, go downstairs and head out to the park. I walk past the line and show the gatekeeper my employee badge. He waves me through. I wonder if I will be able to sell my badge at the end of the summer to someone who could use it to sneak into the park next year. There's no picture on it or anything.

I don't feel like eating in the cafeteria, but it wins out because it doesn't involve anything I'll have to heat up in a microwave or eat out of bag. The park is always interesting this time of day. It features all the telltale signs of a summer vacation: parents in shorts and polo shirts with sunglasses, old people with socks and sunglasses, packs of teenagers in t-shirts with band names on them. Everyone talking and laughing and gaping at all the lights and turning toward every sound. No one paying the slightest bit of attention to their immediate surroundings. Not for the first time, I wish I had the dexterity to be an effective pickpocket. The movies make it look so easy.

I get inside and see, much to my dismay, that it says "Daily Special: Spaghetti" on the whiteboard. There is nothing special about spaghetti. My guess is someone called in sick or the manager is gone, and someone said "fuck it, it's spaghetti day." Nothing else looks even remotely appetizing, so I order a pizza. The girl behind the counter stares at me like I told her I just punched her mother. The lunch rush is starting, and a pizza is one of the few staples that requires effort. I smile at her stupidly and say thank you like I don't notice, and have a seat.

I pick up my phone and call my voicemail. "You have one unread message. New message at: Nine-Oh-Three, a.m." Definitely my mother. When I was a kid she used to always freak out and yell at me if my friends ever called before nine; before that, she assumes, any reasonable human will be asleep, and after that, any reasonable human will be awake. Phone calls before nine are for emergencies only. As a result, my mother often sits down and makes any phone calls she needs to make precisely at nine o'clock.

"Hey, it's Mom," the voicemail starts. "Just calling to see how things are going, but you're probably at work or busy right now, so I'll just leave a message. Your dad says hi. We're doing good. You got some more mail since the last time we talked but I think it's all junk mail. Let me know if you're expecting anything important. If it looks important I'll open it up. It's mostly just credit card offers, I think." There's a pause, and I wonder if there's a limit on my voicemail for how long it will let someone talk before it just ends the message automatically. I check my phone to make sure it's charged decently enough just in case my mom rambles for another ten minutes.

"We had a family reunion; bummed you couldn't come but hey that's life. Your cousin Jake is having a baby. It's going to be a girl but they aren't telling anyone the name yet. His wife seems kind of strange though so I hope they don't name her anything silly. Seems like that's all the rage these days. Anyway, I was just calling because your dad and I tried really hard to get the vacation time that we need to come and see you but it's just not going to work out. He's busy at work and my boss is being picky about when she lets us have time off. I guess we'll see you at the end of the summer. Maybe we can all go on vacation together next summer or something. We'll see. Love you. Bye."

Huh. I guess I should be a bit relieved that they aren't coming – I was kind of dreading showing them around for a weekend and having them everywhere in my life and asking me if I was making enough money and if I'd met "anyone special." Still, they're my parents and I haven't seen them in awhile. I haven't decided if I'll go and see them before I leave for São Paulo or not. I know I should, but it'll either mean spending a lot of money (which I hate doing) or taking a bus to go see them (which I hate almost as much).

My parents aren't coming to see me. Sometimes it feels like I'll never see them again. It makes me homesick but not all that sad. It's just kind of how things go when they're at work all the time just to make ends meet and I'm going wherever I need to to make money myself. I'm doing it so I won't end up like them, but I can't help wonder if they were doing the same thing I was when they were my age. I doubt it – from what little I've heard them mention from the years before I was born, they were mostly working for minimum wage and smoking pot. I doubt they have the wit or the stomach to do anything illegal for money. I wonder what will happen when it's time for them to retire.

"Hey. Hey!" It takes a second for me to realize it's the girl behind the counter yelling at me. "Your pizza's ready."

In my room, I eat the entire pizza, thinking about calling back my mother and putting it off. The food sits heavy in my stomach, and I feel sick. I should have thrown most of it away, or given it away to someone else on my floor. Too late now. I resign myself to getting nothing else done and stay in bed the rest of the day.

* * *

Nicole, Grace and I are at Shitter's. I'm wishing a waitress would come over and refill our drinks, but she's nowhere in sight. Grace isn't at work with us today, but Nicole called her on the way out and invited her to dinner.

"Do you ever think about how much time we'd have to waste at work before they fired us?" I ask.

"Nope," Grace says. "They pay us almost nothing and assume we're screwups, and for the most part they're right. Short of stealing money, injuring someone, or assaulting a customer, it's impossible to get fired. I bet you could get away with assaulting a customer or blowing something up once and keep your job as long as you apologized for it." I think about the heavy glass figurines we sell and imagine Grace smashing one of them over someone's head.

I'm eating a plate of "Asian style noodles with chicken," and letting them do most of the talking. I regret the food I'm eating. It's not bad, but apparently Shitter's idea of Asian food is soy sauce and "a blend of Asian spices." I can't figure out what the "Asian spices" are, and the server has no idea either. The cook in the back probably has a jar labeled "Asian Spices" in Sharpie on masking tape. I wonder how far back I would have to go in the supply chain before anyone could tell me what's actually in it.

"So," Nicole says, "I hooked up with the guy from the Wave Blast. James."

"Who?" Grace asks.

"The hot one," Nicole says.

Grace nods. "Oh, him. I don't know if that's awesome or gross. He's soooo hot, but I heard he's fucked like half the park."

"We didn't fuck," Nicole says.

I have to find out. "How exactly did you find out he's fucked half the park, but you didn't even know his name?"

Grace looks at me like it's a stupid question. Then she looks back to Nicole. "Well, details."

"No, come on," Nicole is smiling as she protests. "We went back to my room, we made out for a bit, then he left. That's all. I wonder if he's going to call me back."

I know it's unfair to blame Nicole for everything that's happened over the last few days, but I went to the Wave Blast hoping to have a few drinks and a few laughs with Nicole and Grace and Dave, and instead someone poured red Powerade in my dresser drawer and will likely continue making life miserable for me for the rest of the summer.

"He's not going to fucking call you," I say. "Even if he does call you, it'll be because he's hoping you'll put out and –" I almost say 'guys are attracted to easy pussy' which I realize in time is the wrong thing to say and will get me slapped. I didn't care so much when it was Margaret, but I do with Nicole. "Guys are assholes who think with their dicks and won't use anything else unless you make them." There we go. It's not you, it's them.

"Geez, you don't have to be so mean about it." Nicole looks sad now, but it's way better than the alternative. Since I'm in a work uniform it wouldn't be my responsibility to get the stains from her iced coffee out of my shirt – the laundry services monkeys take care of that – but I'd rather have as few of my coworkers mad at me as possible.

"Sorry," I say. "I'm just saying, if you think about it, he probably left not too long after he realized he wasn't going to get laid. I'm sure he tried to be subtle about it and pestered you and poked you and did everything he could to try and get you to grab his dick without outright asking for it."

"It's not like that," Nicole says. The look on her face says it was exactly like that, although I'm sure she'll never admit it to me. She can barely admit it to herself.

"Then, once he realized he wasn't going to get any, he got out of there as quick as he could without screwing up future chances of screwing you."

Nicole sighs. "I guess."

"We've all been there, sweetie," Grace says.

The waitress comes over and takes our empty glasses seamlessly to go refill them. She doesn't interrupt us. I'd be impressed with her if she wasn't so slow about getting the job done.

"Why are you so pissed off today, anyway?" Grace asks me.

"You guys left me alone with Margaret the other night and things got weird." They turn on me, the previous line of conversation dropped immediately in the face of juicier gossip. I'm not sure I want to be talking about this, and I'm definitely sure these are the wrong people to be talking to about it, but it's better than hearing an even more detailed account of where and how James the douchebag got to put his hands on Nicole.

"What happened?" Grace asked. "You didn't say anything when I came back for our stuff."

"It happened after that. We were both still drunk and she kissed me. She tried to get me to come up to her room with her."

They look at each other. "She tried to take you back to her room, and you didn't go?"

I realize that between 'two of my coworkers drunkenly kissed' and 'a guy turned down easy drunk sex,' the latter is the more shocking news to both of them. In this moment, I hate them both a little.

"Yeah. You don't think it's just a little weird to fuck someone just because you're drunk? Margaret and I hardly know each other."

They both laugh a little and look at each other knowingly.

Grace says, "Oh, you're such a gentleman." She winks, and makes a clicking noise with her tongue, and punches me in the arm. "So, was it good? Does she like it dirty? Or does she just lay there? Come on, spill it. How are you guys getting it done in the Midwest?"

"Look, I really didn't —"

"I was wondering when you were going to get laid this summer," Grace says. "Dave bet me twenty bucks you wouldn't." She cuts a piece of chicken and sticks it in her mouth, pointing the knife at me and talking with her mouth open. "Good on you for playing shy about it though. Classy."

"Do you know how Dave got his black eye?" I ask. I'm hoping this diverts the conversation.

"Oh, yeah," Grace says. We were all hanging out at the side of the pool and then Dave ran into his ex-boyfriend's new boyfriend. By the time we got over to them they were brawling. Dave threw the first punch."

I wonder how Dave is dealing with it. If he hasn't brought it up with me, I'm not going to bring it up with him. If he wants to chalk it up to everyone being drunk, I'll let him. As for me, I hope nothing from the Wave Blast ever comes up again.

We finish eating lunch and Grace decides to walk home. She's not gone for long when Nicole says, "So? Did you hook up with her or not?"

"No," I say, "I really didn't."

We walk over and stand in a long line of people waiting for the train that goes from the back of the park to the front. We should be able to get on the first train, but it'll be close. The people behind us will be waiting for the next train. Once you've worked at an amusement park long enough you get an eye for these things.

"Do you like her? I mean, it seems like you guys would be a good fit." I wonder what she bases that assessment on, but I don't want to know the answer.

"Not really," I say. "I mean, she's not a bad person. She's just not my type."

"Whatever, why isn't she your type?"

I wish I could say "I'm just not attracted to her." I wonder if it's always been impolite to say that or if it's a recent historical development, but either way I think the world would be better off if people could say that without getting their heads ripped off. It's nothing personal. People can't help who they are or aren't attracted to. It's only because people place personal worth on how many people want to fuck them that it matters at all.

"We just don't get along that well. I mean, we get along okay, but her personality is really abrasive. It'd get exhausting in a big hurry."

"Yeah, I see what you mean. She's cute though." I can't tell if she really thinks that or if she's just being polite.

"I guess. That doesn't last for very long. No matter who you end up with, they seem normal eventually. It's not worth putting up with someone you don't like just because they're cute."

"So what are you going to tell her?"

"We talked already. She was pretty pissed at me. I tried to be a nice guy but she wasn't having it."

"You're a nice guy. It's just normal to be upset when you get turned down. I mean, I'm sure she was feeling pretty good after the two of you spent the whole night together."

"I didn't mean to lead her on."

"That's why I don't tell guys I like them. I wait for them to tell

152

me. Getting shot down after you think you're making the right move really sucks."

The train pulls up and people start getting on. The line shuffles forward and sure enough, only a few people after us are able to get on before the train is full. Nicole and I can't sit next to each other since by the time we get on the train the only seats left are spread out. She sits two rows in front of me and our conversation continues over the head of a small child sitting next to his exhausted-looking mother.

"How did that happen, anyway? I thought all of us were going to hang out together and I got stuck hanging out with Margaret while you guys went off doing whatever."

"I feel bad about that," she says.

"Well, I would have rather been hanging out with you than Margaret. No offense to her." I'm not sure if I'm flirting or just repaying the compliment about me being a nice guy. I'm sure she wouldn't think that if she knew me better. Then again, with the caliber of guys she's used to being around, maybe she would.

"You are a sweetheart, aren't you? Most guys would have slept with her even if they didn't like her."

At this point the exhausted mother perks up. She's looked burned out and pissed off ever since I noticed her, but now it's directed at us. "Hey, some of us brought our kids here, can you maybe watch your mouth a little bit?"

I look down at her kid. He's completely oblivious to the conversation of course. He's got his head down, his focus locked in on the Nintendo DS he's holding. I want to ask her what kind of parent pays $100 to get her and her kid into an amusement park full of rides, games, and shows, and then puts him on a shitty train with a video game. I'm wearing my work uniform though, so it'd be pretty bad if things escalate.

"Sorry, ma'am," Nicole says. "It won't happen again." The pissy mother rolls her eyes, but goes back to half-napping and ignoring her kid.

"I really am sorry about standing you up at the Wave Blast the other night. Dave didn't want to hang around Margaret, so I went with him, then we all kind of wandered off and did our own thing."

I try not to think about the fact that Nicole's "own thing" was James the Hot Guy.

"Let me make it up to you," she says. "There's an aquarium in town I've been wanting to go to, but Grace thinks it's dumb and she won't go with me. You can be my date."

"Okay, sure."

"Text me your work schedule later and we'll go on whichever day we both have off next."

I know my work schedule already, but I don't want to seem like a dork, and I do want a chance to start up another conversation with Nicole later.

"I'll text it to you when I get home."

29

Margaret agreed to meet me for lunch. The line stretches out the door of the employee cafeteria because I was stupid enough to ask her to meet me here during actual lunch time. My thinking was that if there are a lot of people around, she'll be forced to be civilized. Waiting in this line is mind-numbing enough that I almost regret my decision.

I'm finally inside the building but still a solid twenty minutes away from getting through the line. I can see that Margaret is here already, sitting by herself but surrounded by people. They're all laughing and talking and enjoying lunch, and she sits in the middle, smiling disdainfully, not talking to anyone. The seat directly across from her is one of the few empty seats in the place. Even with the place this packed, everyone knows better than to start an argument with a bitchy white girl.

Her saving me a seat is pointless. The line is so long that the people sitting by her will probably be done and replaced by others before I even get through it. I'd ask her if she just wants to go somewhere else, but I want this to seem as little like a date as possible, and she has food already anyway.

I hate when this happens. It doesn't matter where. One person at their seat, the other one in line. If I'm not looking over at her it looks like I'm ignoring her, but if I try to maintain communication through yelling or waving or whatever, it looks ridiculous. There is no way out, and no way to hurry it up.

Several minutes later I'm close enough to tell that the day's special is beef stroganoff, one of the world's most disgusting foods. (Ingredient list: soggy noodles, greasy hamburger, old milk, slime.) I take it as a bad omen.

"Thanks for saving me a seat," I tell her as I sit down, squeezing between a big bald guy in a water park uniform and a girl wearing the turquoise shirt that all the ride operators wear. I bang her elbow accidentally as I sit down. She doesn't even look over. She's so engrossed in her own conversation she might as well be on another planet.

Margaret doesn't look at me. She doesn't look any more pissed than normal though, so I take that as a good sign.

"Thanks for having lunch with me," I say.

"It's fine. Why did you want to have lunch anyway?"

I decide to be honest. Not out of any moral compulsion. I just can't think of a lie that's more convenient or effective.

"I just want to apologize for before." I like that phrasing. I do want to apologize. I'm not sorry for anything I did or said, but I do want the benefits that go with her thinking I am.

"Okay," she says. She still looks pissed at me. I don't know how. I get the flash of anger that comes when someone pisses you off, but I can't hold onto it for days and days like Margaret apparently can. It's not like she's been mad nonstop the whole time since the Wave Blast. It's like she's conjuring up the emotion just to make things difficult.

"You ruined half my wardrobe and there's going to be ants in my room all fucking summer now." It's the wrong thing to say, but I can't help it.

She takes a french fry off my plate and eats it slowly. This is the part where she apologizes. This is the part where everyone in the history of the world knows you're supposed to apologize. She doesn't.

"I'm not sure what you think I have to do to make things right."

Her eyes narrow. "You don't get to *do* anything. I got embarrassed, and I'm pissed off at you about it. It doesn't go away just because you put the bare minimum amount of effort into trying to make me feel better."

We eat silently. Suddenly, I feel someone slap me on the shoulder from behind.

"Hey, dude!" It's Cory from Texas, grinning down on me with his braces and his big Texan grin. He looks across the table. "And hi, uhhh..."

"Margaret," she says.

"Margaret. Right. Hi again," he says. I realize that I never told him what happened after he left her alone in our room. We didn't see each other for awhile thanks to his work schedule, and I just didn't think about it.

Cory tries to get the guy next to him to move over, who looks at Cory like he's a dumbass. There's no room.

"So, are you done eating?" Cory asks. There's still obviously food on my tray. "It's packed in here. I've been walking around trying to find a seat."

I grab my tray and stand up. "Yeah, I think we're just about done here. Go ahead, man. You ready, Margaret?"

"I think I'm going to stay here for a little bit," she says. "He can keep me company." Her demeanor has changed completely – her eyes are softer, and she's smiling at Cory.

"Okay, I'll see you later."

"Later dude, thanks," Cory says over his shoulder.

I don't care at all what they talk about, just so long as it gets me out of having to sit through any more awkward lunch. I look back at them and can see her smiling and leaning toward him. Well, whatever.

30

Sundays aren't nearly as busy as Saturdays are at Wonderments, but it's still the weekend. There isn't enough to do to justify coming two days in a row, but plenty of people do it anyway, hoping Sunday won't be as busy as Saturday. They should come on a Tuesday if they want to avoid the crowds, but their shitty day jobs make fun and relaxation a weekend-only activity.

It keeps the four of us – me, Dave, Nicole, and Margaret – pretty busy. Nicole is running one of the registers and not smiling as she takes money. She thanks customers in short, rushed responses with a "why did I ever take this job" tone sure to make anyone who deals with her thinks she's a bitch. Dave is trying to get something done in the back room, either writing an order for more merch to come in, or finishing the copy of *Us Weekly* he brought into work with him. Every once in a while when the lines start getting really long, Nicole yells his name and he pops out for a few minutes to ring people up until it starts to die down. Then he retreats again.

I help a customer and run out of receipt tape, so I duck behind the register to rummage around for more. I don't understand why people take receipts for the dumb shit they buy. It's not like they're going to return the candy bar or the pocket fan or Wonderments-branded pacifier, and even if they did, the items are worth so little we wouldn't check the receipt anyway. If you're buying a big screen TV or a new car, sure, it probably helps to have a little paperwork. But over stuff less than ten bucks? All you're doing is helping kill trees and adding more clutter to your life.

"Hey!" Someone bangs on the counter, excited. I jump and hit my head on the corner.

"Ow." I cut off the "fuck" I was going to add on just in case whoever is up there would report me to management.

It's Grace. My stinging head distracts me and for a second I do that thing where you see someone and you know you know them, but you can't remember who they are because they're out of context. When my brain lets me know it's her, it occurs to me how uncommon it is to see my coworkers when they aren't in uniform. I mean, I see them often enough out of uniform when we hit the bar or whatever, but it feels weird seeing them in what management calls "street clothes" while they're in the shop.

Grace is wearing some chunky and cheap but trendy-looking jewelry, the kind college girls get by shopping at stores in the mall that were originally designed to cater to pre-teens. She probably got them off Etsy or some other online community where stay-at-home moms sell their crappy arts and crafts for twenty times what it cost to make. It'd be a great racket, except for all the effort that goes into having to make something.

She looks good. She's wearing a knee-length black dress and dark nylons, with freshly painted light blue nails. I imagine a crowd of Wonderments employees with an Asian fetish following her here and leaving a puddle of drool on the floor. I wonder how she figures out which guys like her and which guys just want to fuck an Asian girl.

"Hi, Grace." I rub the back of my head, partially to ease the stinging and partially to remind her to feel bad for surprising me. If she does, she doesn't show it. "Why are you here on your day off? You look nice today, by the way."

She really is beaming. She reaches into her purse and hands me a green flyer with a business card attached. The flyer reads:

ART EXPO – LOCAL TALENT – TWO DAYS ONLY

159

and goes on to list the location, time, and date. The business card reads "Ginny Gervais, Artist Representative" and has a phone number and e-mail address in an obnoxious over-stylized font that makes it hard to read.

"I met with the representative about the art show came straight here after we got everything set up. This is really exciting. I'd love it if you guys came. You don't have to buy anything. It should be nice, though. Just dress up a little, if you've got anything to dress up in. If you don't I guess that's okay too."

"That's cool, I'm happy for you."

She hovers a bit like she's waiting for something. I help an actual customer so things don't get awkward.

"I need the flyer back though, sorry, I don't have any extra copies yet. I'm going to the front office to see if they can make some for me. Maybe I can even get a mention in the employee newsletter or something."

I wonder why Ginny Gervais the "artist representative" didn't give her any extra copies, and hand the original back to Grace.

"So, you're coming right? Please? Come on."

"Yeah, I'll come if I don't have to work, don't worry." I find myself hoping I have to work. I like art as much as the next guy but spending an evening surrounded by a crowd of desperate artists begging for sales does not appeal to me.

"Aren't you going to write down when and where it is, then?" She gives me a severe look, like she caught me in a very serious lie.

"Yeah, I will," I say. "I mean you're going to put a flyer up in the shop right? I was just going to get the information off that, it's easier."

"Oh," she says. "Yeah, I guess that'd be a good idea. I wonder if they'll let me put up flyers in the other stores too?"

I'm nearly certain she isn't allowed to put up anything in any Wonderments store, regardless of whether or not she works in it.

"I'm not sure," I say. "You could put them up on the employee bulletin boards at Knickers and in the dorms, at least."

"That's a great idea, thanks," she says.

I turn to help another customer, and she rushes over to Dave to give him the same news. I can see him sneering at her in a way that I know she'll misinterpret as a genuine smile. Margaret is skulking in the back of the store, keeping herself busy but keeping an eye on Grace, obviously hoping to dodge the announcement entirely if possible. I feel bad for Grace. I don't know much about her parents or her past, but apparently no one ever told her that no one gives a shit about her dreams.

31

It's early in the morning, which is my favorite time to do anything if it doesn't involve people. When you spend most of your time around people in their twenties, no one is awake at seven a.m., except for the occasion that they're still up from the night before. Anything and everything from shopping for food to doing laundry is faster, easier, and quieter, because everyone is sleeping off a long night of doing whatever it is they like to do for fun.

I'm walking through the lobby toward the convenience store looking for my morning Mountain Dew when an idea hits me. I veer over to one of the computers in the lobby and sit down – it's nice to not have to wait. Even the addiction that is social media can't penetrate the college student desire to sleep through the morning whenever possible. I do a quick search online and it's just as I suspect: generic raffle tickets are dirt cheap.

When I was a kid my parents were part of a bowling league, and I'd agree to come along so I could spend the night feeding quarters into whichever arcade game they had in the corner instead of staying home to fast forward through my dad's R-rated movies looking for tits. This was back before every arcade machine in every bowling alley was Golden Tee Golf. Golden Tee Golf is the scourge of bowling alley arcades everywhere, a shitty, useless, invasive species, like European rabbits in Australia, taking up all the space once held by more interesting creatures.

So I'd sit there, feeding quarters into the X-Men arcade, or the Teenage Mutant Ninja Turtles machine, or the Simpsons arcade game. I realize now they were all based on TV shows my parents forbade me from watching because they were inappropriate, but for some reason were totally fine with me playing as a video game, so long as I didn't bother them. While I played my video games, my parents had their own form of fun: the fifty-fifty raffle.

The idea behind the fifty-fifty raffle is simple. You sell raffle tickets – my parents paid a dollar each or six for five dollars – to all the drunk and bored bowlers. Then at the end of the night, half the money made gets given out in cash and prizes. I remember my parents winning a knife set once, and a steakhouse gift certificate another time. The other half of the money goes to the Girl Scouts, or March of Dimes, or whatever other charity out there has decided that they are most definitely against gambling, unless of course they get a cut.

I do another quick search and discover dozens of bowling alleys in the city around Wonderments. I figured I'd find more than a few, but I had no idea there would be so many. Finding one to look the other way for a harmless, fun raffle in the name of helping someone – kids with disabilities, maybe – should be easy. I buy the raffle tickets with a few clicks. I was going to spend the day studying Portuguese or maybe napping at the beach, but it looks like I'll be spending the day buying some enticing raffle prizes instead. Being the fine upstanding citizen that I am, there's nothing I enjoy more than some charity work.

A few more minutes online and I've got my list: a discount electronics outlet, a few local restaurants, and directions to the local Super Walmart to pick up a smattering of cheaper prizes as well. I'd love to just use the Salvation Army instead, but I can't risk anyone getting suspicious just because the stuff isn't in the original packaging. I could add an extra lie and say the stuff was donated, but I don't want to risk it. The nature of the raffle means the "charity" takes half the money anyway, so I decide that the amount of money I'd save by cutting corners on the prizes isn't worth the risk of blowing the whole thing.

I go over to the front desk, where a bored girl is playing a game I don't recognize on her Nintendo DS. "Hey, how are you this morning?" I ask.

"What's up?" she asks. She doesn't pause her game or look up. I wonder if she's emulating the snooty, out-of-touch receptionists that populate eighties movies, then realize she's too young to have seen any of them. She can't be too much younger than me, but it feels like there's a huge age gap between us.

"I ordered something online," I tell her. "How do we get our mail here?"

"It'll come to the main office, and they'll sort it and send it to the desk here. If it's a letter we'll shove it under your door, if it's a package we'll leave a note and you can pick it up here. Just bring your ID."

"Thanks," I tell her.

"Yep." She never looks up at me at any point.

* * *

The aquarium where Nicole has decided to take me on her date is called The Fish Tank. I stare at the sign for a long time, thinking I must be missing some sort of joke, or pun, or something. I try to think of a more generic name for an aquarium. I can't. Underneath the name – which is spelled out with light blue bubbles on a white background and difficult to read – the sign claims, "biggest Aquarium in the State!" I forget about the questionable capitalization and try to guess how many aquariums there even are around here. I can't help myself.

"Hey," I interrupt the redheaded teenager who is selling us tickets and explaining the map of the various attractions. "Your sign says, 'biggest in the state.' How many aquariums are you competing against, exactly? Who certifies that sort of claim?"

"What?" the kid says.

"I mean, who can we contact to verify the claims of this fine establishment?"

The kid furrows his brow and stares at me, like he's trying to figure out if I'm serious. Nicole loops her arm around mine playfully and laughs. "Come on," she says, and drags me away by the arm. "Don't pick on the kid."

She looks back at him as we walk away. "I wish I had red hair," she says.

"Why?" I ask. "He looks like a confused carrot."

She doesn't disagree with me. "Red hair looks good on girls, though. Don't you think I'd look hot with red hair?"

I think she looks hot now. "I guess," I tell her.

I let her pull me into the first room and I have to admit it's sort of interesting. The room forms an arch so you're sort of walking through a wide tunnel, but it's entirely made of thick plexiglass so the fish tank is on both sides and above you all at once. The water is a sort of artificially vibrant blue you see in brochures for exotic vacations, and the fish are, for the most part, equally vibrant. I look for any dead or sick ones, but I don't see any. It's well maintained, which I didn't expect given the shitty exterior on the place.

Nicole watches the fish with a sense of genuine awe, oblivious to the fact that I'm spending most of my time watching her. She's wearing a pair of old jeans and a t-shirt with a cartoon penguin sporting a handlebar mustache. She still has the perfect hair and the perfect makeup, and I wonder if she spent time making herself look nice to come out with me, or if it's just so automatic she'd look like this no matter where she was going. I have no way to ask her without ruining the mood, so I just keep looking at her out of the corner of my eye, and looking at the fish whenever she looks over at me.

We walk through the next few rooms – decidedly less impressive in scope – and I see a sign with an arrow pointing to a side hallway. It says "undersea documentary." I plan to ignore it but Nicole walks that way without asking me, and I follow her. The hallway is damp and designed to look like a cave. It's cold, a refreshing break from the summer. I'm impressed they pulled off something this unique in such a small amount of space. I reach out and touch the rock wall as we walk. It's real.

The hallway quickly opens up into a large viewing room, with seats set in rows facing a screen. No one else is here, and we sit near the center. The documentary is already in progress – it must just run on a loop. A man with a British accent narrates about biodiversity over footage of what he says is the Great Barrier Reef.

"I'm glad you decided to come with me," Nicole whispers. She doesn't need to whisper, since we're the only ones there, but I don't say anything. She leans close to me when she whispers, and that alone makes it a great idea.

"Me too," I whisper back to her, leaning close to her ear when I say it. "This was a great idea. I don't know if Grace would be jealous, but she should be."

"I doubt she would be. She's got her own thing going on I guess. Too busy to come out to some tourist trap like this. But I like it."

We sit in silence for about ten minutes as the documentary finishes. The screen goes dark for a few moments, then the documentary restarts. The opening credits make the thing look at least twenty years old.

"Well, that was about as much fun as an educational film can be, I think." She slaps me on the leg above the knee, and stands up. "Let's go see some more actual live fish, and then maybe grab some lunch or something." I follow her out of the cave-theatre. My leg feels warm where she touched it.

The next room has a fish tank with hundreds or maybe thousands of tiny fluorescent fish swimming around in it. There's a plastic bubble in the bottom of the fish tank with a space so a child could crawl under the tank and stick their head up, giving the illusion that they were inside the tank. We look at the tiny fish for a few minutes, each one darting around seemingly at random.

"I'm going for it," Nicole says.

"What?" I say.

"Hold this." She hands me her purse and drops down to her hands and knees to crawl through to the bubble. I strongly doubt that she or any other adult could fit, but her attempt makes it impossible not to notice her ass, so I don't say anything. It really is stunning, but I realize there is absolutely no way to for a straight male to compliment a girl's ass that doesn't sound creepy, so I keep my mouth shut. She gets through to the bubble pretty easily. I must have misjudged the size of the bubble or the tunnel, or both.

"Take a picture of me!" she says. Her voice is muffled by the thick plastic. I give her a confused look. "Use your phone, dummy."

I take out my phone and fiddle with it for a minute to figure out how to take pictures. I snap one. It doesn't look bad, for a camera phone.

She crawls out from inside the bubble and takes my phone to look at the picture. "That's pretty cool," she says. "Send that to me later."

"Yeah, sure."

"Let's take one together, too."

"I'm pretty sure we wouldn't both fit inside the bubble." I imagine being in a relationship with her, years later. We sit with some other couple and tell the story of how we first started dating, and the time we tried to squish ourselves into a tiny photo op at an aquarium.

"Yeah, you're probably right," Nicole says. "In front of the tank, then."

We stand in front of the tank. There's no one else there, so I hold the phone out at arm's length to snap the picture. It doesn't come out nearly as well as the first one, since we're blocking so much of the view.

We walk through to the next room, and reach the official end of the aquarium. All that's left now is the unnamed gift shop and "The Blue Lagoon Diner," which is a small counter and a second bored kid standing in front of a fryer. The advertised special: fish and chips. I'm sure they just wanted to keep things fished themed, but it's just creepy. All the tables are empty.

"Do you think our kids are going to ask us someday why there's an arm obscuring one side of every single picture taken by our generation?"

"Our kids?"

I didn't mean it like that. I'm not sure if I should laugh or just dismiss it, but I can feel the blood rushing to my face.

"Yeah. Like, the world's kids. Our generation. All the kids yet to be born. Our parents and our grandparents had all these faded vintage photos, black and white even. In thirty years, 'vintage' is going to be shitty cell phone selfies."

"I guess I never thought of it," she says. "Send me that one too."

"It doesn't look as good as the other one."

"Yeah, but it's got you in it," she says.

I suddenly wonder how many other pictures she has on her phone that are pictures of her out on dates with guys this summer. I don't ask.

32

Dave asked me to come out to Knickers for dinner, which really means coming out to Knickers to get drunk. I should have known better, but I'm a sucker sometimes, so I said yes. I'm eating a burger and Dave is barely touching a plate of nachos, preferring to save as much room as possible for tequila shots. We're listening to the music on whichever radio station the servers decided to put on, which usually means shitty pop music. Since Dave's drinking, he has an opinion on every song. "Baby" doesn't even finish playing before Dave starts up.

"All I'm saying is, when he tells everyone he's gay, no one is going to be surprised," Dave says to me. He leans in and then yells too loudly like we're in a crowded bar on a Friday night. We're not. It's a Tuesday, and we're just about the only ones here. Almost everyone else is either still working or out in town discovering there's nothing to do in town. But Dave's drunk, which means he's going to be loud enough to talk over a rock concert until he passes out.

"It happens all the time," he says. "Sure it's not cool while he's popular because warming up girls' crotches sells records, but once his career is done, he'll admit it. Ricky Martin did it. That kid from Hanson did it. Lance from N'Sync did it. I mean his name is Lance for fuck's sake. We knew before he did."

I want to complain to management for playing Justin Bieber and starting this conversation.

"I'm pretty sure no one in Hanson is gay," I tell him.

"How do you know?" he asks. "You knowing that is so gay."

It could be worse. I know eventually Dave will find out I went on a date with Nicole and grill me for dirty details that don't exist, and then give me bullshit about it when he realizes they really don't.

"Are you going to Grace's art thing?" I ask.

He lets me change the subject. "Fuck no," he says.

"What? Why?" I wasn't planning on going either, but I expected him to be more polite about it.

"That's the problem with people these days," he explains. "Everyone just wants to be an artist or a pop star or be in movies. No one wants to buckle down and do hard work."

I wait for him to crack a smile or something, but he seems serious in that intense drunk way. "You're pretty much the laziest person I know," I point out. That's not actually true, but he is pretty lazy, so I don't mind the hyperbole.

"Yeah I guess, but I'm honest about it. I don't spend all my time pretending I'm going to be special or some shit. That's the problem with your generation. You just can't get over yourselves."

"What do you mean 'my generation?'" I ask. "You're the same age as the rest of us."

He dismisses my question with a hand wave which he also uses to call the waitress over to get more drinks. I give her a glare that says "please don't give this guy any more drinks" that she either ignores or just misses entirely.

Dave looks up at the waitress bleary-eyed. "Honey, if I were straight I would slap you on the ass right now." Then he looks at me. "Dude, you're straight, slap her on the ass."

The waitress just laughs and leaves to go get the drinks. I wonder how much unfiltered harassment the average waitress has to put up with per shift.

"I don't want to go either," I tell him, "but it's the nice thing to do."

"Fuck that," he says. "We barely know each other. The place

will be busy. She won't even notice I'm not there."

In the background, the song finishes on the radio – a song called "Save Tonight" I forgot even existed. I try to remember who the artist is, but I can't.

"A guy I know lost his virginity to this song," Dave says.

I don't ask for details.

"I'm the one that took it," he says with a grin. He holds his fist up to me and I bump it.

* * *

Learning Portuguese still eludes me. I've learned a lot of the words – bathroom is "banheiro," dinner is "jantar," hotel is "hotel" with an accent, stuff like that – but I'm still speaking English, I'm just substituting in Portuguese words. My thoughts are all English, and the sentence structure is way off. It bothers me – I was hoping to sound better than a tourist that picked up an English to Portuguese dictionary on the plane ride over.

My phone chirps and I check the text. It's from Nicole. "Have lunch with me :) Cafeteria 20 min." I get up and get dressed. I'd like to take a shower first, and I wasn't planning on leaving anyway, but I find myself smiling when I get ready. I assumed she'd wait for me to call her first. I text her back that I will be right there and leave.

The meal of the day is a wet burrito. It will probably be okay because it follows two basic good ideas of cooking with crappy ingredients: wrap it in something or cover it in sauce. If you can do both, even better.

"Okay, what do you want?" the girl behind the counter asks. She's chubby with short, dirty blonde hair inside a hairnet. Her white apron makes her look formless. She's not wearing any makeup, and her cheeks are red, hot and sweaty from being in the kitchen. Before I respond, I notice a streak of flour on the side of her face near her ear, and she strikes me as beautiful.

"I'll have a chef salad, I guess." I don't want to order something messy in front of Nicole. It's the first time I ever recall changing my food order to impress a girl.

Nicole orders after me and gets a salad as well. I wonder if she actually wants one, or if she's doing the same thing I am. I try to remember the kinds of things I've seen her eating before, and can't remember ever seeing her eat something that was particularly messy.

We pay and sit down. There's plenty of room, so we sit across from each other at an empty table.

"So, I had a really nice time at the aquarium yesterday," Nicole tells me.

"I did too." I smile at her, and it feels like the insincere grin I give people when I'm pulling one over on them. I really did have a nice time. I just trust my ability to fake it more than I trust her ability to interpret a real smile.

"I was worried it'd be small and boring, but it was nice."

"I thought so too. Aquariums are always kind of quiet and peaceful. São Paulo has one of the biggest aquariums in the western hemisphere. I'm sure I'll go while I'm there."

"Wait, São Paulo?"

"Yeah. São Paulo, Brazil. Once the summer's over I'm going to visit there for awhile. I've been saving a ton of money."

"That sounds amazing. I'd love to go. Just warm sun and beaches, not a care in the world. I'd lie to everyone about who I was, and just lie there until even I forgot who I was, and just be someone else."

"São Paulo isn't really known for their beaches. It's landlocked."

"Oh." Nicole frowns, and it might be the saddest that I've ever seen her – a deep, penetrating frown, mourning the loss of a place that never existed.

"I've heard Rio Di Janeiro is beautiful though. They have a ton of beaches."

She nods and smiles, and her troubled look dissipates.

"Well, we should hang out more," Nicole says. "Even if it is only until the end of the summer. You're off to see the world, and I'm back home to finish up college I suppose."

It occurs to me that I've been making small talk and hanging out with Nicole at work all summer, and she has never mentioned college before, or her major, or anything she might be interested in as a career.

"Yeah? What do you want to do?"

"I have no idea," she admits. "I chose psychology as my major my sophomore year and my parents have always been supportive, but you have to get at least a master's degree to do anything with it. I don't want to do any more school at this point."

I wonder how much money Nicole's parents are paying for a degree she's never going to use.

"Well, I'm sure you'll find something interesting."

"Maybe I'll just work here forever," she says. "It could be nice. Simple. Not much to do, no real expectations, no real responsibility. Long hours for low pay, but enough money to get by. Just stay in the employee dorms and live off cafeteria food."

"When you put it that way it sounds like prison."

She laughs.

"It'd get old after one or two summers," I tell her. "You're meant for a lot more than this place." I don't really believe it. I'm not sure anyone our age is meant for anything more.

33

The sunlight streams through the dirty window above my dresser, splashing a little puddle of light onto it. It occurs to me that I should have gotten some better curtains at some point, instead of the thin, transparent ones provided, worn even thinner by years of washing and about one more year away from being fit for use as a prop in a haunted house. Cory is asleep above me, snoring softly, one foot hanging off the end of his bunk, oblivious to the sunlight. I try to remember the last time I saw him when he was awake, and count it as good fortune that it was long enough ago that I can't.

There's a neon pink paper on the floor by our door, with a smaller, dull yellow piece of paper on top of it. I pick them up.

The yellow piece of paper reads "A package is here for _____" with my name handwritten in. The second line advises, "Bring ID to front desk to collect your package!" I'm impressed; I expected it to take longer for the raffle tickets to show up.

The pink sheet of paper is so bright it's almost hard to look at. It says:

!!! Employee Dance Party !!!
!!! This Friday at Knickers !!!
Employees Only
Bring A Date and Boogie Down

The rest of the paper is decorated with music notes and a clip art cartoon dancing guy. I had no idea anyone used clip art for anything in the last decade. The whole layout just agitates me on some level: no date, no time, off-center formatting. My guess is that they had a party just like this one last year, and whoever was responsible for sending out fliers just deleted the dates and hit the print button.

I go downstairs to the front desk. The same neon pink sign is taped to the front of the desk, and another one is pinned on the notice board by the door.

"Hey, I have a package to pick up, please." The girl behind the desk isn't the same one that helped me before, but she's equally uninterested in doing her job. She pauses her iPod and takes the slip. She doesn't ask for my ID. She leaves the iPod while she goes into the closet behind the desk to look for my stuff. I recognize Zooey Deschanel, but I can't tell what movie or TV show it's from.

The girl comes back and hands me my package. She still doesn't ask me for my ID.

"What movie is that?" I ask her.

She's already back to watching it, headphones back in without so much as a goodbye. She pulls one of them out and looks up at me. "Huh?"

"Never mind," I say. She doesn't argue and sticks the headphone back in her ear.

Once I get back to my room I stick the flier for the dance party on Cory's desk. It seems like something he'd be interested in. I open the package, which has the raffle tickets and a printed off receipt. I drop them in my top dresser drawer and go take a shower in the single upstairs bathroom. Someone comes in without knocking and takes a piss in the urinal while I'm in there, but it's better than having to go all the way to the main showers.

When I get back, Cory is gone. I don't think he's avoiding me or anything, so I just accept my continued good fortune at not having to deal with him, get dressed, and go to lunch.

* * *

I'm sitting in my room trying to work up the resolve to study when my phone chirps with an incoming text message. It's from Nicole. "U going to G's show?"

I text back, "idk. Maybe."

She texts me again. "y not?"

"Do you want to meet for dinner?" I ate already, but I'm willing to fake it if it means not having to have an entire conversation by text message.

"Ok, be at my place in 20."

I'm five minutes late getting to the lobby of the girls' dorms, and five minutes after that, she comes downstairs. She's wearing a bright pink tank top that matches her lipstick. It's garish, but I don't say anything. It reminds me of the obnoxious fliers for the dance party. I wonder if she spent the time after our texts getting ready, or if she was just sitting around in her room, makeup already matching her outfit, just in case.

"Hey," she says. "Where's dinner?" I wait for her to apologize for being late, or reference it in some way, or anything. She doesn't.

"I don't care much. Want to hit the cafeteria?"

She makes a face. "Not unless we absolutely have to," she says. Then she lights up. "I know. We should totally go to '52! I've been meaning to go all summer, but no one else wants to go."

I've heard that before. I'm starting to wonder if she likes having me around because she likes me, or if I'm only around because she has a checklist of stuff she wants to do here this summer, and going with me is better than literally her only other option, which is going alone.

"Like with the aquarium?" I ask.

She frowns. It's never occurred to her before that it's possible to be selfish in a benign way, and it bothers her to see herself as "selfish," even though it's harmless. That's one of the things that separates me from other people: At least I can be honest with myself about when I'm taking advantage of someone.

"Come on, it'll be fun. The aquarium was fun. I mean, we don't have to go if you don't want to. Where did you want to go?"

"It's cool, let's go to '52," I say.

'52 is the flagship tourist trap restaurant for Wonderments. It might be a chain, but I'm not sure. If it is, it only exists in amusement parks. The whole idea is 1950s kitsch – classic cars, waitresses in skirts on roller skates, jukeboxes playing Elvis. All the girls trying to look like Grace Kelly or Jackie Kennedy, all the guys wearing white folded soda jerk hats. If there's one thing Americans love, it's their nostalgia for the good old days, whether those days were ever real or not.

We go inside, and a blonde girl with a beehive hairdo zips up to us. She has on a knee-length lime green skirt with a white shirt, and white roller skates with matching green wheels. Girls must trip and fall at least occasionally thanks to the skates. It's got to hurt like hell.

"How many times can you fall on those skates before they fire you?" I ask her.

She holds up two menus. "Welcome to '52! Just the two of you?"

"Yes please," Nicole says. "Ignore him."

She skates us over to a table, and I watch her skirt flounce as she does. I wonder if the girls are issued matching lime green underwear for when they inevitably fall on their asses, drop a plate full of burgers and malts, and sprawl out in front of a family of four.

We look over the menu, and I'm impressed by how blatantly they rip people off to eat here. All the food is really generic. Hamburgers, hot dogs, chicken fingers, french fries. You wouldn't want anything on the menu that wasn't certified 1950s. Everything is double the price of anything else in the park, which is already marked way up.

While we're deciding what to order, another fleet of employees dressed like waitresses and line cooks skates out of the back room and outside. Once they're there, they do a little choreographed dance featuring a mash-up of fifties music, starting with "Chantilly Lace" before moving on to "Great Balls of Fire" and ending with "Johnny B. Goode." A crowd gathers and watches the show, all staring stupidly, not really enjoying it, just letting it happen to them. Afterward the performers line up and take a bow and skate back into the restaurant, past the people at the tables and into the back room.

"That was pretty cool," Nicole says.

"I like the Back to the Future version better," I say.

"Huh. I never saw it."

The jukebox clicks over to the next song, "Bye Bye Love." I resolve to see if I can get a look into the kitchen and find out if the cooks are required to wear skates as well, or if that's just for the show cooks that go out and dance for the crowd. I realize the food is probably marked up so high as a way to cover their liability insurance.

Our waitress skates over.

"Hi there. What can I get for you here at '52?"

"I'll have a cheeseburger and french fries and a chocolate malt," I say. I'd also like to know if the staff is required to rhyme everything they say with "'52."

"I'll have the same thing," Nicole says.

"Sure thing, coming right up," the waitress says with a smile. She turns and starts skating off.

"Oh, wait!" Nicole says, and the waitress whips around expertly with a flourish. "Can I get a strawberry malt instead of chocolate?"

"Sure thing, hon," she says, and skates off again.

Nicole then says to me, "So you're really thinking about not going to Grace's art exhibit? I wanted to go."

"I don't know," I say. "It could be cool I guess."

"I'm sure it will be," Nicole says. "If nothing else, it always feels good to get out of the park for a little while."

Truthfully, I don't mind being in the park. It's convenient to have such a self-contained little world. It's scenic, almost peaceful, so long as you know when to avoid the crowds.

"Grace put you up to this, didn't she?" I ask.

"No!" Nicole says, trying to look offended. It's not very convincing. She gives up. "Okay, yeah. She really wants everyone to be there. I think she's pretty nervous about it."

"Yeah, I get that."

"But I really do want to go. I think it'll be fun."

"Okay, I'm in."

"I mean, it's no cute girls on roller skates, I guess, but it'll be nice to do something that's a little bit more cultured than getting drunk."

"I said I'd go and I want to go," I tell her. "You can stop convincing me."

"Great," she says with a sincere smile.

The waitress skates out holding a giant tray with our order on it. Sets our plates and drinks down in front of us with expert precision. Nothing wobbles or shakes.

"How do you keep from falling down constantly in those things?" I ask her.

"They make us work in the back on skates for at least a week before we're allowed to do any of the serving or the choreography. It's worth it, though."

I'm not sure if she's serious or screwing with me. It makes me appreciate her answer even more.

We eat our overpriced food, and it seems like Nicole is having a genuinely good time. It's hard for me not to be cynical. Her selfishness blends so smoothly with her personality that it wouldn't be fair to call her malicious. I can't tell if she even realizes she's manipulating me to do what she wants. It's just in her nature.

"Let's pay and get out of here. I want to take you somewhere," she says.

We split the bill and leave. Outside, the sun has gone down, and the place is lit up by the lamps along the walkways, the shops, and the lights on the carnival games. It feels comfortable to walk around, even if it is a bit crowded.

"Come on, we have to hurry. They might shut it down soon."

I follow her through the crowd, trying to guess where we're going. It's not long before we arrive at the giant Wonderments Ferris wheel, lit up and sparkling with a thousand colored lights. It surprises me. During the day it's a smooth white. I barely ever looked at it before. With the lights on it looks totally different.

"I want to see what the park looks like in the dark," she says. "There's hardly any line."

"It's always what you want to do, isn't it?" I ask her. It's a serious question, but I say it with a smile.

"Tell me you're not having fun and I'll let you go home."

We get in line. The Ferris wheel isn't popular, and it holds a lot of people. We only wait a few minutes before we get on. It's standard to seat at least four to a car, but the ride operator assumes we're on a date and sends us up, just the two of us.

Nicole ignores me, looking over the side of our gondola at the park below. I lean back with my eyes closed. The sounds of the park seem far away. I like it.

"It's nice up here," she says suddenly.

"No one can hear us up here," I say. "It feels good."

She stays quiet.

"It feels like a place for secrets," I explain. "Tell me something about yourself. Something no one else knows."

"What, like truth or dare?" she says mockingly.

"No," I roll my eyes. "I'm not in high school. I'm not going to dare you to show me your tits or make out with me. I just want to know one of your secrets."

My skin feels warm. I can't imagine what she might tell me. That's what makes the question intoxicating.

"You first," she insists.

"I tell you mine, you tell me yours, kind of a thing?"

"Sure."

I think for a moment. I don't want to tell her anything that might get me in trouble, but I don't want to cheat, either.

"When I was in high school I learned how easy it was to steal stuff. If you don't look nervous no one suspects you – as long as you're white, I suppose."

"It can't be that easy." She doesn't seem too surprised to hear this story from me. That worries me, but I keep going anyway. "I used to steal food at the grocery store I worked at all the time. Just take a sandwich off the shelf in the deli and stick it in your pocket. No big deal. No one's watching. Once I even got caught. I just pretended I lost my receipt, and that was the end of it."

Nicole still looks like she doesn't believe me. "That's really all it takes. Really?"

"My friends and I used to play this game, where we'd try and walk out of the store with stuff without paying for it. Not hiding it, not sticking it in our pockets, just walking out carrying it in our arms to see what would happen."

"What's the most expensive thing you ever stole?"

180

"No, that wasn't the point. The point was to walk out carrying something big. Something obvious. You sneak out with a piece of jewelry or a digital camera or whatever, it might be worth money, but it's not difficult to steal."

"I don't get it," she says.

"Once I walked out with a three-foot-wide bright yellow exercise ball. I could barely see where I was walking when I was carrying it."

"No one stopped you?"

"Nope. Just walked right out the front. The dumb thing sat in my parents' basement until I moved out. Hell, it might still be there."

I enjoy watching her face, the conflicted emotions of amusement, admiration, and judgment. Judgment wins out. "Stealing is wrong."

"A lot of things that are wrong are pretty fun."

"I guess I wouldn't know."

I don't believe that for a second.

The Ferris wheel lurches to a halt as they load more people on. The lights on the rides flash and sparkle beneath us. If someone described it to me I'd think it sounded beautiful, but being here, it isn't. My eyes strain, knowing that if it was daylight I could see an amazing view of the park, but now, all I can see is the thick, inky blackness of night.

"Okay, it's your turn," I say. "Tell me something I don't know about you."

"I don't know," she says.

"Oh come on," I say. "There's got to be something." Honestly, the thing that annoys me most is that now I feel tricked: she got me to reveal something with no plans to share anything herself.

"I really don't know," she says. "I'm boring." I can tell it depresses her. She wants to share something. She just can't imagine anything interesting enough about herself to share. It annoys me even more.

I want to like Nicole so much. I'm attracted to her. She just seems so... empty. Sometimes it feels like everyone is either so bland there's nothing worth finding out about them, or trying so hard to not be bland that they're obnoxious instead.

181

"It's okay," I tell her. I keep waiting for her to volunteer something, anything. Just pick a cliché. When was the first time she got drunk? The first time she lied to her parents? The time she lost her virginity? Just pick something from the catalog of human experiences that feel intense and unique but really aren't. Everyone has them.

She doesn't, and we finish the ride in silence, staring into the dark.

34

Silver Pines Bowling Alley is turning out to be the perfect place for the fifty-fifty raffle. It's a run-down mom-and-pop kind of place, but still busy. The only employees are the kid behind the counter handing out shoes, a couple waitresses rushing back and forth to make sure everyone stays fed and drunk, and the old guy who owns the place and won't go home because there's no one there. No by-the-book business types. Just a few overworked charitable spirits totally willing to overlook local anti-gambling laws in the name of a good cause.

Everything is going well, but I'm still nervous. I decided to come in on a league night to get as much money as possible, and the place is packed. The waitresses are helping me sell tickets (two bucks apiece or three for five dollars), but I've still spent most of the night chatting with people and selling tickets myself. The old guy had a microphone with a portable speaker on it for who knows what reason, so I've been using that to remind people about the drawing whenever I get the chance, as well.

I've just put down the microphone and gotten ready to maybe take a piss and get away from the crowd for a few minutes when a middle-aged man walks up to me. He's tall and a bit muscular with gray hair and a crew cut that suggests he's either ex-military, or wishes he was. He shakes my hand.

"Officer Tony Baker," he says. "You look beat, son. We appreciate the hard work you're doing tonight."

"It's no problem, sir. It's worth it for the kids." I didn't want to use a local charity since there's the off chance I could run into someone from the organization and get in a shitload of trouble. In a moment of panic I suppose I could always say I was working independently and planning on giving the money as a donation, but that's hardly ideal. I just went with the Make-A-Wish Foundation. Few things inspire charitable giving like sick children.

"I don't suppose you have a police officers' discount on those tickets?" he asks, half joking.

"Sorry," I say. "I wish I could help you out. It's for a good cause, at least."

"True enough," he says. He opens his wallet and pulls out a twenty dollar bill.

"I really appreciate it," I tell him. I quickly count off the tickets and give them to him before he can think to ask for change. "Good luck, the drawing starts at 8 p.m."

"Thanks," he says. "Anything I can do to help." He reaches into his pocket and hands me a business card. It's cheap and amateurish, probably printed off on his printer at home. "Give me a call. There's an annual police fundraiser next month. Maybe we can get some more donations for Make-A-Wish."

I take the card. "That sounds great. I'll have my boss give you a call. It sounds like fun."

"What did you say your name was, again?" he asks.

"Josh," I tell him. "It's good to meet you."

Josh is one of my favorite aliases. Josh was a kid I knew in high school. He had it all, at least in the sense of pointless high school popularity. He was tall and handsome, got good grades, good at basketball and football, and good at talking to girls. Every guy in school envied him and every girl in school had a crush on him. That's probably not true, but it's how it felt at the time.

One day, Josh's mom died. It was a random car accident in the middle of winter – no one's fault, and no way to see it coming. He was missing from school for a week surrounding the funeral. I remember that when he came back, he just sat in his desk empty-eyed, not even really there, just starring off into space with a glassy look. Why none of the teachers pulled him out of class and sent him back home, I'll never know.

Anyway, we were all there in fifth period U.S. History, and our history teacher, Mr. Roberts, stood in front of the class, lecturing us about American involvement in World War II. He asked a question, and when no one raised their hand, he called on Josh. I don't know what he was thinking. I remember wondering immediately, "What kind of dumb fuck calls attention to someone their first day back after their mom dies?"

Josh didn't answer. He didn't shrug, he didn't apologize, nothing. It was like he hadn't even heard the question. The teacher asked the question twice, getting no response. Then, for whatever reason, Mr. Roberts decided today was the day he wasn't going to let one of students blow him off. "Hello? Josh? Joshua? Anybody home?" he asked, waving at Josh as he badgered the kid.

The whole class just sat there, feeling uncomfortable. Everyone in the room but our Mr. Roberts realized how out of line he was. After a minute or so of awkwardness, he gave up. He turned back to the board and said, "I'm sorry for your loss, Josh. Just remember, God never gives us more than we can handle, and he helps those who helps themselves. You have to keep moving forward, even when it hurts."

Josh didn't say a word. His vacant expression never changed. He stood up, walked silently to the front of the room, and punched that asshole in the face. Just one punch. It knocked Mr. Roberts to the floor. One kid in the back of the room said, "Oh, shit!" but the rest of us just sat in silence. Josh didn't even look back at us. He just walked out of the classroom without so much as a word. I heard later that he'd walked down to the main office to tell the principal what he'd done. He never came back to school after that day, and I never saw him again. We assumed he'd been expelled.

I'll always remember that day. I use his name as an alias to remind myself not to do something stupid in a fit of emotion.

I wish I could meet him today and ask him if the punch was worth it.

The night continues, and I chat it up with the locals, wearing my "nice guy" smile the whole time. People are drinking, the waitresses are busy, and I've sold a ton of raffle tickets, but most importantly, no one is suspicious of anything. The whole con is a fantastic idea that I'm annoyed I didn't think of sooner. Since the entire thing looks identical to real charity work and the theft comes later, there's just no way for things to go wrong. Worst case scenario, someone gets too nosy and I just give the money to charity. I'm having a great night. I've given away a ton of stuff already and everyone is happy. No one suspects anything is amiss. I check my phone for the time. 9:28. Close enough. I pick up the microphone.

"All right folks, you know what time it is! Every half hour on the half hour we're giving something away until it's all gone. Thank you so much for supporting the Make-A-Wish Foundation. This charity means a lot to me, and it means even more to the kids and their parents that just want to make a dream come true. We're selling tickets all night, just talk to me or ask a waitress. Don't forget to tip, though. They're working hard tonight."

I go over to the pile of prizes. There are still a ton left. I either need to start giving out more during each round, or start giving them away more often.

"Remember, we can call you to get the cash prize at the end of the night, but you have to be here in the building to claim the other prizes. Let's see if we can find a winner for.... a gift certificate to Bubba's Bar and Grill! Thanks for supporting our local businesses."

I reach over to the counter and reach into a giant plastic fish bowl I brought with me to put the tickets in, and pull out one of the tickets. "Okay, ticket ending in number 7, 7, 6, 0, 1. That's number 7, 7, 6, 0, 1. Come on up for some Bubba's Bar and Grill on the house!"

There's a moment of silence as conversation dies down and everyone checks their ticket stubs. A few people don't have any and they're just ignoring me, but most people have at least a couple, and a few people have big handfuls of tickets. One guy I see must have fifty or more. The desire to win is so strong in this guy that he'll pull a hundred dollars or more out of his wallet so he can have a shot at winning a fifty dollar gift card or forty dollars' worth of concert tickets.

He doesn't win, though. After a few seconds I hear a woman's voice shouting, "it's me, it's me! I win!" I see her running toward me. She's wearing a pair of faded, frayed jean shorts with a Def Leppard t-shirt advertising a recent concert tour. Good for them. I, like most of America, assumed they disappeared decades ago. She has a deep tan and bleached hair. When she gets close, I'm blasted with the overpowering smell of cigarette smoke.

"I won," she says. She hands me the ticket forcefully, like she's expecting that I won't believe her. I make a point of checking it deliberately, since that's what she seems to be waiting for.

"Congratulations," I tell her. "Thank you so much for all your support tonight." I hand her the gift card and she goes back to her friends, no doubt spending fifty dollars on booze to celebrate winning.

I go through the whole process again. This time I call out numbers and no one comes to the front, so I drop the ticket back in the bowl and pull out another, ultimately awarding a set of Ginsu knives to a middle-aged man who likely has never cooked a day in his life. The next half hour, an overweight guy in his twenties wins a Target gift card, followed by another middle-aged guy who wins lawn care service from EnviroClean Lawn Services. I keep giving away prizes until 10:30, and I notice the crowd starting to thin out.

I approach the counter where the old guy is still hard at work, mostly collecting and spraying down shoes at this point. "Hey, I just had a family emergency come up," I tell him. I make sure I use a low voice and keep a concerned look on my face. "Is there any way I can have you finish up the night for me? I know you're a trustworthy guy, I can just give you the prize money and you can do the announcing."

"I don't know," he says. He looks genuinely torn. He wouldn't want to keep me from something as important as family. "I'm not much of a big talker. You've done a great job tonight." I agree, it turned out well. Mostly I just channeled my various memories of radio DJs. "I guess I can have one of the girls do it," he says.

"Thank you so much," I say. "I really appreciate it. This has been great. I'm so sorry I have to leave early."

"It's okay, I understand," he says. "You have to be there for family."

I pull out the money and divide it into two piles, then I pull out the list of everything I bought to give away as prizes and deduct that from the prize pool. I'm not sure exactly how much is left over, but it's a lot, and it feels like even more since it's almost all in small bills.

"This was a lot of fun," I tell him.

"We'll have to do it again sometime," the old man says, shaking my hand with a firm grip.

I pocket my half of the money head out the door.

35

Nicole and I get off the bus, looking for Grace's art show. We don't see anything.

"Are you sure this is the right place?" I ask.

"That's what the directions said." She looks doubtful. After we look around for a minute and don't spot anything other than a strip mall and a McDonald's, Nicole punches the address into her phone and it gives us walking directions.

"Okay, I guess it's about a third of a mile away from here. I don't think it's on the main street."

I follow her and we walk down a residential street. It's quiet. I don't see any kids playing outside. One guy is mowing his small front lawn with an expensive-looking riding lawnmower. It's peaceful here. I'm having doubts we'll find anything resembling an art show, but there are worse ways to spend a summer evening than wandering through suburbia.

"Turn right in twenty feet," Nicole's phone advises us. She gets to the corner before me and says, "Oh. Right."

We see a sign in the middle of a large front lawn. It says JEFFERSON HIGH SCHOOL, then, underneath it in cheap black block lettering:

ART SHOW TONITE!
OPEN FOR ALL
JHS SUPPORTS LOCAL ARTISTS

Under this at the bottom of the sign, Nicole and I discover that Jefferson High is apparently "Home of the Scorpions."

"I wonder why no one said anything about it being at a school," Nicole says.

"Because 'high school gym' doesn't exactly sound like a classy place for an art exhibit, does it?"

"You'd think they'd at least rent out a hotel banquet hall or something," she says. "I fucking hated high school."

I silently agree with her. I fundamentally mistrust anyone who says they enjoyed high school.

There's a middle aged-woman standing in the lobby greeting people as they come in. She's dressed in a dark gray pantsuit with a blue tie and carefully-done hair. She's obviously taking this very seriously. I wonder if this is the woman who interviewed Grace for the show.

She gives us directions to follow the yellow arrows placed on the floor to get to the "exhibition hall," which I have no doubt is going to be the gym. We follow her directions. It's clear they've tried hard to make the place inviting, but it still feels creepy in the way that all empty schools feel creepy. When the summer ends the place will once again be packed with teenage angst, confused sex drives, and feelings of inadequacy, but for now everything is quiet, like the building itself is thankful for a moment's rest.

There's an open door and a sign taped up next to it that says "exhibition hall." It's the gym. We go inside and I immediately wonder how long we have to stay before it would no longer be impolite to leave. There's no air conditioning and there must be a hundred people perusing the artwork. On top of that are all the "local artists" lined up along the walls, practically elbow to elbow with each other, like a grade school science fair. I wonder if Grace exaggerated to us about how exclusive it was, or if she was genuine and the agent exaggerated to her. For her sake, I hope it's the former.

We walk from stall to stall, pretending to admire each person's artwork as we pass. Most of it is terrible. We meet an elderly man who is showing fifteen different paintings of fruit in bowls, then a high school girl – maybe a freshman in college, but I doubt it – with paint splashed angrily and seemingly at random on the canvas, like she was painting something else but then went berserk and threw paint over the original work. We meet a husband and wife pair selling sculptures made from stuff they cleaned out of their shed.

Nicole and I don't talk much. I don't know why she's quiet. I am because if I open my mouth anywhere near this mediocre "art," I'm going to say something that pisses off a lot of people. So I just nod and smile and hope we find Grace soon.

The place is so crowded that we're almost on top of her before we see her. She's talking to a disheveled but happy young couple, and the first thing I notice is that Grace looks fantastic. She's got on the same knee-length black dress I saw her in before and a simple diamond necklace with diamond earrings. I wonder how much she spent getting dressed up for this.

Her paintings are impressive, at least compared to the other stuff we've seen tonight. Most of the paintings are scenes from inside Wonderments – the giant Ferris wheel, the boardwalk at sunrise, a roller coaster towering above a tree line, stuff like that. But it's the centerpiece that grabs my attention.

It's a large canvas – maybe four feet tall – and it's a headshot of Nicole. Half the face is cut off. The Nicole in the painting stares straight ahead with a penetrating stare, lips pursed, not really smiling, not really sexual, but alluring. The painting explodes with color. The single eye is a mix of vibrant blues and pinks, surrounded by thick lashes much longer than Nicole's real ones. The face is stark white underneath, splashed with color. Yellows and oranges greens, the paint applied liberally and left to run. The hair is a billowing shock of orange-red with yellow highlights, reminiscent of a fire or a sunset. In the end, it's not really Nicole. Nicole would never be so unkempt and wild. It's inspired by her. It's her face, her eyes, but it's not her. It's something so much more. In a way, the picture of her seems more alive and dynamic than she does.

"Wow," I say under my breath.

The disheveled couple moves on without buying anything. Grace turns around and then squeals with delight when she sees us, giving Nicole a hug and kissing her on both cheeks. I have never seen them greet each other this way before.

"It's going great," Grace says with a big smile. "I've sold a few pieces already and there is definitely some more interest. This is so exciting."

She doesn't seem to notice that this is all taking place in a high school gym. She's just happy to be recognized for her work. Since I can never tell anyone the way I spend most of my free time, I get it. I decide not to spoil it for her.

"I never saw the finished picture of me," Nicole says, looking a little shocked by it. "It's really good."

"It's the first one I sold," Grace says. "I've had people asking about it all night long. I should have priced it higher, I guess."

I look at the corner of the stand where Grace has a small card with her name and the name of the piece, "A Summer Afternoon." There's no price that I can see, just a placeholder card that says "SOLD" on it.

"Has Dave or Margaret showed up yet?" Nicole asks.

"Not yet," Grace says. "But I can't say I'm surprised. Still disappointing. Whatever." She says the whole thing smiling, like if she stops looking cheerful for even a moment, security will swoop in and toss her out of the building.

"This stuff is actually pretty good," I tell her.

"What's that supposed to mean?" she asks. "What were you expecting?"

Nicole puts a hand on her arm and says, "Ignore him, sweetie. He's a boy. He's going to say dumb stuff sometimes."

"I said I liked them," I tell her. I really do like them. I'd love for her to paint me something like the painting of Nicole, or I would if I had anywhere practical to put it. Nothing else she has is like that piece. I want to compliment it, but I don't know how without embarrassing myself. Anything flattering I say about the painting will come off as me trying to flatter Nicole.

Grace ignores me as she and Nicole shift into polite small talk. It's one of the things I enjoy about having Nicole around: it saves me the trouble of having to socialize. I can just let her do all the talking and take credit by proxy.

I look at the paintings more closely while they chat – she's got about half a dozen, most of which are marked in the fifty to hundred dollar range. I don't know too much about painting, but I'm not even sure that would cover the cost of materials, let alone the time invested.

Eventually Grace and Nicole hug again, I tell Grace goodbye, and we head toward the exit. I appreciate that I didn't have to ask Nicole if she wanted to keep looking around.

We leave the school. It's dark and quiet. The fresh air makes me realize how warm and stale it was inside the gym.

"I wish I had brought a blanket or something," Nicole says. "It's a nice night out."

"Next time, I suppose."

She looks at me for a moment with a smile, but she doesn't say anything. It starts to feel awkward, so I keep talking.

"That was a pretty good time, but I'm happy to be away from the crowd a bit. Grace was glad we showed up, anyway. And hey, you got your wish for red hair, in a way."

"Yeah," she blushes. Or, she's trying to look like she's blushing, anyway. Between the twilight and her makeup, I can't tell. "I didn't tell her to do that," she says. "

"Well, it was impressive. I'm glad I came."

"Me too," Nicole says. "This was a lot of fun. We should do something like this again sometime."

I know better than to miss the opportunity if I want another date with her. "There's the Wonderments dance party thing coming up pretty soon. I'm sure Dave will be going. It'd be fun if you came along too."

She raises an eyebrow at me. It's high and perfect, as though she's practiced the gesture in a mirror to get it just right. "You like dancing? You don't seem like the type."

"I hate dancing," I admit. "But we can have a few drinks and hang out. Dave will ditch me as soon as a cute guy comes along, so it'd be nice to have someone else there."

"How can you not like dancing?" she asks. "I love dancing. It feels good."

"I'm clumsy. I look like the awkward old guy in a night club."

"Well, we're going, and when we go, you're going to dance with me."

"Does Wonderments give us medical insurance?" They don't. "I'm not paying for your broken toes. If my dancing turns into your disaster, I'm not picking up the tab."

"Maybe I'll just send you out alone and watch. Or send you out with Margaret, if she's being bitchy and needs her toes stepped on a bit." She laughs, and I laugh along with her. I hope she's not serious.

* * *

Dave is standing next to me doing jack shit while I refill our wall of stuffed animals.

"Can you at least pretend to do a little bit of work?"

He scoffs. "Why do you care? You don't sign my paychecks."

"I don't," I tell him. "But if you stand around all night looking like you're doing nothing, one of the girls will bitch about it later and I'll have to stand there and listen to it."

"They talk about me behind my back?" he says. "Skanks."

"They talk about how lazy you are, because you're lazy."

"Fine, fine." He takes over the job of putting up stuffed animals and I switch to reorganizing shirts. Dealing with clothes in retail is the worst. Everyone wants to have a look at the clothes, which means they want to touch them, which means they take it off the rack. No customer in the history of clothes shopping has ever taken the time to put clothes back how they found them, which means twenty minutes after you finish stocking any sort of clothing, it looks roughly like you were visited by an angry wolverine with a vendetta against fabric.

In the front of the store, we can hear Grace banging around behind her register. She must be looking for more register tape or maybe more bags, but it's definitely more violent than strictly necessary.

"Wow," Dave says. "I wonder what kind of bug flew up her ass tonight."

"Her art show was last night."

"Oh, that. Did it not go well then, I take it?" He manages to cram the last stuffed animal – a purple turtle with big, glued-on plastic eyes – into a precarious position on the shelf and goes back to not doing anything.

"I'm pretty sure it went fine," I say, "But you didn't show up. Margaret didn't either. I'm pretty sure she was looking forward to seeing you there."

Dave rolls his eyes. "Oh come on, she cannot possibly be mad about that."

"Did you tell her you were coming?"

"I mean, I told her I was coming." The stuffed turtle falls onto the floor, and Dave scoops it up. "I had to be polite. She was really aggressive with those invites."

"I'm just saying, that's why she's pissed. You should probably go talk to her about it."

"No I shouldn't," Dave says. He puts the stuffed animal back on the shelf in the same spot, where it is destined to fall again in a few minutes. "If she wants to go off on me I'll take it. I'm a big boy. But like hell I'm going to go looking for it."

In the front of the store, it looks like Grace might be coming this way, and Dave ducks around a corner. The turtle falls over again. I look at the wall. It's pretty sloppy, but it is full. I could rearrange the wall and find a place for the turtle, but I decide to toss it back in the closet instead. If there's one thing people love to touch more than t-shirts, it's stuffed animals. If I kept the stuffed animal wall looking orderly, I'd never do anything else.

She comes back to me, ignoring Dave. It's not like The Jolly Tinker is big enough for him to hide anywhere.

"Hey, I just wanted to say thanks for coming last night." Then she adds, loudly, "Unlike some other assholes."

"Yeah, Dave says he's a huge asshole and he's really sorry he didn't come," I say, also loudly and clearly directed at Dave. "He wasn't doing anything important, he's just very stupid. "

Grace laughs. "I guess I can get over it," she says. "It went amazingly. I actually sold most of the stuff I painted. I wasn't expecting to."

"Wow, you sold it all?"

She scowls at me. "Don't act so surprised."

"Sorry, I just mean, there were a lot of artists there. It was good work, it's just a tough market." I knew there was never a chance that I was going to get the painting of Nicole, but I'm still sad that I'll never see it again.

Dave comes out from around the corner and saves the awkward moment. Grace says, "Apologize, asshole."

Dave holds his hands in front of him like he's praying. "I'm really, really sorry," he says.

"Well, I don't believe you," she says. "Buy me a few drinks next time we're out and try again and maybe it'll work."

I wonder if she'd be so quick to forgive if the show had gone poorly, but Dave seizes his good fortune.

"Okay, that sounds good to me. I'm happy for you, and I'll pick up the bar tab the next time we're out."

"Awesome," I say.

"Not you, just her. Jerk."

With any luck, that's the last I'll have to hear about it.

36

It's standard procedure not to count down the register where any customers can see. It's a convenient rule for me, since it lets me skim the change I've been stealing all night without anyone noticing. It's also standard procedure to have two people count down registers together, but no one follows that rule. Everyone wants to get home, there's no way two of us are going to do a job one of us can.

I'm separating out the $118 I pulled off customers tonight. I actually took $118.30, but I leave the extra thirty cents in the drawer. They don't even have us count down the change, just the bills. The office workers will count every penny, but minor screwups happen all the time. They just don't say anything if it's only a few dollars. It'd look strange to them if my register wasn't off.

I'm sticking the money in my pocket when the door opens. I panic. I can feel myself go cold, then feel my face flush as blood rushes to it. I've seen it on people a thousand times when they feel guilty. If it's someone who pays attention to their surroundings at all, I'm fucked.

It's Nicole. I am not fucked. "I need you to meet my parents," she says.

"Aren't you going to say hello or something first? You've got to ease into something like that." I finish putting the money in the ammunition box, put the count slip on top, and close it up. It feels very deliberate. I'm still holding my breath a little wondering if she saw me. Luckily, it seems like she's wrapped up in her own shit. It suits me that she's a little bit self-absorbed. Spending time with her is so much easier than it would be with someone who wanted to know every detail about my life.

She sighs. "I told them about a boy I was seeing earlier this summer." I wonder if it was the guy with the picnic basket. Probably not. He didn't seem to get very far. "Now they're kind of expecting me to show up with him. It'll just be a lot less awkward if I show up with someone."

"Hey Dave!" I call out the door. "Can you go with Nicole to meet her parents?"

"Only if she has a hot brother," he calls back. I chuckle, but Nicole just glares at me.

"Come on, I'm serious. It won't be terrible, I promise."

The way she's looking at me is familiar – that pleading, desperate sort of look that lets me know I can ask for a favor. I think for a moment and realize there's nothing useful Nicole can give me. It annoys me because I still feel compelled to help.

"I can do it," I say. "But I'm not really cool with lying to your parents. I'm not a good liar," I lie. She looks at me like I'm an adorable puppy.

"Look, they won't be here for a few weeks. If I can find someone else to go instead, I will." She pauses. "I haven't really been seeing anyone lately though." Another long pause. "Have you?"

"Nope," I tell her.

On the other side of the door I hear Dave bidding goodnight to the last customer. He says, "Have a nice night," but in a tone that says "get the fuck out of my store so I can go home."

"Well, I better get back out there," Nicole says. "We can talk more about it later."

"Sure," I say.

She leaves and I breathe a sigh of relief at not getting caught. I don't like the idea of meeting Nicole's parents, but it shouldn't be too bad. Maybe a few awkward moments, but I can do a few hours of fake smiles. I try to imagine what they look like, but it's tough. Everyone over forty looks the same to me until they're old enough to be put in a nursing home. Then they still look the same, just all used up.

I think about my parents in a nursing home. It'll never happen. They don't have the money for it. I realize I have no idea what happens to old people who have no money and no family. I can't recall ever having seen a geriatric homeless person. I guess most people who have no money and no family end up dead long before they get to that age. I shudder. Being old is the only thing worse than being broke. When you're broke you can always steal more money, but when you're old, there's no way out except in a box. I wish I could live forever.

37

The four of us – Dave, Grace, Margaret, and me – close up shop
and get ready to head to the second Wonderments movie night. I
didn't expect Margaret to come along and I can't recall anyone
inviting her, but she's walking with us. She's not saying much but
that seems pretty normal for her. Dave and Grace dominate the
conversation talking about things I don't care about even a little bit.

Nicole got sent on ahead by Dave to save us a spot while the
rest of us closed up. It struck me as a phenomenally stupid
decision on both of their parts – if they got caught she could easily
get fired for leaving her shift early, and he could get fired for letting
her. Of all the things to possibly get fired over, "slightly better seats
at a free shitty movie" has to be somewhere near the most trivial.
Then again, we're talking about a guy who habitually steals candy
worth less than a buck and a girl who hasn't come back from a
lunch break on time once all summer, so I guess I shouldn't be
surprised.

Her original text said "@ dippin dots" which isn't helpful in
any way, because by the time we've gotten there, the crowd has
spread out over so much of the main walkway that she could
realistically be near any of three different Dippin' Dots carts. We
text back and forth and figure out that she's near the one closest to

the movie screen. We shove our way through the crowd while *Hitch* booms over us, still in the opening scenes where we're establishing that the generic female lead across from Will Smith absolutely does not need a man, before we watch the rest of the movie, which is about her getting a man.

Nicole got here early enough to get us close to the screen, which means now the ground all around her is packed. The four of us wade through the crowd trying our best not to step on anyone. Normally I'm not too self-conscious about how I look, but it's hard not to feel clumsy when you're shoving your way past hundreds of people and getting in between them and the thing they're collectively watching. Once we find her it just gets more awkward. She may have saved enough room for all of us originally, but the more people showed up, the more her saved spot has shrunk. She still has a halo of empty space around her, but I have serious doubts there's enough room there for five of us. This doesn't stop anyone else from sitting down though, leaving me to sit down last and mash myself between Dave and Nicole. I stumble and my hand lands on her knee as I try to position myself on the blanket.

If it sounds cute or romantic or erotic, trust me, it isn't. It feels like that moment when you get shoved up against a hot girl on the bus and you feel ugly because she's so far out of your league that she assumes you must be trying to cop a feel, mixed with that moment in middle school gym class where you have to do chin-ups in front of everyone because your shitty school only has one chin-up bar, and you can't do any.

I readjust and try to settle in. No one seems to notice how awkward I looked, and I remind myself it was probably all just in my head. I can feel Nicole's leg touching mine, and under normal circumstances I'd move over to stop touching her, but there's no room between me and Dave. I take a breath and try to relax.

"It's a good thing you didn't bring a date this time," Grace says. "What a crowd."

"Yeah, I guess," Nicole says.

I hope someone will jump in and change the conversation but it looks like I'm on my own. Margaret is watching the movie, and if Dave does jump in, he's likely to make things more awkward rather than less.

"This is a pretty decent movie, for a romantic comedy," I say.

"I heard the female lead was supposed to be white, but the producers thought that a movie with an interracial couple wouldn't sell, so they cast Eva Mendes instead," Grace says.

"Isn't she Hispanic?" I ask.

"I guess so," Grace says.

People say racism is dead in America, but you can still hear it in the language. "Interracial couple" is still code for "someone who isn't white dating someone who is." People don't bat an eyelash if it's a Latino and an Asian or an African American and a Filipino, but as soon as the white girl wants to get with someone who isn't white, it's all pitchforks and torches.

"You ever date a black guy?" Grace asks. "I never have."

"Nope," I say.

She gives me a look. "I meant Nicole."

"You're into black guys?" Dave says to me.

"No," I tell him.

"A couple times, I guess," Nicole says. "Nice guys."

"I bet," Grace says.

Their conversation strays to their past dating exploits. They're being as cryptic and self-restrained as possible, like a weird sort of party game where the first person to reveal specific details about themselves or their romantic history loses. I do my best to ignore them. My hand is cramped from the way I'm sitting, but it's going to be impossible to move until the movie is over.

* * *

It's almost three a.m. and I can't sleep. I lie in my bed in the dark and listen to Cory snoring deep, gasping snores. I've never heard anyone so young snoring so loudly. He must have a cold or something. That's not what keeps me awake.

Sometimes I just get this craving for intimacy with other people. Not sex, and not spending time with someone I already know, either. I want to meet someone and find out all about them. I want to hear their dirty little secrets, about the time they accidentally smashed their parents' windshield and blamed it on someone else, or the time they snuck into a cemetery at night as a kid and caught a couple making out there. Secrets that really don't matter in the grand scheme of things, but that they've never told anyone, anyway. I want to tell them my secrets, too. Once they've told me all their secrets, they're used up. We can still be friends, if it comes to that, but they can no longer quench my desire to know someone *more*.

I know I could go down to the lobby or out into the hallway and read a book if I wanted to. I could just be a dick to Cory and turn the light on and read in here – he probably wouldn't even wake up. I could put in my headphones and try to learn some Portuguese. That's what I feel like I should be doing.

I should just sleep. I have to work tomorrow. It always goes the same way when I feel like this: there's no one awake at this hour, so I'll stay awake for hours wishing I could meet someone. Eventually exhaustion will win and I'll fall asleep unsettled and anxious. When I wake up, the feeling will be gone. I wish I could skip the obsessing part and fall asleep. Same results, less being exhausted all damn day tomorrow.

I pick up my phone and look through the contacts. I consider calling Dave, but decide not to. I have no doubt that he has an unending litany of stories of drunkenness, gay sex, and drunken gay sex. The problem is it's not a secret – he'll tell anyone who wants to listen. It wouldn't make me feel any closer to him because I know the homeless guy on the corner can hear the same stories. It's almost like if they don't feel vulnerable or naughty by telling me, it's not worth hearing. If they tell me something they can only say in a whisper, then I feel closer to them. Otherwise, it doesn't matter.

I realize why it's bothering me. I'm still feeling a bit cheated and vulnerable from when Nicole extracted something personal out of me but didn't give anything back. I know on an intellectual level that she doesn't "owe" me anything. But it still feels like she does.

I send her a text. "Hey. Are you awake?"

I drop the phone next to me on the bed and keep it close, just in case she texts me back. I know she won't. It's not her fault. I don't think she's avoiding me or anything paranoid like that. I just know that at this hour, anyone reasonable is asleep.

I wonder how she would react if I told her who I really was. What I thought about her, about everyone we work with, in the most biting and explicit words I could use. I wonder how she would react if I told her about all the little ways I've been stealing money this summer, and how I did it in the last place I lived, and the place before that, and how I plan to do it again wherever I go next, and that I don't feel bad about any of it. Would she tell a manager? Go to the cops? Blackmail me somehow? I've never told anyone. If the internet age has taught me anything personally, it's that braggarts get caught.

I decide that if we do meet up, and she does get closer to me and share secrets with me, I'll tell her. Maybe not everything, but enough so that she can get an idea of who I really am. Maybe leave out all the stuff I'm doing now and just tell her about how I started as a kid, stealing baseball cards and comic books, or stealing my parents' cigarettes to sell to my friends.

I lie in bed imagining how the conversation would go. Sitting on a bench inside Wonderments in the dark, her sitting close to me, cold in a long-sleeved hoodie. Listening to the stories of my childhood delinquency, with me watching her so I can stop telling her before it goes too far. Stories of how she felt with her adolescent boyfriends or when she accidentally killed a class pet and felt horrible or how she always wanted to be famous but gave up on her dream. I have no idea what she'd tell me, and that's the point.

It takes a long time but eventually I fall asleep, listening for a text reply that I know isn't coming.

38

I'm standing at my register doing nothing, staring at the girl in the back of the shop. I can tell from the way she holds herself that she's not American, but it's impossible to know much beyond that. Russian maybe, or Czech. She has dirty blonde hair that falls to her shoulders in a simple straight cut. She probably did it herself. She has the thin but curvy body with the smooth, clear skin that every European that works in this park seems to have. She doesn't wear any makeup though, and the work uniform makes her look dumpy and forgettable. She'd be the perfect candidate for one of those teen movies where the plain girl gets a makeover so she can get nailed by the quarterback. They always stop the story before the quarterback fucks her once and never talks to her again. I wonder what would happen if Grace and Nicole gave Margaret a makeover.

"Hey. I said, hey!" Nicole snaps her fingers in front of me. It's a clear, loud snap that only some people can pull off. I want to compliment her on it but I can't think of a way to say it that doesn't make me sound ten years old.

"Hey," I say.

She follows my stare to the girl in the back of the store. "Got a thing for leggy blondes, huh?"

"Not really." I look at the girl's legs, and they don't seem longer or any more impressive than any other pair of legs. It's not her fault. Even the hottest legs in the world would look dumpy in the Wonderments work-issue khaki shorts. "What's up?"

"Did you text me last night? You texted me. I was asleep already."

Dave sticks his head out from around a display case. I didn't even know he was there. "Sounds like someone was after a booty call." He comes over and holds his fist up for me to bump it. Neither of us do. "Come on, you can tell me. Did you give up that booty?"

"No!" Nicole says. The denial has a high shriek of embarrassment.

"It wasn't anything like that," I say.

Dave looks at Nicole and takes her hands in his in mock sympathy. "He was boring in the sack, wasn't he." He clicks his tongue at me disapprovingly. "We kind of knew it would turn out that way though, didn't we."

Nicole laughs. I want to tell Dave to fuck off, but I know anything I say will just make things worse. "It's really not like that," Nicole says.

"You two are no fun at all. He –" Dave points at me, "– really needs to get laid. You could help a guy out you know."

"Don't be an asshole," I tell him.

Dave holds his hands up defensively. "Hey, just trying to help out." He winks at me and goes back to whatever he was doing before he came over looking for gossip.

"So uh... what did you text me about?" She leans in closer than absolutely necessary. She smells like something sweet. I search my brain frantically, trying to place the smell. I can't.

"It was nothing. I just couldn't sleep and wanted to see if someone wanted to hang out."

She raises an eyebrow at me. "Okay." She touches my arm for a second. "Well, if you decide you want to tell me what you were really thinking, you can do that."

No, I can't. I don't know what I was thinking before.

Dave comes back over holding an animatronic hamster dressed in whatever karate uniforms are called. When you press the left hand, they make karate chop motions and sing "Kung Fu Fighting" in a voice reminiscent of Alvin and the Chipmunks.

"The battery is dead on this one," he says, demonstrating by squeezing the hand repeatedly. Nothing happens. "Fucking kids." The box has a big arrow with the words "Try Me!" on it, and at least a few times an hour, someone does. I've never seen anyone buy one, but people sure do love touching them. Nicole rolls her eyes. I'm not sure if she's rolling them because of Dave or because we're all going to have to hear a hamster sing "Kung Fu Fighting" a hundred more times this week.

"I'm going to go to the back and help Legs, so I don't have to hear whatever disgusting thing Dave is going to say to you next." She waves at me and I watch her leave.

"Seriously, you're going to tell me when you guys start fucking, right?"

"It's not like that, and even if we did, I wouldn't."

"I'm going to know anyway," he says. He would.

I watch Nicole walk away from us. Her legs are just as bland and chunky-looking as everyone else's in a work uniform, but they charm me nonetheless.

* * *

I've had a lump in my throat for the last few hours. I think everyone should know their limitations, and I'm pretty good at knowing mine. Yet, here I am at Knickers, which has been turned into a shitty dance club for the night. I am certain I will make a fool of myself.

"You need to relax," Dave says. "Seriously. You're going to give yourself a brain hemorrhage if you don't calm down. I'm waiting for your nose to start bleeding."

"Whatever." If anything, Dave noticing makes me even more nervous.

Dave calls a waitress over. "We need some tequila shots. On second thought, you better bring a bottle. Just whatever is cheapest. Bring four glasses. We have more people coming."

"Is that really —" I start.

"Yes," Dave says. He shoos away the waitress with a hand

wave. "Two things. First, stop looking at the door. She's going to show up." If I have been looking at the door, it's been unconscious. I can't tell if I'm really doing it or if Dave is just trying to read into the situation like he always does. "Second, you need to start drinking. Like right now. You can have fun tonight if you want, but you need to get out of your own way."

I don't know what to say, so I just nod. I try to smile and laugh, but it sounds forced.

Grace and Nicole should be here by now, but I guess it's not much of a surprise that they're running late. Margaret said "she might be around" but it sounded to me like a polite way to avoid coming out. I have the urge to check my phone for messages from Nicole, but I don't want Dave to accuse me of being nervous again, so I leave it alone.

The bottle shows up and the girls aren't here yet. We start drinking anyway. Thanks to Dave, I've done more drinking this summer than I have at any other point in my life. When I was in high school my friends drank shitty beer, but I never joined in. I never got pressured to drink that often – turns out most drunks are more than happy to have someone along who will clean up the puke and drive people home.

I always assumed the worst would happen to teenagers who drank alcohol. They'd get in car accidents, or get in fights, or say something that would ruin their lives, or get caught and get in huge unspecified amounts of trouble. In retrospect, they were having fun, and I was missing out.

I'm choking back the second shot when Nicole and Grace show up to the table. Grace shoves Dave to make him move over, and Nicole slides into the booth next to me.

"This guy cannot hold his liquor," Dave says, filling all four shot glasses.

"Ugh," Grace says. "Tequila? Really? Do you *like* throwing up?" This does not stop her from taking one of the shots.

"I can hold my liquor just fine," I say. "It's just getting it down that sucks."

"Don't be a whiner," Dave says, sliding two of the glasses over to Nicole and me.

The waitress comes back over when she sees our table has filled up.

"I'm starving," Grace says. "We should split something. Fries? Nachos?"

"Damn you and your Asian metabolism," Dave says. "They do sound good though."

The waitress writes down an order of fries and nachos before waiting for confirmation and says, "Anything to drink?" The girls order margaritas and the waitress disappears back toward the kitchen.

"Not too many people dancing," Grace points out.

"We should fix that," Nicole says. "Let's go."

"He's not drunk enough to have fun yet," Dave says.

I take another shot and hold it up in his direction. "I'll drink to that," I agree.

I enjoy spending time with these people, and I'd rather not ruin it by making a fool out of myself. Maybe if I'm lucky I can get away with just drinking and chatting all night, or, failing that, I can get us all drinking enough that no one remembers anything tomorrow. The nachos come and we eat, drinking and bitching about work. Time passes slowly, more drinks are had, there's a drunken arm wrestling contest at one point (Grace beats Dave, Nicole beats Grace, and I let Nicole beat me to claim the title). The tequila makes it easier to enjoy the moment.

The more I have to drink, the less I take part in the conversation. I'm not upset or anything. Being drunk with friends is just... pleasant. I can listen to them without feeling like I need to participate in the conversation, and they let me listen without expecting me to join in. No one says anything important. It just feels good to be part of the group.

Knickers is dark except the strobe lights and the disco ball on one side of the room, which has had the pool tables pushed aside to make room for a dance floor. The DJ is blasting 90's music that came out when we were in grade school. Everyone loves it.

In my mind, I think, "Why do they have a disco ball?" but out loud, I'm singing along to the chorus of the Counting Crows song "Mr. Jones." I'm screwing up a lot of the lyrics but I'm okay with that. I loved this song when I was a kid. Fuck it, I still do.

I'm bobbing my head along silently when the verse is playing, but when the chorus starts I just belt it out.

"Mr. Jones and me tell each other fairy tales," I sing to Dave. "Stare at the beautiful women. She's looking at you. Ah, no, no, she's looking at me." Dave just nods to me with a smile and doesn't say anything.

I can hear my own voice, and it sounds loud. I realize that if I wasn't drinking, I'd be mortified. I'm still me, I'm just a version of me that's willing to relax a bit. This is why alcohol is awesome.

"Okay," Nicole says. "You're drunk enough." Between the music and my own singing, she pretty much has to yell at me. Her voice seems far away.

I squint. "What?"

"I said, 'you should dance with me' and you said, 'I can't dance, I'm too sober, ask me when I'm drunk.' Well, now you're drunk, and I'm collecting my dance."

I stand up immediately and pitch forward, barely catching myself before I fall into the table. I grab Nicole's hand and the sensation of touching her jolts pleasantly up my arm into my brain. I'm sober for exactly one second where my thoughts are, roughly, "fuck fuck fuck fuck fuck what am I doing" and then I'm pulling her toward the dance floor with the Counting Crows as my wingmen.

The song fades out and is replaced by Wonderwall by Oasis. I normally hate this song. Now it seems awesome. I resolve to never be sober again.

I shove our way out to the middle of the dance floor. Everyone is having a good time. No one notices that I dance like shit. I don't know any dance moves and I have no rhythm, so I'm swaying back and forth out of time with the music. I've already bumped into people twice, but no one cares.

Nicole is a much, much better dancer than me. Her hips sway with the music and the rest of her follows along. Her hair has become slightly disheveled, and I realize it's the first time I've ever seen her that way. Everything about her outfit matches. Her loose red top matches her lipstick perfectly, with a red and white belt tying in the khaki capris. Even her shoelaces are red. I marvel at

210

them for a moment. Tennis shoes for dancing seem out of place to me. Then I realize I've been staring at them, and the floor, for a long time.

"Hey now," Nicole says. She touches my chin and pulls my face up until we make eye contact again. "Don't fall asleep on me."

"You have pretty shoes!" The words blurt out of me without consulting my brain. When I say it, I bump into someone again, hard. Thankfully the guy is too interested in his own dance partner to make a scene.

Nicole laughs. "You're terrible at this." She turns with her back facing me and slides in close, our bodies touching. I realize we've never been this close. I feel weak. I am doing my best to not pull away but absolutely not get any closer. "You have to go with the music!" She takes my hands and puts them on her hips. I'm trying as hard as I can to make my dancing match hers, but it's hopeless. Her rhythm is perfect to me, but my hands can't capture the motion. I can't predict how she'll move next; only recognize it as perfect after I feel it.

She doesn't give up on me, and we keep dancing. I put my hands on her shoulder, on her hips, her back. We dance through a few faster songs ("This is How We Do It" and "Hey Ya!"), which I butcher. Nicole laughs at me. I let her. Another slow song comes on (I'm not sure if I should hate the DJ or hate Whitney Houston directly for breaking up the moment), and we stumble off the dance floor with our arms around each other.

We get back to the booth, where Dave is chatting it up with a few guys I've never met before. Nicole puts her head on my shoulder, and I put my hand on her knee, eyes closed, listening to the second half of *Saving All My Love For You*. We sit like that for a long time, dozing while the world hurries on around us.

39

We stay at Knickers until the dance party officially stops at 3 a.m. The lights come up and the place suddenly looks depressing. Everyone leaves in a hurry. Grace and Nicole say goodnight and I walk home with Dave.

"So, straight answer time," Dave says.

"Don't you mean, gay answer time?" I'm still drunk. I can feel the delay between when a thought pops into my brain and when it comes out of my mouth. I like it.

"No, because you're straight, and you're the one doing the answering. When you ask me a question, then it's gay answer time."

"Fair enough."

"Why aren't you going home with Nicole right now?"

"Huh." It's surprisingly difficult for me to come up with a good answer. "I don't know. We're both drunk."

"I guess," Dave says. "All straight sex is awkward, though. I don't see what difference a few drinks makes."

We stumble along in the dark for a bit without saying much. I can feel my thoughts slowly pooling in my brain. It takes concentrated effort to get them out in a way that makes sense.

"Plus, how much longer am I going to be around her, really? I like her a lot, but I don't want to be one guy on the long list of

212

guys she did it with this summer."

"It's not that long of a list, dude. I think you're imagining things," Dave says. I look at him, and I think he's serious.

"I don't know. I guess on some level, I'd rather be the one that got away instead of just another one."

"Bullshit," Dave says. He sits down on a bench and leans his head back. "If you want to be loved and lost, you have to be loved first."

"Who said that?" I ask.

"I don't know," he says. "I probably saw it stitched on a pillow or some shit." Then he adds, "I should have drunk more water. This hangover is going to fuck me up." He sits there quietly. "And anyway, if anyone is going to be the one that got away, it's going to be her, not you."

I hope Dave is wrong about the severity of the impending hangover.

"She's not going to make the first move," he says. "She just won't do it. But if you do, she'll go along. Trust me."

"Did she tell you that?" I ask. "Or are you just pulling it out of your ass?"

He shrugs.

"You think it's too late for me to text her?" I ask.

"Yeah it is. By now she's back home and probably asleep. That opportunity is gone for sure."

I nod.

"Cheer up though. She likes you. You'll have other chances, if you take them."

I stand up and help Dave up from the bench, and we walk home.

When we get there we can hear at least three different parties going on upstairs. Predictably, the girl behind the front desk is sitting there doing her very best not to give a fuck about any of it. She doesn't even look up when we come in.

"I guess not everyone was ready to stop the party," Dave says. "I'm going to get a bottle of water from the store. You want something?"

"No," I tell him. "I'm tired, and I'm going to bed." I've had enough to drink at this point that I can pass out through any amount of shitty European club music.

Dave gives me a clumsy fist bump, and we go our separate ways.

I head up the stairs and the music blasts me from all sides. Techno coming from one room, Lady Gaga from another, hard rock in another. Plenty of room doors are wide open, and people are wandering up and down the hallway. I wonder if security has been contacted already, or if someone is waiting to call them, or if they've just given up entirely.

I get to my room looking forward to trying my best to get to sleep, and notice that my door is open. I jog over to see what the hell is going on. The song "Shake Ya Ass" is blaring out of the room, and at least a dozen people are inside. There's a guy in a tight pink shirt dancing on top of Cory's dresser, and a girl in a black lace bra and blue jeans dancing on top of mine. Some frat boy with no pants is passed out in my bed, and a couple sitting on the top bunk looking like they're trying to figure out if it's poor etiquette to fuck right there.

Cory is standing over in a corner holding a shitty beer and ogling the dancing girl like he's never seen a bra in real life before. Most of the other people in the room are holding the same shitty beer. There are two cases of it in the corner; one of which appears to be empty. I can't tell how many of the people here are under 21, but I'd guess most of them.

Alcohol isn't allowed in the employee housing. If anyone enforced that rule, they'd have to fire just about everyone. It's just one of those rules in place so Wonderments has plausible deniability when a teenager ends up in the hospital with alcohol poisoning.

"What the fuck, man," I say to him.

"Hey, you want a beer?" What an idiot.

"What's going on here? I kind of live here, you know."

"Shit, did I not tell you?" he says. "Obviously they won't serve me beer at Knickers, so a bunch of us just decided to do our own thing tonight. I thought it was weird that you didn't show up."

I do my best not to get angry. The music pounds in my brain and makes it hard to say anything. I have to yell over it.

"You didn't tell me shit," I tell him. "I was going to go to bed. In my room. But I can't, because there's a guy with his dick out passed out on my bed."

Cory looks over. "Sorry about that, man, but I don't know what to do. I'm not touching that." I stare at him without saying anything, so he adds, "Hang out with us. It's good times. Have a beer dude."

"I'm drunk already," I tell him. "I was at the real party tonight. Is there anyone here that can legally drink? Where did you get this beer?"

Cory shrugs. "Everyone here is legal, if you know what I mean." He gives me a big grin. "You sure you don't want to stick around?"

I close my eyes. I wish I was more drunk so I could throw up on him. "I just want to sleep."

Cory says, "If you say so," then after a minute, he taps a guy on the shoulder.

The guy turns around, beer in hand. Greasy black hair, dark vacant eyes, and a black t-shirt with white letters. It reads, "I hate your smile." Cory leans in and whispers in his ear for a minute, then the smile-hating kid says to me, "Hey, my room is next door, you can crash there if you want." He turns back to his other conversation. I think about it a minute, and then ask him, "Which room is it?" He turns around and looks at me like I'm a dumbass. It doesn't occur to him to that there's a "next door" on both sides of us.

He looks at me like he doesn't understand why I'm asking him, and it bothers me. This guy will spend the rest of his life thinking that I'm stupid. He won't ever think about this conversation again, but he'll just see me somewhere later and think, "I met that guy once, he seemed kind of dumb."

"It's 202," he says. "We good?"

"Try not to puke on my stuff," I tell him, and walk out.

Room 202 is two doors down from us. The door is shut, and there's no light on under the door. I knock and there's no answer. I knock again, louder, just in case. There's still no answer, so I open the door and go in. The room is dark and I don't turn on the light. I crash in the lower bunk. The pillow smells like cheap cologne.

40

I have an intense feeling of not knowing where I am. It's not because I just woke up in someone else's room – they all look more or less identical. It just happens when you travel a lot. I get out of bed and stumble out in the hallway, which is covered in more trash than usual. I have no idea if security ever even showed up last night, or if they just let the parties burn out. I bet cable news would give serious air time to an exposé of the rampant underage drinking on the premises of one of the largest amusement parks in the United States.

I notice immediately that my door is still open. That's not a good sign. Inside the room, Cory is passed out on the floor, he's alone, and the place is trashed. There are beer cans everywhere. All the stuff on his dresser was shoved onto the floor at some point, and one of his drawers is open. Cory's mirror survived the night, carefully placed in a corner. There's a smashed bottle of some sort of alcohol along one wall, but it doesn't look like there's any puke, piss, or broken furniture, so I guess for a teenage party it's a good result.

I look down to see if anyone drew any dicks on Cory's face. No one did. How disappointing. At least he should be sore from sleeping on the floor all night.

I turn back to my bed to inspect the sheets, and that's when I notice my dresser drawers open slightly. I pull the second drawer open quickly and dig through everything. It's clear that someone has been here. I rip everything out and dump it on the floor, shaking each piece of clothing as I do just in case. I stare at the empty drawer, then close it and rip open the top drawer. I kick Cory, intending to wake him up but kicking him harder than absolutely necessary. "Hey man, get up." I dig through my top drawer as well, and then even check the bottom drawer that I never put anything in. They're both empty.

I hear Cory groaning as he sits up.

"I'm pretty sure we were robbed," I tell him.

"What?" He says. "What did they take?" He looks around the room in a vague panic, even though the place is such a mess it'd be impossible for him to notice anything missing at a glance, anyway. "You don't have a laptop here do you? I don't even have anything worth stealing."

"Of course you don't."

I dig through my clothes on the floor a bit and then sit on the edge of my bed, eyes closed. "You fucking idiot," I say.

"Hey, cool it man," Cory says.

"I was talking about myself, but you're a fucking idiot too, now that you mention it. You never even told me all these people were going to be here, and now I'm out a lot of fucking money."

"Shit. How much is it? I can pay you back."

All the time spent stealing change, selling counterfeit merchandise, everything I've worked on and worked for this summer... gone. There were a few uncashed Wonderments checks in the envelope that I'm sure I can get re-issued, but the rest of it is gone. Even if Cory had that kind of money, which I'm sure he doesn't, there's no way I can explain to him how I had thousands in cash in my dresser drawer.

"You don't have that kind of money," I tell him. "Forget it."

"Well, I'll ask around about it. I'm sure it'll turn up. " He doesn't get it at all. If I thought I could take him in a fight, I'd punch him right now.

"You do that," I tell him. "And maybe ask someone to teach

218

you how to respect other people's fucking property."

He stands in front of me silently, not making eye contact, looking guilty. It's a stupid, childlike guilt, like he believes that if he demonstrates that he feels guilty, that absolves his wrongdoing.

I stand up, standing over him while he's still sitting on the floor. There's a split second when I'm sure I'm just going to bash his head in, and from the look on his face, I think he's expecting it. Instead, I walk out the door and slam it as hard as I can. The doorknob comes off in my hand when I do it. It's cold and heavy, heavier than I would have expected. The glass is smooth, with no imperfections. I toss it on the floor in the hallway with all the leftover garbage from last night's parties. I hate this place.

* * *

Wonderments might be the worst place in the world to nurse a hangover. The clangs of rickety amusement park rides and the flashing lights and sirens of half-rigged carnival games mix with the summer sun to make me wonder if it's possible for a headache to be fatal. I just want to go back to sleep at this point, but I also don't want to go back to my room, so I keep walking through the park. I pass the line for the novelty train that will take you to the back of the park, and regret my decision to walk as soon as I'm far enough away that it doesn't make sense to turn back.

Going to Brazil probably can't happen at this point. I could go, but it would be a much shorter trip than I planned. I hate the idea of going and then leaving after a few weeks when I was planning on staying for six months. I imagine running scams in São Paulo to stay afloat, but that's a horrible idea. Being in a foreign country, without knowing the language well, and needing to be a success to make rent just adds up to too much pressure and too much that could go wrong.

The idea of moving back home with my parents horrifies me. It'd be fine for the first few days, and then the hints would start about getting a job, moving out, paying rent.... My parents love me, but we don't do well living under the same roof. Given the option of living with them or being homeless, I'd flip a coin. The most realistic option for me at this point is probably to just pick some

219

other shitty American town, move there, and keep saving up money.

I find a park bench in the shade. Luckily, since the back of the park doesn't have any of the premier roller coasters or the water park nearby, it's relatively quiet. I lie on the bench and close my eyes, putting my arm over my eyes for good measure.

It's after noon before I wake up. This time I take the train back to my room. When I walk back in, I see that Cory has cleaned. All the trash is in a garbage bag propped up outside the door. All the beer cans and evidence of a party are missing. Even my clothes are stuffed back into the drawers. He's not in the room, and there's no note. He had to work today, I suppose. I have to work the late shift tonight myself, so I pull on my uniform. It's wrinkled and smells like dried sweat, but at this point it doesn't make any difference to me.

41

Grace, Margaret, and I are working alone. Three people is not enough people to do a decent job at any of the things we need to do to keep the place clean and well stocked. It's going to be very, very late before we get to go home tonight. Dave was supposed to be working tonight as well, but he called in "sick" since being honest enough to call in hungover would get him in trouble.

When the shift manager said on the phone that Dave was sick, she said she'd "make some calls" and see if she could find a replacement for him. We knew immediately that we were screwed: if there was someone available to fill the shift, they would have been sent here already. It's going to be a busy night. Both the girls will be in a pissy mood over it. It bothers me a lot less; they pay us by the hour, so it doesn't matter to me what they have us doing. Either way it's just trading time for money and waiting to go home. I don't want to be here tonight either, but having Dave here or not having him here doesn't make any real difference.

Just the three of us working means there's not much being said, even if we could find a few minutes to pry ourselves from our registers to chat. They won't interact with each other unless they have to, and I'm not about to get between them. As long as the store stays busy, it keeps the peace by necessity.

I'm skimming people's change again, more out of habit than anything else. I can't make enough money to make up what I lost thanks to Cory's party, but more money is always better than less, so I go through the motions anyway. Being shorthanded makes it the perfect opportunity – fewer employees to notice what I'm doing, and more time trapped behind my register ringing people up. I make a mental note to complain about it later. With any luck it will be a good way to unify the girls and get out of here without any drama. I suspect that most people hired into middle management are socially inept assholes for the same reason: retail workers always produce more when they have someone on the outside that they can hate. Dave is more useful when he's gone than when he's here.

"Oh, hey!" the guy at the front of my line says as he puts three Wonderments themed t-shirts and a tube of $20 sunscreen on the counter. "Everything good with the family?"

It takes me a second, and the silence gets awkward. Then I recognize him: the cop from the bowling alley.

"Oh, yeah. I mean, we're getting by. It's Officer.... Baker, right?"

He hands me the money for the shirts. I give him his correct change.

"Sure is. Just Mr. Baker for today, I suppose. Spending some time with the wife and kids."

"It's a beautiful day for it. Do you have season passes?"

"Nah. We probably should. The water park alone would be worth it on hot days. Didn't know you were working here for a day job. How is it?"

"Yeah, just for the summer. It's pretty fun, and they work us really hard, so the money's good."

The line behind him is starting to get long.

"Well, looks like I should leave you to it. It was good seeing you again.... damn. James? Jeremy? Josh? I feel bad, I can't remember."

He looks at my name tag. "...Nathan."

He gives my face a long, hard look. "Well, you have a good day now." He scoops up his bag and he's gone.

222

I've been here too long.

42

The last customers of the night – a pair of teenage girls who pay $30 for a pair of cheap matching friendship bracelets – leave the store, with Grace following so close behind them I wonder if she'll literally shut the door on their asses.

The door clicks shut and she says, "Okay, I know we were short tonight and this place is fucked, but let's hurry up and get it clean and get out of here. I have stuff to do."

Margaret walks by with an armful of folded t-shirts to restock some shelves and mumbles, "yeah, right."

"What was that?" Grace says.

"I'm sure it was nothing," I say deliberately. "You're right. Let's just clean up and get out of here."

We all work in silence for a few minutes, sweeping the floors, restocking the shelves, tying up trash bags. Grace is the one that breaks the silence. "You know what, fuck off."

So much for getting out of here in a hurry.

"What did you say to me?" Margaret says. She has a hard, feverish look in her eyes, the look of someone who got picked on as a kid or got cheated on by their first boyfriend or yelled at every day by their parents, and has just stayed pissed off for years and years, waiting for just the right moment to spit it all out at once.

"You might not have anything to do tonight except go home and sit there and be lonely or whatever it is you do by yourself all the time, but I actually have things I'm passionate about, that I'd rather be doing than sitting here all night long."

I can see the news headline already: "Girl Hospitalized After Amusement Park Assault."

"You don't know anything about me," Margaret says, "and you never will."

"I know enough about you already," Grace says.

Margaret looks for a second like she's going to hit her, but then she breaks off her death glare and goes back to stocking a shelf. She's setting things down hard enough that the shelf rattles. I'm waiting for one of them to give out and dump merchandise all over the floor.

Grace follows her. "No, we're not done. You're not going to sit there and start shit and then pout about it for the rest of the night because someone put you in your place."

"Come on, Grace," I say. "Let's just finish up here and then we can go home."

Margaret cuts in. "I don't need you to defend me, especially when these cunts have you so pussy-whipped you'll do whatever they say." The memory of the word "cunt" hangs in the room.

I put my hands up in surrender. "Not getting involved," I say.

"You think I don't know you," Grace says. "But what you say about me couldn't be more wrong. You've spent this whole summer wishing you were like the rest of us, wishing you were prettier, and funnier, and more interesting, brooding around and being all cynical because you think it makes you special. It doesn't. No one likes you."

I'm considering calling a manager at this point, but they'd never get here in time. Margaret has gone pale, and her lip is quivering.

"I'm going home," she says quietly.

"Fuck you. I'm not doing your work. Cry on your own time." Grace says.

Grace might be smart in a lot of ways, but apparently she never learned when arguments are over. When someone goes from loud to quiet, you let it drop. When someone wants to storm off, you let them. Just take the win and let it go.

Margaret walks up close to her. They're standing so close their noses almost touch.

"Back up, bitch," Grace says, but she's the one who takes a step back.

"I might be a loser," Margaret says. "Yeah, you think you're super popular and everyone loves you. Yeah, your airheaded friend can pick up any guy in the park, and decided to go after the one guy I paid attention to this summer. Whatever. I'll get over it. But deep down you know you'll never be a success. No one is ever going to pay attention to the art you try so hard at. It's shitty amateur hour stuff and you know it. That's why you couldn't even get your friends to show up."

She pauses and looks at me accusingly. "This guy showed up, sure. He'll do anything a cute girl tells him to. If he didn't think he was going to get laid, he never would have been there in the first place."

Grace lets out a deep hiss like she's been punched in the stomach. She shoves her way past Margaret to the center closet, goes inside, and slams the door. The toys nearby rattle on their hooks on the wall, and a bag of plastic army men falls to the cement floor with an impotent "whap" sound. It would be so much more dramatic if it had been something breakable.

"That was way over the line," I tell Margaret.

Margaret gives me the finger. It looks ridiculous, childlike. I just stare at her. After a moment, she turns around and pulls on the door to leave. It's locked. She pulls on it angrily again, and after nothing happens, she unlocks the door clumsily and storms out.

I clean the store for awhile, count down my register, and restock the shelves. My phone says it's almost 1:30. The park officially closes at 11:00 on week nights, which means most of the time people are actually out of the park by midnight. On a good night, we're finished closing and on our way home by 12:30. I can't remember ever being here this late. If we don't call a manager to close us up soon, someone is going to show up on their own, and they're going to be pissed. Part of me thinks I should throw Margaret under the bus – she'd almost certainly be fired for leaving a shift early without permission – but if it came down to it, I know

226

I'd cover for her. It's just the sort of thing you do for your coworkers.

I close out Margaret's drawer as well. The temptation to steal the money is strong. Margaret would get fired for leaving her shift early, but they'd still trace the theft back to me. I don't take anything. If I was going to risk getting caught, it'd have to be enough money to actually make a difference. Margaret hates working the register, so there's almost nothing inside.

Eventually there's nothing else I can do. Grace is still in the center storeroom. I have the urge to call the manager, tell her we're done, lock up, and go home, and let Grace drag herself out whenever she's good and ready. I won't do it, even though it would amuse me. If covering for your coworkers is the right thing to do, it's also right to not lock your coworkers in a closet overnight.

I knock on the door softly. There's no answer. I knock again, a bit louder. Still nothing. I open the door, half expecting to find her asleep or dead. She's sitting on a stool facing away from me. Definitely not asleep. Probably not dead.

"Are you okay?" I ask. "It's getting late. It's just you and me. We should close up and get out of here."

She turns around. Her makeup is blotched and her eyes are red. She's been trying to make it look like she hasn't been crying – an impossible task.

"You don't care about me at all. Don't pretend."

"How am I supposed to respond to that? I don't have a problem with you. I like when you're around. Mostly I just want to go the fuck home."

"We've barely talked all summer," she says. "We don't really hang out. When you hang out with me it's because Nicole is around. I mean, I get it, she's cute and you like her and all that."

"It's not that I don't like you, it's just that I don't know you very well."

"You're supposed to say you do care, dumbass. Lie if you have to. I'm so pissed at you right now."

I wonder if there's a word in Portuguese, or in any other language for that matter, that can convey what I said without making me sound like a jerk. There certainly isn't one in English.

"See, this is why I hate people," I say. "If I lie you get pissed, if

227

I tell the truth you get pissed. We have fun when we hang out. That can't be enough?"

Her anger is burned out. Now she's just unhappy. Tears well up around her eyes and she's sniffling. She looks around for something to wipe her nose on, but can't find anything. I don't have anything either. I could offer her my sleeve, I guess, but that seems too intimate. Plus, I don't want someone else's snot on my clothes. I try to muster up genuine concern, but really, I'm more curious about her makeup. I've never seen a girl cry in makeup, except in movies. It doesn't streak or smear as much as I thought it would. I wish there were a way to ask her if that's because she's cleaned it up, or if movies are full of shit.

"Tell the truth, then. If it wasn't for Nicole would you have come to the art show? Would we talk to each other at all, even?"

"Of course we'd still talk," I say. "I see you here every day. As for coming to your art thing, you're the one that asked Nicole to bring me along. I guess that kind of says it all."

"Do you think I'm going to make it? You know, as an artist?"

I have a vision of one of the supervisors showing up at the door to discover us here. An hour late, everyone else gone home, the two of us alone in a supply closet. It wouldn't look good. I walk back out onto the sales floor and talk to her through the door.

"I doubt it," I say. "It's not your fault. Almost no one makes it. You could be the most talented painter in the state and you probably wouldn't make it."

It looks like she's going to start crying again.

"I really did like the painting of Nicole. And not just because it's of Nicole, before you ask. It's something special. If anyone deserves to make it, it's you. It's just that most people don't, whether they deserve to or not."

"Shut the door," she says.

"We have to go. Someone is going to get pissed pretty soon."

"Get out!" she screams at me. Her voice is high and shrill. The room is small and the piles of boxes, stacked floor to ceiling with the shelves between them little more than a formality, muffle the sound.

I just stand there. She wipes her eyes. "I mean it. Go home. I'll finish up here."

I'm not sure what else to do, so I shut the door. I grab my cash box and Margaret's, and head up to the front office to turn them in. The whole time I'm walking I'm expecting to notice Grace following me. She isn't. I'm expecting someone to ask me what's going on, since I showed up without manager approval. No one does. I punch out, walk home, and look forward to being asleep.

* * *

The light in my room is on. I stop outside my door and take a deep breath before I go in and have to deal with Cory. He's sitting on his bed goofing off on his phone. If they ever figure out how to convert the energy spent playing shitty flash games into scientific research, we'll have cancer and AIDS cured inside a month. Most mobile games would be called "This Game is AIDS" if they were honest anyway, so a research game would fit right in.

"Hey, what's up," Cory says. I can't tell if he was waiting for me to get home, or if he just spent the whole night goofing off. I'm not sure which is worse. I hope he was just playing games all night and my getting home now is unrelated. At least then he's keeping his time wasting contained to himself.

"Shitty night at work," I tell him. "Two of the girls I work with can't help but fight every chance they get, and then they want me to patch it up. It's stupid and I'm sick of it."

"Sounds hot," he says. "Which two?" I can't tell which I think is more annoying: the fact that he describes two girls bitching at each other as "hot," or the fact that it doesn't occur to him to stop playing his game to have a conversation.

I'm tired, so I give in to his vernacular. "The Asian and the plain one."

His phone makes a sad sound which I assume is his character dying and/or his game ending, and he sits up.

"Why bother with them if you don't like them? There's plenty of girls out there, am I right?" He grins.

"I spend all my time with them. It's where I work. Things go shitty there and my whole summer gets weird." I pause for a moment. "Actually, that's not it. I like spending time with Nicole, and if Grace gets pissed that fucks things up."

He stares at me blankly.

"I like the hot one, and she's friends with the Asian one."

He nods. "Nicole is the hot one?"

"Yeah."

"How's that working out?"

I hop up on Cory's dresser to sit, since apparently this conversation isn't going away. "I like her," I say. My mouth feels strange when I admit it out loud, like it's someone else shaping the words. "I really do. I haven't wanted to go on a real date with a girl in a long time."

"Do you think she likes you? I mean, like that?"

"I have no idea," I confess. "I guess. It feels like she does, sometimes anyway. Then she talks about exes and cute guys around me and it just gets weird."

"Well, you should get ahold of her if you want to get ahold of her, if you know what I mean. The summer isn't going to last forever."

"I'm not sure I want her to be a random hook-up," I say.

It hits me. My money is gone. São Paulo is out for sure. I just sort of assumed Nicole would be gone forever at the end of the summer, and I'd be in Brazil. But now that I can't go, what if I moved back to her hometown after the season was over? If any town is as good as another, I could just choose the town she's in.

The idea makes me feel warm. I check my phone, thinking about texting her and telling her how I feel. There's an unread message.

"Is it her?" Cory asks.

I look at the message. It's not Nicole. It's Dave. "Drinks at Knickers after work" it says.

"It's Dave," I tell him.

He gives me a blank stare. "Who's Dave again?"

"The manager at my store," I tell him. "The gay guy. I'm sure you met once."

He snaps his fingers and gives me a smile. "Oh yeah, I remember that dude."

"He wants to meet me at the bar," I say. I wasn't planning on going out, but maybe it'll help me take my mind off stuff.

"Cool, I'm coming," Cory says.

"You can't even drink there, can you?" I'm hoping he'll take the hint.

He shrugs. "Nah. But not every night can be a party right? It's not like the last party turned out all that great, anyway." There's an awkward moment of silence, then we leave for Knickers together.

43

Cory and I find Dave sitting in the same booth he always sits at, if it's open. It gives me a vision of him being in a sitcom. Of course since he's gay and we live in America he'd probably have to be a quirky sidekick instead of the main character, but that's not so bad. No one in our little group of friends would make a convincing lead anyway.

"I didn't know you were bringing a date!" Dave says. There are a few empty shot glasses in front of him, and I wonder how many drinks in he is already.

"Oh, no, we're not —" Cory starts.

Dave laughs harder. "Calm down bro, I know."

We slide into the booth. "I don't know how you plan to get through this sober," I tell Cory. He looks sadly down at his hand, which has an obnoxious purple stamp on it marking him as a minor. He's rubs it compulsively. It doesn't come off.

"I texted Nicole for you," Dave says. "I was bored and the rest of you fuckers were still at work. But let's pretend I did it for you, because it makes me seem like a better guy."

I inspect the booth more closely. Dave's drink is there, but it's the only one. No purses, no jackets. As far as I can tell Dave is here alone.

"Uhhh.... where is she?"

"She said she'd come out after Grace got home from work, and they'd come out together."

"Oh. Shit."

"What?" Dave says. "You've been working with those two all summer. I know they're hot and everything, but you can't still be nervous with them at this point. You need to grow a pair."

The waitress comes over just in time to overhear Dave's advice about growing a set of testicles and ignores it in expert waitress fashion. I order a whiskey sour, and Cory orders a Coke and burger. I'm surprised he doesn't try to pull one over on the waitress and get some alcohol, but I suppose his braces and dopey smile keep him from ever passing for over twenty-one.

"It's not that," I say. "Grace is pretty pissed at me right now. If they're talking to each other, that conversation is not going well."

Several minutes go by, then the waitress shows up with Cory's burger. She also does that annoying thing waitresses do where they wait until the whole order is ready to bring out my drink, but it's not worth getting pissed over. Cory is most of the way through his burger and I'm thinking the girls aren't going to show up at all, when they do.

"Incoming," Dave says.

Nicole and Grace come over to our table. They don't sit down. "I didn't know he'd be here," Grace says to Nicole.

Nicole looks at me accusingly for a moment. "I didn't know either," she says.

"You stay here and have a fun time with the guys," Grace says. "I'm hitting the bar. Far away from here." She turns without another word and disappears into the crowd.

Nicole slides into the booth next to Dave. "Real smooth, assholes." Then she looks at Cory, who looks like he's stupid enough to respond. "Not you," she says. "You didn't do anything other than guilt by association."

"I didn't mean to piss her off, and I didn't know she was going to be here tonight," I say. "I feel shitty about the whole thing at work."

"Well, you should feel shitty, because it was some shitty stuff to say," Nicole says.

"No offense, guys, but I'm with her on this one," Cory says. "I can tell when a conversation is going to get super awkward. I'm going to go chat up some girls on the other side of the bar. Wish me luck."

He gets up and leaves, taking his Coke with him. Dave helps himself to some leftover fries immediately.

"That kid has no chance," I say. "What an overeager little dork."

Nicole sighs. "I thought you were a nice guy," she says.

"Huh?"

"I mean, first I hear about you going off on Grace for no reason, then you're ragging on that kid for no reason. He's barely out of high school. All he wants to do is hang out and make some friends. Then the second he's out of earshot you're a huge dick to him."

"He is kind of a dork," Dave volunteers.

"You don't know the whole story. Just drink your drink."

Cue an awkward moment of silence.

"That's it," Nicole says. "I thought you were nice, but really, you're just quiet. You're not that sweet, are you? You're just an asshole who can't speak up."

"Won't speak up," I clarify.

"What?"

"I'm not an asshole who can't speak up. I'm an asshole who knows when not to speak up."

"Oh, well, that settles it then."

"I think we need some more drinks," Dave said. "Don't let whatever catty thing Margaret and Grace have going on get into whatever you've got going on, and definitely don't involve me in it."

"Don't be pissed at me," I say. "You don't know the whole story between Cory and me."

"Feel free to fill me in," Nicole says.

"Yeah he will!" Dave says. He reaches into the table for a fist bump that no one returns. Nicole gives me a disgusted look.

"See?" I say. "Everyone is an asshole."

"Well, you guys are friends," Nicole says. "If everyone is an asshole, why have friends at all?"

The waitress shows up again and brings a round of shots with her. It looks like Jägermeister. "From the guy at the bar," she says. We look over and Cory is at the bar, still holding his Coke. From the look of things he's working up the nerve to talk to Grace, but hasn't gotten there yet. He's just kind of hovering near her and the small crowd of girls that has converged around her for some sort of drinking game. He sees us get the drinks and holds his glass up.

"Jäger is disgusting," Dave says. "You can always tell someone isn't old enough to drink when they try to order it." He picks up one of the shots, smells the glass, and wrinkles his nose. "Free drinks is free drinks," he says, then knocks it back.

"You can be friends with someone even if they're a jerk," I tell Nicole. "Everyone is an asshole. Friendship is just knowing someone is an asshole, and staying quiet about it."

"Hear hear," Dave says. He passes one of the Jäger shots to Nicole and takes mine. "To assholes." They both drink.

"Well, I'm going to find a nice guy to be with someday, and some nice people to hang out with," Nicole says.

"You need to get over it and get over yourself. There's no such thing as a nice guy or a nice person. Not really."

"I'm a nice person," she says.

"I doubt it," I say.

"Woah buddy," Dave says, putting his hand on my shoulder. "Maybe we need to scale it back a little bit here."

"It's nothing personal," I tell her. "You're not worse than anyone else. But I mean really, I don't know anything about you. No one does. We work together all summer long, and I really like you, and really pay attention to you, and I don't think I can say even one single thing about who you are. I don't know your college major, or your hobbies, or what music you like. Everything is just so surface level with you. Maybe if you had a bit more personality guys would be interested in hanging around with you instead of just trying to get laid."

She doesn't say anything.

"One thing's for sure, though: no one is that guarded about who they are without hiding some serious shit underneath." I pause for a moment. "I think I like you more because you're so good at it."

Nicole's lips tighten. For a moment it looks like she's going to say something, then she stands up instead. "You know what? Fuck this. We'll talk later. Maybe." She slides out of the booth and storms off, not looking back. It occurs to me I may have gone too far to try and make my point.

"That," Dave holds up his glass, toasting me, "is an impressive number of things in a row that you should not have said."

"Ah, shit. She told me her major when we went to the aquarium," I tell Dave.

He puts on a sarcastic smile. "Yeah, *that's* why you're in trouble right now."

* * *

I've got my arm around Dave and we're walking through the park, although I'm not sure where we're headed. He's doing most of the walking, and I'm just sort of staggering along where he guides me.

"Is it really so hard to be around girls? They seem so easy to, easy, until you try, and then it gets all fucked up, you know?"

"Mmm-hmm," agrees Dave. "That's why I go for boys. Easier to deal with."

My stomach doesn't feel good. I double over. Dave jumps back. Without him supporting me I'm pretty sure I'm going to fall over, but instead I just puke everywhere.

"Well, that was a close one," Dave says. When he's sure I'm done he pulls me upright and puts my arm around him again. "I'm going to get you home, and get you a nice big glass of water, and tuck you into bed. What I'm not going to do is let you throw up on my new outfit."

I swing my head to look over at him and he does have a nice outfit on. Pale, button-down yellow shirt and gray slacks with matching shoes. I get the urge to puke again.

Dave can see me eyeing his shoes. "Don't you do it," he says. "I'll dump your ass right here. It's summer. You'll probably still be alive in the morning."

Somehow we manage to lurch and stumble our way back to the

employee housing. I've given up trying to hold my head up, so I notice the carpet as we walk in through the front doors. It's even uglier and dirtier than I remember. I'd swear I remember being woken up at least once a week by the sound of vacuums in the hallways, but the lobby carpet looks like it's never been cleaned.

"I should have saved it," I say.

"What? Never mind."

"To puke on the carpet. It'd match."

We head up the stairs with Dave doing most of the lifting. He doesn't complain at all. I'm aware on some foggy level that this is an inconvenience for him, but I don't know how to make that stop, so I just go along with him.

I see it as soon as we round the corner to my hallway – there's a bright pink scrunchie on the door.

"Whoa, whoa, whoa. We can't go in there. Not allowed."

"What are you talking about?" Dave asks. "Oh shit, did you lose your keys?"

"No, no. There's a scrunchie on the door. That means no entry allowed. Girl over. Naked time."

"You have got to be kidding me," Dave says.

"Nope. Can't go in there. Scout's honor." I stand up straight, make a peace sign, and salute with it. I stumble, but the wall keeps me from falling over. I have my face on the wall, feeling vibrations from loud Russian club music coming from one of the other rooms on the floor . I'm not sure how long we stand there.

"Well, shit," Dave says. "Come on then. You can come sleep in my room on the floor."

I look at him and give him a wobbly smile. "Nope. Can't fool me. I might be wasted but I'm still straight. You're not getting any man love from me tonight, buddy."

He seems genuinely dumbstruck by my comment, so I fill the void by laughing.

"Well, okay then. You're drunk, so I'm just going to ignore the fact that you're assuming I'd even want to fuck you, and implying I'd just date rape a sloppy drunk dude if I had the chance. You'll pay for it later, but if I hit you now you probably wouldn't even feel it."

"You're right," I say. "I got a face like a rock."

"Sure thing. Back downstairs with you." He slaps me on the cheek softly. I wobble, but the wall catches me.

We head back down the stairs, and Dave makes me walk in front of him, presumably so that if I slip and fall it only kills one of us. We walk by the front desk again over to the small lounge. I don't think I've ever been in it before. I saw a couple making out on the couch here once, but generally it doesn't get much use. I wonder what kind of gross shit must be on that couch right before Dave dumps me on it. I discover the couch is quite comfortable; I forgive it for whatever diseases or illnesses it's communicating to me right now.

"Hey!" I hear. It's the girl who was sitting behind the desk. "He can't sleep here."

"Well I don't know where to put him, so he's either sleeping here, or he's your problem."

"Hey!" I get the impression she's talking to me now. "You can't sleep here. You have to go to your room."

I close my eyes and pass out.

44

I'm still on the diseased lounge couch when I wake up. The TV is on even though no one else is around. It's some cartoon I don't recognize. The volume is turned almost all the way up, and when the character onscreen talks – some sort of blank-eyed dog or maybe a bear – it pierces my brain. I look around thinking there must be some asshole sitting behind me watching the TV, but the room really is empty. I wonder if this is the receptionist's passive aggressive way of trying to get me off the couch. If it is, it's working.

It hurts my eyes to open them. There's a small, empty trash container next to my head I don't remember getting, but it's empty. My hair is damp with sweat, and my mouth tastes like vomit. My neck is sore from sleeping with it at a weird angle. I resolve never to get drunk again and know immediately that there is no chance of me keeping that resolution. I try to roll off the couch and hit the floor. I notice some sort of old food under the couch with ants crawling all over it. It's going to be a great day, I can tell already.

I check my pockets and discover I still have my wallet and keys, and I wonder if the fact that I wasn't robbed demonstrates there's still some good in the world, or if it's just that no one noticed I was out cold. I'm not sure what time it is, but there's light coming in through the windows. I have to work today. Chances are either I still have plenty of time to get to work, or I'm late already and things are fucked up. A few minutes of panicked rushing probably won't change much either way.

I head over to the convenience store next to the lobby and buy a bottle of water. The clerk behind the counter is a young guy who is looking pleased with himself.

As he rings me up, he says, "Need a bottle of aspirin there too, champ?" I must really look like shit.

"No," but I take his advice and buy some Tylenol anyway.

I walk upstairs to my room and find the door locked, which is a relief, since it means Cory is either gone or asleep. I open the door and the room is empty. As usual our room looks like a dump, Cory's dirty clothes on the floor and boots kicked wherever. I wonder what kind of girl he managed to get in here that didn't take one look at the place and run for it.

I grab my toothbrush, towel, and shampoo and head for the second floor bathroom. Mercifully, it's empty. I ignore the fact that someone took a dump and either clogged the toilet and didn't fix it, or just decided not to flush. I'm not going to be the one to find out which. I turn on the shower and just let the water run over me for awhile. I brush my teeth there so I don't have to see the nasty bathroom sink, and then head back to my room, ready to get the bad news about the time.

It's just after one thirty and I don't work until three. I still have the urge to call in sick, but from what I remember of last night everyone is going to be pissed at me anyway, and I don't want to compound that by missing my shift. I consider going to get some lunch but I want to avoid seeing anyone for as long as possible.

Instead I set my alarm for two thirty and fall asleep almost immediately. I don't feel any better when I wake up. I hit the snooze button once, and end up ten minutes late to work.

* * *

"You're late," Dave says as soon as I walk in the door. I can't tell if he's serious or kidding. He's been late just as (or more) often than the rest of us, but he *is* the manager. He's supposed to report late employees, but as far as I know he never does. I wonder at what point upper management will get suspicious that, on paper, Dave is running the first perfect store in the history of retail. My guess is they look the other way so long as the place doesn't burn down.

"Sorry," I tell him.

I wait for him to laugh, or say he's joking, or do anything to clue me in to the fact that he doesn't actually care that I'm late, but he doesn't. Instead, he puts his head down on the counter and groans aggressively.

"Hung over?" I ask him.

"Hell yes," he says. "You aren't?"

I don't feel that bad at this point, or at least, I don't think I feel that bad, but whenever I close my eyes everything feels much better, and it seems like a very good idea not to open them again.

"I wonder if anyone would notice if we just locked the doors and slept all night."

Margaret walks up from the back, slamming down a box of small tiki gods. They hit the counter with a loud bang and Dave and I both flinch. I can't tell if it was an accident or if it was deliberate. I'm a bit surprised to see her – it wouldn't have surprised me to find out she'd been fired for leaving work early. I guess Grace never said anything, and no one noticed. She appears to be pretending nothing happened, and I'm inclined to let her.

"See?" she says. "This is why I don't go out drinking when I have to work the next day."

I want to call her a hypocrite, but thinking back, I can't recall her ever showing up to work hung over. I'm sure she must have at least once, but I can't think hard enough to remember.

"You can go home and do nothing if you want. At least we're making memories." It looks like she's about to get pissed, so Dave adds, "The stuff I can remember, anyway." This seems to draw her sympathy, a little bit anyway.

The night drags on so slowly that I half expect to be paid for twice as many hours as normal on my next paycheck. It's a slow night, but hot. Normally the weather is cool (for summertime, anyway) since we're on a lake, but today the wind is dead and the air is hot, sticky, and stifling.

It's quiet for most of the shift. Thankfully Margaret leaves us to our misery, and we keep to ourselves. The store runs more smoothly with two of us feeling like shit than when we're all feeling fine. The store cools down a bit once it gets dark, and I start feeling a little better. There's not much going on, so I approach Dave.

"Hey."

"Hey," he says. He's sitting up now, but he's taken to wearing an overlarge pair of dark sunglasses he got from the back room.

"I wanted to say sorry."

He tilts the glasses down and raises his eyebrows. "I really don't care that you were in a bit late, like, not even a little. As fucked up as you were last night, it's a miracle you made it in at all."

"Not about that," I tell him. "I made a pretty big ass of myself. I didn't mean all that shit I said."

"It's fine," he says.

"Really? Come on."

"Yeah, it really is. I mean, yeah, you kind of implied I was a creepy slut, but you were really drunk, and you weren't exactly having a great night before that, either."

"Yeah, I screwed up pretty bad," I admit. "I guess you're not the only one I should apologize to."

"I'm not letting you off the hook that easy," Dave says. "You owe me one, big time. Next time I'm that drunk, you're the one that's dragging my ass home, instead of the other way around."

"Okay, that's fair," I say. "I'll be there."

He leans back against the wall, and if I had to bet I'd say his eyes are closed behind the sunglasses. I let him rest and we finish the rest of the shift quietly, both looking forward to sleeping off the rest of this hangover.

45

It's starting to rain as I walk home, which is a relief. I like the rain. Being wet is better than being hot. I'm sure management is disappointed it didn't start raining until after the park was closed. When it rains people go inside, and people who are inside buy stuff, especially comically overpriced umbrellas and ponchos. You'd think good weather would be better for business for an outdoor amusement park, but actually, the opposite is true. Good weather means people spend more time enjoying the rides and attractions and less time shopping.

I get back to the dorms and the whole place smells like wet dog with a faint undercurrent of fungus and mold. There's a bucket in the lobby which is slowly filling from a drip in the ceiling.

"This place has like, four floors, doesn't it?"

"Yeah, so?" the girl behind the desk says.

"So, we're on the bottom floor. Where is the water coming from?"

"It's raining outside," she says.

For a second I stare at her like she's an idiot, and she stares at me with the same look. I break first and go upstairs.

Cory is there. I walk in and change out of my soaked work clothes and text Nicole. I still need to apologize to her. "We need to talk, I'm stupid," I send.

"Dude. Thanks for last night," Cory says.

"What?"

"Last night, man. Pretty wild stuff. I thought I was going to go the whole summer without getting any."

"Oh, no problem," I say. "The couch in the lobby is pretty shitty and I probably have a disease now, but I was drunk, so I didn't notice."

"Well, I officially owe you one," he says. He hops down from his bed and high fives me.

I check my phone. Nothing. I don't know if Nicole is ignoring me, or if she just hasn't gotten the message.

"How you manage to work with such hot girls all summer without hooking up with them is beyond me, dude."

"Wait. You hooked up with Grace? No offense, but I thought she was classier than that."

He looks confused. "Wait. Shit. I thought Grace was the Asian girl."

"She is. How are you fucking girls without even knowing their name?"

"Grace would hardly even talk to me, dude. Her friend is the one who jumped my bones. Nicole."

My mouth goes dry. "Stop fucking around," I say. "Not cool. Did she put you up to saying that?"

"Nah man. I don't know what you said to her but I was trying to talk up Grace when she came over all pissed off. I just listened to her for awhile, asked her about where she was from, and told her how pretty she was. She couldn't wait to drag me back here."

My phone chirps with the sound of an incoming text message. I ignore it.

"I told you I liked her."

"You told me you weren't going to make a move, man. Besides, I didn't go to her, she came to me. If she wanted to hook up with you, why didn't she?"

I don't have a good answer. I'm not sure she ever liked me at all.

Cory frowns. He looks genuinely conflicted. "Look, I'm sorry.

If I had known you were chasing after her I would have left her alone. Honest. I'm not the kind of guy who chases after someone else's girl." I believe him. I don't think loyalty and stupidity are always connected, but in Cory's case I'm sure it is. "It's just that you never said you wanted to hook up with her, and every time I asked you about it you seemed wishy-washy about it. Then she was chatting me up and even told me flat out you guys weren't together."

"I know," I say. "We're not. I kind of thought we would be, but I guess I was just dreaming."

"Plenty of fish in the sea, right?"

I shake my head. "Don't worry about it. It's not your fault. I'm pissed, but not at you. At her, maybe. At myself."

"Shrug it off, bro. It's not that big of a deal. I'll back off, I promise."

I want to explain to him that the fact that Nicole would sleep with someone like him makes her unattractive to me. That I feel like if she hooked up with me now, I would always know her standard for guys included someone like him, and somehow, that would make me less of a person. That even though I believe him, and know he really would back off, that I'd always wonder, no matter what happened, about the two of them. Logically, I know it was nothing, or at least that they would both say it was nothing and try their very best to mean it. But I'll always know that that's not how they felt last night, in the middle of it, in my room. No matter what happens, I'll know they'll just be revising their own personal history to make things less awkward.

I check my phone. It says, "u can come over if u want. Not coming 2 u. Rm 408."

It sounds like a terrible idea. I know I should give myself a few days to let myself think about this.

"Okay, I gotta go," I say. "Do you have an umbrella?"

"No," Cory says. "I'm a man, and I'm from Texas. I might have a hat or something you can wear."

I try to imagine situations where I would be desperate enough to wear a cowboy hat and come up empty. "Never mind, I'll get one downstairs."

"Good luck, dude." In my mind, he adds, "Say hi to Nicole for me." Of course he doesn't say that, and I have no reason to think he would say it, other than the fact that I'm apparently just as much of a dick to myself as I am to everyone else.

* * *

I buy an umbrella at the convenience store downstairs. They're the same exact ones we sell in the park – plain, cheap plastic in black, lime green, or clear. I grab a clear one and head out into the rain.

The first thing I notice when I get to Nicole's dorm is that even though it smells a bit wet and moldy just like the guys' dorms, it's nowhere near as pungent. It could be that girls just take better care of where they live than guys do, or maybe this place was just cleaned better and more recently. Most likely, neither building has ever been thoroughly cleaned, and the guys' dorms are just older. It seems like the sort of thing a nearby university could get a research grant to study.

I walk up three flights of stairs to get to her floor and stop for a minute to catch my breath. While I'm standing there I try to imagine where Wonderments houses its disabled employees. There are no elevators in the dorms or anything, and no rooms on the main floor. Come to think of it I don't think I've seen one disabled employee all summer. I wonder if it's discriminatory hiring practices, or just me not noticing them around. After all, Wonderments does have thousands of employees, and I don't know most of them.

I head down to Nicole's room. I knock on the door, and Nicole answers. Something immediately seems off. Has she been crying? Is she sick? After a moment I realize that this is the first time I've ever seen her without makeup. Even when we went to the Wave Blast, she wore makeup to the water park.

I expected her to be alone, but her roommate is there as well, sitting on her bottom bunk, ear buds in, watching a movie on an iPhone. Nicole's roommate is a petite redheaded girl who has more freckles than I've ever seen on one person before. She's wearing pink pajamas with long sleeves and legs that go to the ankle. She distracts me because I've always thought pajamas were sexy. I guess she's not wearing a bra, but she's too thin to be able to tell, so it doesn't really matter.

I've never seen the two of them hanging out together, and realize that up until now I assumed that Nicole and Grace were roommates. There was no real reason to think that, I just did since I saw them together so much. I reach out and shake her hand. She shakes my hand and says "hi," with that odd inflection someone gets when they're trying to talk over the sound of their own headphones. She doesn't get up from the bed. Her indifference somehow makes her more attractive to me.

"I wasn't expecting you to come over," Nicole says. "I was getting ready to go to bed."

"Well, I guess I get points for braving a storm to come see you," I say. I mean it as a joke, but it comes out flat.

"Not really," she says. "I was just being polite."

Nicole's roommate pulls one of the ear buds out of her ear and says, "Did you guys want me to leave? It's really not a big deal."

I start to tell her that would be a great idea, but Nicole speaks up over me. "No, that's fine. He's not going to be staying very long, anyway."

Ouch.

I don't have much experience with girls, but if there's one thing I know for sure, it's that when a girl insists on keeping her friends around instead of talking to you alone, it's never a good sign. I wish I had spent some more time thinking about how I wanted this to go before I came over.

"Say whatever it is you wanted to say," she says. She's pissed. She was pissed before I even got here. She didn't want to make up. She was never planning to. She just wanted another chance to be angry at me. I can hear it in her voice.

"You fucked my roommate," I blurt out.

Nicole's roommate sits up without taking her ear buds out of her ears. "Okay, well, I'm going to go be anywhere else now," she says.

She stands up from the bed and puts on a pair of tennis shoes. It makes the pajamas look ridiculous. "Send me a text message when you're done with whatever this is," she says to Nicole. Then she turns to me. "Nice meeting you." Her voice still has the weird

247

too-loud sound as she talks over the movie that only she can hear. She walks out and shuts the door behind her.

"You're not my boyfriend," Nicole says as soon as the door clicks shut. "What I do and who I do it with is none of your business, and even if you try to make it your business, you have no say in the matter anyway."

I come into the room and sit on her roommate's bed. Nicole doesn't sit down. It feels strange and vulnerable with her staring down at me, so I stand up again.

"It had to be him?" I say. "I mean, really. Of all the guys in the bar, all the guys in the park, you hook up with him? He's a dorky fucking kid. All he's thought about all summer is getting some girl, any girl, into bed. He has to be the most shallow person I know, and after a summer of working where we work and knowing the people we know, that's saying a lot."

"See, this is what I mean when I say it's none of your business. I have my reasons for sleeping with him, and you don't get to hear them. That's what 'none of your business' means."

"I want to hear them," I say. "Because it blows my mind that someone as pretty and popular and fun to be around as you, would sleep with a guy like him."

Her eyes narrow. I think my compliment was lost on her.

"We started talking, and he was nice. We had a fun time. He made me laugh. It wasn't planned. Being around him made me feel good, so we just went with it."

"Are you going to see him again?" I ask.

She throws up her arms in frustration. "Is this what you came all the way over here for? To grill me about my sex life, which, apparently I need to point out again, does not include you in any way? If you must know, I don't know if I'll see him again or not. What I do know is that you don't get any say in that decision."

I take a deep breath and there's a little quiver to it. I wasn't expecting that. I can't tell if Nicole noticed or not.

"He's my roommate," I say. "This is a decision that affects me."

"What makes you think me sleeping with someone who isn't you, is somehow all about you?"

"You slept with my roommate. Of course it's about me."

She stares at me for a second like she's seeing me for the first time, and not in a good way.

"You are such a self-centered asshole," she says. "How did I go this long without noticing?"

"I'm usually better about keeping my mouth shut," I say.

She walks over to her door and opens it. "Maybe you should practice a bit more before we talk again," she says.

She stands there, hand on the door handle, waiting to shut the door behind me after I leave. "Well?" she asks.

"I don't know," I say. "I know I should say something, but I'm not sure what."

"Just go," she says.

"Give me a second," I say. I stand there and think. The silence makes things feel awkward in a way I know there's no coming back from. "Okay, look. What you do and who you do it with is your decision and your life. I get that. But don't stand there and pretend like it doesn't affect me at all. I've liked you this whole summer. You're not stupid. I know you know I like you."

She won't look me in the eye. I assume it's an admission of guilt.

"We've had a lot of fun together. We've hung out together in situations that with any other guy you'd assume it was a date, but we've never hooked up. I think you're hot, and fun to be around, and comfortable. I feel like I screwed up by not telling you sooner. I don't know why we're not making out on your bed right now. I don't know how I let things end up like this."

She's still, and takes a deep breath before she says anything. "Thank you for saying that," she says.

I smile. It feels like something good could happen here. I should kiss her. Her roommate is gone. I can see it in my mind: I kiss her, she shuts the door, we fall onto the floor to make out, and everything is okay.

"Please don't tell me you're thinking this is going to turn into some sort of messed up booty call," she says. "That's not how this works."

"Of course not," I say, trying my very best to look offended. "I actually came over here to apologize. Well, I was going to, anyway.

Before I found out you fucked my roommate. Now I don't know."

"Not exactly the smoothest apology of all time," she points out.

"Yeah," I agree. "Sorry."

"For which part?" she says. "For saying I'm a terrible person? For saying guys only hang around me because they want to get some? For the mean shit you said to Grace? For apparently being a dick all summer? For implying I slept with your roommate as a weird way to get back at you? I'm starting to lose track of all the shit you're supposed to be sorry about."

"Sorry for being so bad at apologizing."

She sighs in disgust. "Just get out," she says.

"Okay. Good night."

She doesn't say anything as she glares at me while I stand there, waiting for something, anything, to happen that will make the situation better. Nothing does. I nod softly and walk out. She shuts the door the instant I'm in the hallway. I take it as a good sign that she didn't slam the door too hard. I realize I left my umbrella in her room, and there is no way that I am getting it back.

The walk home from Nicole's is cold, with the rain picking up and blasting against me, the wind blowing hard enough that it changes how it feels to walk. I'm soaked immediately, and I can feel my hair clinging to my face as the rain runs down the back of my neck and drenches my clothes from the inside out. I said rain was better than hot weather; I stand by it.

The lights are out in my room when I get back. I hear Cory shuffling around in bed when I walk in, but he doesn't say anything to me, and I don't say anything to him. I could turn on the light if I wanted to. I don't. I don't want to be here anymore. I don't want to see Nicole every day at work. I don't want to listen to Grace and Margaret spend the rest of the summer bickering with each other instead of figuring their shit out. I don't want to listen to Dave crack jokes about how my summer melting down isn't that big of a deal. I definitely don't want to come back to my room every day and hear Cory talking about trying to hook up with his random crush of the week.

I strip down into my boxers in the dark and leave the wet

clothes in a pile in front of my dresser. I grab my towel and dry off a bit, then lie down in bed. It feels good to be out of the soaked clothes, even though the summer heat and the lack of air conditioning in the dorms means I'll always be a bit damp from sweat if not the rain. The rain smashes against the window and adds some pleasant white noise to the room.

I still need almost six thousand dollars to make my trip to São Paulo work. I doubt my parents or anyone else I know for that matter has even held onto six thousand dollars at one time. Maybe it's time for another round of selling fifty-fifty tickets in a bowling alley. I'd hoped to pull it off at least a few times, but my brush with Officer Baker is a bad sign. The dumb thing is that if I'd given him my real name to begin with, meeting him at Wonderments wouldn't even have been a big deal. Over a million people a year come here – if it hadn't been him, it would have been someone else. I can't blame myself.

My mind is blank. The room is dark except the sliver of light that shines under our door from the hallway. I stare hard into the dark, and convince myself I can just make out Margaret's warning. I realize that, in some weird way, the whole thing with Nicole is Margaret's fault. If she hadn't stirred shit up with Grace, Nicole and I never would have fought at Knickers. I don't know if I can keep Margaret from finding out, but I hope she doesn't. Imagining her smug smile pisses me off all over again.

A light comes on somewhere above me: Cory's phone. It chirps in the dark as he gets a text message, and sends one back, and gets another, and another. I wonder who it is. I can't decide if it would be worse if he was texting Nicole and trying to hook up with her again, or if he was texting some other girl to try and hook up with her instead. I could tell him to go out in the hall. He'd listen to me. I could be alone in the dark, and fall asleep. I don't say anything. At one point I hear the "click" sound that they add to phones so it sounds like an old timey camera when you take a picture.

I reach over to check my phone. No messages. Well, one message; an old pleading message from my mother asking me to keep in touch. I should just either call her back or delete it, but I can't quite bring myself to do either one. I think about what her and my father must have been like when they were young. I wonder if they wanted to travel and see the world and just never got around to it, or if they're living the life they really wanted. Their teenage dreams must have been bigger than where they ended up.

Above me, I hear Cory say, "Hey dude, you awake?"

"Yeah," I say.

There's a pause and then the light from his phone disappears.

"Well, goodnight," he says.

"'Night."

46

It's after four a.m. when I hear the sound of an incoming text message. I reach for the phone. The blue glow of the screen is the only light in the room. Nicole felt bad about our last conversation and now she's trying to patch things up, I suppose.

The text says simply, "You there?" It's not Nicole. It's Margaret.

"Yes," I text back. It's automatic. I should have just ignored it.

"Sleeping?"

"Not anymore."

"Hi." Of course, she didn't text me at 4 a.m. to say "hi." As usual, she doesn't want to tell me what she wants, she wants me to pry it out of her.

"Hi," I text back.

"Want to hang out?" she asks.

"Now?"

"Yeah."

"It's raining." I resolve not to go out in the rain for a second time in the same night, even though it's not Margaret's fault I went out in the first place.

"I'll come over."

"OK."

I go down to the lobby to wait for her. The girl behind the desk gives me a dirty look. I don't know if it's because she's pissed I fell asleep on the couch down here, or if she's judging me for meeting up with someone at four in the morning, or if she just always looks pissy and I never noticed it before now.

Margaret shows up dripping wet from the rain. She doesn't have an umbrella, or a hoodie, or a hat, or anything. It makes her a lot more attractive. Her hair is darker and doesn't look thin and wispy when it's wet and sticking to her face. Her loose-fitting dark t-shirt clings to her and reveals curves I never noticed. It's all ruined by the dim light and dirty surroundings of the dorm, but it's still a wild improvement over her everyday look.

A version of the conversation ahead fills my mind. I tell her she looks cold. She says she is. I offer her a change of clothes, and she comes up to my room to get them. From there both of us know what's going to happen, and it happens anyway.

"Wow, it's pouring out there," she says. She stands there in the entryway, dripping, waiting.

"I warned you," I say. "The employee shop is around the corner if you want to buy a towel or something."

She walks by me without saying anything else and I go sit down on the couch. The TV is on, as usual. More cartoons. Who the fuck is watching cartoons at four in the morning, that this is successful programming? I consider turning it off, but I don't see a remote anywhere, so I leave it on.

Margaret comes back a minute later with her hair wrapped up in the towel, and any allure she may have once had is gone. She sits on the couch next to me, sure to leave an unflattering wet butt print when she stands up again.

"Kind of late for a chat, isn't it?" I ask her.

"More too early than too late," she says. "I was going to get some breakfast, but the cafeteria doesn't open for another hour and I didn't want to microwave something. Your store is even shittier than ours, by the way."

"I'm not surprised," I say.

Breakfast at the cafeteria doesn't sound appealing to me, even if Margaret is still around an hour from now. I like caffeine in the morning, but when I want some I just stop in the store and pick up a Mountain Dew or a Coke. No reason to make a whole meal out of it.

"Why didn't you go out with me this summer?" she asks. Right to the point. It seems unlike her, and it catches me off guard.

"Do you really want to talk about this?" I ask.

"Yeah, I do."

"Why?"

"I don't know," she says. "Because it's the middle of the night and I was thinking about it and I just want to know."

I can think of a lot of reasons. She's abrasive, plain, condescending. She doesn't think things through, and she's petty. I can't say any of that. The only reason that's socially acceptable is some variation of "It's not you, it's me," that doesn't sound anything like "It's not you, it's me." This aspect of human relationships has always bothered me. The real answer is always the same, and always obvious: either you're attracted to someone, or you're not. Thinking about Margaret doesn't turn me on. It doesn't make me miss her or want anything sexual from her. But there's no way to say that without it sounding like an insult, so no one ever says it.

"I guess you're just not my type," I say. "It's nothing personal."

"It's pretty personal to me," she says.

"I don't mean to be mean. There's nothing wrong with you. Well, there is, but there's not more wrong with you than there is with anyone else."

"You like Nicole," she says. It's an admission of defeat.

"I guess so, but I didn't hook up with her, either."

We're quiet for half a minute while a commercial for bathroom cleaner comes on TV. I'm still not sure who's out there watching cartoons at this hour, but apparently it's someone interested in household cleaning supplies.

"Why do you like her instead of me?" she asks.

Margaret is a real sucker for punishment. I want to tell her that everyone else figured out to stop asking stuff like this when they were teenagers, and there's a good reason why. I want to tell her the answer won't make her feel any better and won't resolve anything.

I think about it for a minute. "She thinks the world is a good

255

place. She thinks good things happen to good people. She thinks there are good people to begin with."

Margaret snorts. "She's wrong, you know."

"I know."

We sit in silence, watching the last few minutes of an episode of Spongebob Squarepants. The end credits roll and it shakes Margaret out of whatever she was thinking about.

"Well, I'm going to go get that breakfast."

She doesn't ask me to come along, and I'm grateful.

"I'm going back to bed," I say. Breakfast doesn't even start for another half hour. She'll be waiting in the dark and the rain alone for at least twenty minutes if she leaves now.

"Okay, goodnight," she says.

"Goodnight." I stand up.

She stands up with me. It looks like she's going to say something more, or maybe hug me. I can't tell. Instead, she unwraps her hair, folds up the towel, and walks out into the dark without saying anything else.

47

The next morning the rain has stopped, but everything is still soaked. There are puddles everywhere along the park walkways despite the frequent grates, and the grass glows a vibrant green. The clouds overhead are dark and thick, enough so that it feels like dusk even though it's mid-morning. It'll rain again soon. Already the air is heavy with humidity, so that walking outside leaves me damp even without the rain. The day is perfect.

I came out this morning to sit on one of the park benches near the pond and enjoy the weather, but they're all still dripping wet from the rain. I consider just wiping off one of the seats the best I can and sitting anyway, but I decide to compromise instead and go sit on a bench near the Wizard Arcade, because the arcade has benches under the overhang of building, so they should be dry.

I do my best to ignore the sounds coming from inside. I can hear at least a dozen arcade games, plus the clangs of pinball machines and the wooden sound of skee-ball machines in heavy use. Most of the rides get shut down when it's too wet out, and it's not late enough in the day yet for lunch, so the arcade is packed.

Amusement parks are pretty much the only place arcades still survive in America, and it makes me a little bit sad. When I was a kid my dad would take me to an arcade on the other side of town called The Fun Factory. They had arcade games, mini golf, go karts, all that kind of stuff. It's one of the few times as a kid that I really connected with my dad. We were going to go for my thirteenth birthday. We pulled up and discovered that they had closed down. There was a sign on the door thanking everyone for their business over the years. I can't remember what we decided to do instead.

I googled Fun Factory when I was older, hoping they were a chain, or had turned into some other arcade, or just that someone else on the internet remembered the place. It turns out Fun Factory is a German sex toy manufacturer. They specialize in vibrating dildos.

I decide to go inside to play some games. A pimple faced kid with glasses takes five bucks from me and hands me Wonderments-branded tokens to play with. A black and white printed sign advises me that Wonderments employees cannot exchange game tokens for cash.

I walk past a row of outdated Daytona racers and a separate row of Bust-A-Move style puzzle games, unable to decide what to play but not really minding, when my phone vibrates in my pocket.

It's Nicole. The text says, "can u still meet my parents."

I text her back. "dont know. we need to talk."

She texts back. "okay come over meet downstairs."

Her text annoys me. I'm the one doing her a favor. She should be the one coming to me. I pocket the coins for now and hope I get a chance to come back here soon and use them. A beautiful day is about to go to waste.

* * *

Nicole is sitting on the couch in her lobby. Not exactly private, but close enough. I go over to her and sit down on the coach, leaving a space between us. The couch here doesn't smell as terrible as the one in my dorm, but it's still cheap and looks like it was bought secondhand twenty years ago. They have a TV as well but it's turned off, which feels odd to me since the one in my lobby is on twenty-four hours a day, whether anyone is there to watch it or not. Nicole turns toward me and tucks her legs up in front of her, wrapping her hands around her knees. It's a bad sign.

"I don't know," she says.

Always a quality way to start a conversation. I sit in silence and do my best not to fidget or check my phone. I'm starting to wish the TV was on, so it would at least fill the room with some noise. I can't take the silence for long.

"Sorry," I say. "I thought you were going to say something. I didn't want to cut you off."

"I feel like I should say something, but I don't know what," she says. "I can't apologize for the stuff that I did. Not really. I feel bad for fighting with you, but I don't regret the things that caused the fight in the first place."

"That's fair," I tell her. On an intellectual level I know I should appreciate her honesty and accept it. It doesn't erase the bitterness I feel when I think about her.

"I wasn't trying to lead you on or anything," she says. "I just enjoyed spending time with you. I didn't want to overthink it."

"You never thought about it? I mean, you and I in a relationship or whatever?"

She shrugs. "Not really. I mean, don't get me wrong, I didn't write you off or anything. I just figured if you wanted to hook up you'd make a move."

"I guess I should have done that awhile ago," I say. The whole conversation feels like it's happening to someone else, and I'm just watching from the outside. A different person would lean over to her now, touch her hand, pull her into an embrace, kiss. A different person, but not me.

"The summer isn't over yet, you know." She smiles.

"It feels like it is for me."

She frowns. I can see the frown in her whole body as she curls up tighter on the couch, almost recoiling from me. "Look, I get it if you hate me. You don't have to pretend. I won't make things weird at work. Just be straight with me one time this summer." It feels like she blames herself for this, in some way. I know it's not her fault, but it's not in my best interest to convince her of that.

"I don't hate you. I'm angry at how things happened. That's not the same." It's far from the whole truth, but it's as good as she's going to get. No one gets the whole truth from anyone else, not really. There will always be some unspoken desire, or cynical thought, or cruel joke. There will always be covered insecurity. No matter how often or how loudly someone insists that they want to hear everything, there's always something that can make them think, "Okay, this just got weird." Some private place where the truly offensive, truly vulnerable pieces of ourselves lie. Relationships only work because both people agree not to probe into that truly private place.

"Look, you don't have to meet my parents," she says. "I shouldn't have asked you to do it in the first place. They're both stupidly overprotective anyway. I just thought if I showed up with a decent guy maybe they would lay off for once. I'll meet them by myself."

"I can go," I tell her. "It's not a big deal, it's not like this is the first time I've had to fake dating a girl to make her parents happy." That's a lie. I'm not sure why I said it. Just to know that I could, I guess.

She laughs, "You're going to have to tell me that story sometime." She pauses and hesitates. "Are you sure you're not pissed at me?"

"I'm going to get over being angry," I tell her. It's not a lie, exactly. I just don't know if it's true or not. I do know for sure I'll pretend not to be angry, and that's good enough.

"Really?" She asks.

"Yes," I say. I try to make my voice sound reassuring. She looks reassured. It gives me the same thrill as when I con someone into giving me money, and I know I can never look at her the same way again.

48

Some people don't like dressing up, but I don't mind. People just look better when they're dressed up. What I do mind is spending money when I don't have to, so I'm wearing khakis and a polo shirt to meet Nicole's parents. It's as nice as I can dress given that I replaced most of my clothes at the Salvation Army.

For the first time all summer, I look in a mirror. I look like shit. I haven't cut my hair since before I showed up at the park, and I didn't bother to bring a comb. I have a week's worth of patchy, uneven facial hair that's against the Wonderments grooming policy, which no one enforces. My shirt is wrinkled and it doesn't fit quite right. I'm not ugly, but I'm nothing special, either. Nothing special mixed with sloppy personal care isn't a good combination.

Nicole is waiting for me by the front desk in the lobby. Her disapproval is both obvious and justified.

"Really?" Nicole says to me, looking me over. "Sneakers? And don't you at least own a shirt with buttons?"

"I came here to work at an amusement park for less than minimum wage," I remind her. "I wasn't planning on going on any job interviews. This is the best I've got."

She reaches over and fixes my collar, brushing the front of my shirt in vain to try and get out some of the wrinkles, and sighs.

Nicole looks much better than I do. She's wearing a vibrant yellow sundress with a pattern of dark pink roses on it. The pink roses have green stems and leaves which match the straps of the dress. She's also wearing matching pink lipstick and barrettes in her hair with pink ribbons on them. Her beauty stuns me momentarily, and I want to kiss her. If I had bothered to find a nice shirt and a jacket, she might have let me.

I snap out of it. "Hey, there's still time to call Dave. I bet he cleans up nice."

"You'll do. If they even let you in."

"What?"

"Dinner is at The Velvet Room, didn't I tell you?"

Oh. Fuck. I really am under-dressed. The Velvet Room is easily the most upscale restaurant in the park, inside the hotel and as far away from the corn dogs and cotton candy and screaming kids as they could figure out how to put it. It's small, exclusive, and caters to the genuinely wealthy. I wonder how long this has been the plan – I've heard you have to book reservations weeks in advance to get in.

"No, you never mentioned," I said. "I thought we'd go to Spoon's or something. I should have bought a jacket, I think." I hope my admission of failure will be charming and placate her a bit.

"Yes, you should have. Let's go."

We take the train back to the hotel, and the whole ride there Nicole alternates between ignoring me and picking at my hair or my shirt. She even pulls my foot up to the seat next to her to try and scrape some dirt off the top of my shoe. I'm wishing I had at least shaved. At this point I'm worried she might claw my face off in the name of grooming.

At the restaurant, the maître d' is equally unimpressed. He looks me up and down, considering carefully whether he should let me in the door. I'm confident that without Nicole there he wouldn't think twice about booting my ass out of the hotel. He frowns disapprovingly, but relents.

"Can I get you a jacket, sir?" he asks. I wonder why he has so much disdain. He's basically a glorified bouncer for a place where you don't call a hamburger and hamburger and you have to pay ten times the normal price once it shows up.

"I don't need –"

"Yes, please," Nicole says, digging her nails into my arm. "Thank you."

He leaves and we wait. Nicole is visibly nervous. "Don't screw this up with my parents, okay? I don't want to have another 'we're disappointed in you' lecture from them."

"Aren't you like... twenty-five?" I ask her. "Shouldn't you be over this song and dance by now?"

"I'm twenty-two."

"That's not any better."

She gives me a dirty look, but the maître d' saves me by returning. He holds up two different suit jackets. He doesn't hand them to me, like he's sure I'd just mess it up if I tried to put one of them on myself. He chooses one without consulting me, the rattier and more plain of the two. Then he steps behind me and puts the jacket on and turns me to face him. His face shows that he thinks this is entirely unacceptable, but there's nothing he can do.

"Enjoy your evening, *sir.*"

I wonder what I'm getting into.

The dining area of The Velvet Room is dim. It's filled with small, round tables with a lit candle on each and a soft overhead light illuminating each table. I'm easily the worst dressed person in the place. Long slinky dresses are common, and every man but me has on a tie and a button down shirt. Some have jackets on. It's the middle of the summer. Everyone in this place would rather be miserably hot and well-dressed than put on casual clothes for even a minute.

A couple stands up when they spot us. Calling them middle-aged would be generous. They must have been at least in their mid-thirties when Nicole was born, maybe older. Her father is dressed in a dark suit with a thick, dark blue tie and a white shirt underneath. Her mother is wearing a long red dress, and I notice she's loaded with jewelry – diamond earrings, pearl necklace, diamond bracelet. It's a summer night at an amusement park, and these two are dressed to go to a wedding.

"Mommy!" Nicole runs forward to hug her mother, and I hang

back and shake hands with her father silently. Then we switch, and her mother kisses me briefly on each cheek. She's even wearing perfume, expertly applied so you don't notice it until you're in close. It smells like cloying fruit mixed with vanilla.

As soon as we sit down her father says, "So, how long have you been dating my daughter?"

I'm not sure how to answer. "Well, we aren't really –"

Her mother cuts me off. "You're embarrassing them," she says, putting an affectionate hand on her husband's shoulder. "Leave them alone about it. There's nothing wrong with a little summer romance." The way she says it, I imagine that if she tells her country club friends about me later, she'll use the word "quaint." I remind myself that once I get through this, I never have to see these people again. Just smile and nod. Don't make a scene.

The waiter, who is also better dressed than me and sports a pencil mustache, presumably because he believes fancy waiters should have pencil mustaches, comes over to our table, handing each of us a menu. He hands me mine last and looks down at me sternly, as if the maître d' warned him to watch out for that hooligan in the borrowed coat.

Just in case patrons haven't figured it out yet, the menu is entirely in some very wavy, almost unreadable font reserved only for the most pretentious of businesses. Nothing on the menu has a price next to it. I order a glass of red wine because Nicole orders one, and I order a plate of chicken parmesan, because I estimate that it's the cheapest thing on the menu that I can order without looking like I'm concerned about the price.

We make small talk. I make eye contact without smiling too much and apply the principle of speaking when spoken to. I notice her father using the same tactic, content to let Nicole and her mother carry the conversation.

"So, did you and Daddy go into the park at all?"

"Oh no, dear," Dear seems to be their pet name of choice for Nicole. Both her parents use it. "Of course not. We're not young kids anymore. I'm afraid the hotel bar is a bit more our taste these days."

"Has the vacation been fun at least?"

"We've enjoyed ourselves," she says. "We did some antiquing along the coast and went to a few charity auctions as well. I found some jewelry and some furniture that is simply stunning. We couldn't be happier." I wonder what Nicole's parents do or did for a living. The price of buying, shipping, and insuring antique furniture must be obscene. My parents would probably have to work for months or even a year to make what these two spent casually on vacation.

"How about you?" her mother asks. "Have you enjoyed your summer away? Is he keeping you out of trouble?"

"It's been a great summer. I like working here and making my own money. I'm happy that you guys help out, but it's good to be out on my own."

"I keep her out of trouble the best I can, ma'am." When someone calls my mother "ma'am" she is always quick to correct people by saying, "I'm no ma'am, call me Rose." Nicole's mother does not correct me.

Nicole's mother delights in updating Nicole about their family. Her two older brothers (who Nicole has never mentioned; I thought she was an only child) are having success on their startup business. Nicole's uncle from California is running for some seat in local government. One of Nicole's cousins is getting ready to start her freshman year at Berkeley. Another cousin is getting married.

After going through the list that contains more relatives than I knew could exist in one family, her mother says, "Enough about that, dear. Have you managed to get by without your clothes? We brought the things you asked for."

"Great," Nicole says. "I've been wearing my work uniform almost all the time here. I appreciate you sending out my stuff. I didn't think you'd come all this way. The post office still exists."

"Nonsense. We were out anyway for our little trip, and I never miss a chance to see my daughter when I can."

"I'm going to go try them on now," she says. "I'm so excited." She grabs my hand and pulls me out of my seat, and her father turns a disapproving stare on me immediately. "He can wait here," he says. "Call me an old-fashioned prude if you like, dear, but I won't have some young man watching my daughter undress in my hotel room."

"Oh, Daddy," she says. "It's not like that. You should know me better. I'll change in the bathroom. I just want his opinion on what I should keep here and what I should send home."

He doesn't seem convinced, but her mother hands Nicole the electronic door card. "We're up in room 813. We'll have some dessert when you get back. Don't be too long."

"No funny business," her father adds.

"No funny business, sir," I promise, and Nicole leads me away by the hand before I can say anything else

.

* * *

We walk into the hotel room and I'm immediately flooded with envy. There's a king size bed along one wall, with a big screen TV on the wall across from it, and a giant wardrobe next to that. A full length mirror with a small table next to it holding an iron and a hair dryer. Artwork on every wall – not prints or cheap reproductions, but real paintings. There's a couch big enough to lie down on and probably more comfortable than my bed. Ornate lamps sit on small bedside tables, and under one of them, a small but fancy safe with a digital key pad. I'm equal parts impressed and disgusted, both for the same reason: this place is far nicer than anywhere I've ever stayed.

"Just how rich are your parents? I mean, damn."

If Nicole heard me at all, she doesn't answer. She's already got the wardrobe open, taking out dresses and blouses and skirts and piling them up on the bed. When she has more clothes on the bed than I even own, she shuts the wardrobe and turns to me.

"I'm going to try these on," she says.

"Ummm..... okay?"

She raises her eyebrows at me like I'm an asshole. I wait for her to explain why.

"Wait in the bathroom."

"Oh. Right. Sorry." My skin feels warm.

The hotel bathroom is large and extravagant. Fresh, fluffy towels. Individually wrapped sample size shower gel and hand lotion. Large spotless bathroom mirror. His and hers sinks. All I can think of is the shithole I live in now, with its dirt-encrusted toothpaste splatters. Inconsiderate neighbors blasting techno music through thin walls. Buying flip flops to keep from getting foot fungus from nasty disease-ridden showers. I think about the shithole I lived in before I lived here, and the shithole I'll live in after I leave here. I think about my parents not being able to afford to retire, and the friends I grew up with feeding their kids macaroni and cheese every night because it's all they can afford. I think about counting every penny I make because it's the only way to make sure that I don't end up like them.

"You can come out now," Nicole calls after what seems like forever.

I open the bathroom door and see Nicole standing there, looking at herself in the full length mirror. She's taken off her shoes and traded the sundress for a long, dark blue evening gown that shimmers around the bottom. She really does look beautiful. The dress is as breathtaking as it is impractical.

"It doesn't fit right," she says. "It fit me better at the beginning of the summer. I'm getting fat."

If she has gained a few pounds since the beginning of the summer, it doesn't matter. "You look amazing," I tell her. It's true.

She brushes off the compliment, fishing for it first but then discarding it once received. "It's missing something," she says. "I wonder."

She goes over to the side of the bed, holding up the dress to keep the hem from dragging on the floor. I wonder what she's after. She bends over the safe and punches in the code: 1-2-0-6-2-5. It opens.

"It's the days my brothers and I were born. They use the same code for everything." She doesn't turn toward me as she explains. I'm not sure if she didn't see that I saw, or doesn't care.

Inside the safe there's a small but deep mahogany jewelry box and a small black drawstring bag. Nicole ignores the bag and pulls out the jewelry box. She opens it and I mask my surprise: Gold, pearls, diamonds. I try to guess how much is in there, but it's not something I'm used to handling. There's a small sign on the front of the safe that says, "Please check valuables with the front desk. Do not leave valuables in the room safe."

Nicole digs for a moment, hardly noticing the contents of the box, then pulls out a single necklace. "They brought it!" she says. "I can't believe I left this at home when I came out here. I've regretted it every day."

"That stuff looks like it's worth a fortune," I say.

She dismisses it with a hand wave. "They find stuff like that at auctions and estate sales all the time. They'll take it back with them, mark it up a ton, and put it in their antique store."

She hands me the necklace. "Take a look." I take it and turn it over in my hands. It's a small, lopsided star shape hanging on a simple white gold chain. The inside of the white gold frame is filled with diamonds. It's small and delicate, weighing almost nothing. It has to be worth hundreds of dollars.

I look up at Nicole and I'm struck by how *different* she looks. I've known all summer that she was remarkably beautiful, but as long as she was in her dumpy work uniform, working long hours and complaining, she was one of the rest of us. Now, she's some other sort of creature entirely. Something utterly foreign. Unrecognizable.

"It's my lucky star necklace," she says.

I laugh.

"What? Why is that funny?"

"It's nothing," I tell her. "My good luck charm is a cheap leftover chess piece from a broken chess board."

"I've had it ever since I was a kid. I saw it in a jewelry store when my dad was shopping for Valentine's Day for my mom. I loved it so much. He wouldn't buy it for me. I begged and I begged. I begged my mom the next day. He gave in and went back to the store and bought it for me. He told me he would always give me everything he had, and that I could be whatever I wanted to be. It's always made me feel safe."

"You shouldn't be working here," I say. "You could be back home with your parents, working for them, or just living at home, spending money without a care in the world. Your parents have more valuables in that safe than my parents have at all."

She looks away from me. "I like it here. It's good to get away. I can't help who my parents are."

"Your parents love you a lot." I don't know what else to say. "And you really do look very beautiful. But we need to go back downstairs before your dad thinks I'm stealing your innocence on his bed."

She laughs, but puts her shoes on anyway. "Okay, okay." I hand her back the necklace, and she puts everything back in the safe and locks it. Her clothes and phone are still in a pile on the bed. "Let's go, then." She walks out ahead of me and I notice the room key card lying next to the other stuff. I pick it up and slip it into my pocket, and follow her out the door.

49

When we re-enter the dining room, I see Nicole's parents are sitting there talking quietly, looking content, with the charm of a first date and the security of years spent together. My parents love each other, but if someone who didn't know them saw them together, I don't think they'd see it. They'd just see a tired, bickering couple.

When Nicole's mother spots us she stands up and says, "Oh, there's my girl! Look how beautiful she is in this dress. Simply stunning." The Nicole that works in the amusement park is the fake one, as far as her parents are concerned. This dolled up girl, dressed far too well for the riffraff around her, is the real one.

Her father turns in his chair to look and nods approvingly. "Takes after her mother. Lucky girl."

We sit down and he levels a hard look at his daughter. "So, you needed a boy to come with you to help change out of your dress?"

Nicole smiles coyly. It's the exact look I imagined her using to enchant boys all summer long. I can remember her using it on me at least twice. "Oh daddy, it's not like that. I made him wait in the bathroom while I changed."

He looks at me. "It's true," I say. I'm not sure why he waits for me to answer. He has that look in his eye that says he's already decided whether he believes his daughter or not. Nothing I say is going to change his opinion. I suppress the urge to lie to him and paint a sexually depraved picture of his little girl. I wonder if he'd yell, or leave the table, or punch me, or maybe just have a heart attack on the spot.

"Oh stop it," her mother says. "You know Nicole is a good kid. She doesn't get into half the trouble we did when we were her age."

Nicole's father shoots his wife a look I imagine says, "Don't talk that way around our daughter," but she either ignores it or doesn't notice.

"Who wants some dessert?" she asks.

"Oh, me," Nicole says. "I've been careful about what I eat all summer, it'll feel good to cheat a little."

We pick up the dinner menu and read in silence for what is probably a minute but seems like a lot longer. The Velvet Room is fancy but they're still in an amusement park, and their dessert list is extensive.

Nicole orders the Neapolitan Banana Split pictured at the top of the page. In the photo, at least, it has three different flavors of ice cream next to a banana, with each scoop covered in its own little swirl of whip cream, nuts, and a cherry for each. There are three little metal cups on the side of the plate with different kinds of syrup, as well.

"It's way too much, but it just looks so good. Who's helping me eat this?" She looks at me. "You. You are so helping me eat this."

Nicole's mother orders tiramisu, and her father orders a black coffee. I order a coffee as well, and for a moment he looks at me sternly, like he's going to take it as a personal affront that I am not capitalizing on his generosity by only ordering a coffee.

Before he can say anything, I say, "Apparently I'm having some of Nicole's banana split." I hope he takes it as sexual innuendo.

The waiter takes our order and we make small talk while we wait. The restaurant has gotten busy by this time, however, and it seems like a long time passes without hearing back from him. I consider that it's just the awkwardness of the situation, but as soon as there's a lull in the conversation, Nicole's mother fills it by saying, "Hasn't it been a long time? How long have we been waiting?"

None of us answer, and she raises a hand to flag over the waiter, who is carrying a giant tray of food. He sees her and nods once, serves a family of five the food he was bringing them, and then quickly scurries over to the table.

Nicole's mother asks, "We've been waiting for our order for awhile now. Is there a problem?"

He exaggerates a look of shock and concern. "I'm so sorry," he says. "Let me find out what the problem is. I'll be right back."

As soon as he leaves Nicole's father starts up. "See, this is why I can't stand all these low class workers. They should really get some better help in here."

I break my speak-when-spoken-to strategy. "I'm sure it was just a mistake in the kitchen. It probably wasn't even his fault." It's one of the reasons I'd hate to be in any position that relied on gratuity. There are so many things that can go wrong, and the waiter is the one that'll get punished for all of it. I can't imagine how much this meal cost, but it has to be enough that it'll be a pretty big deal to the waiter if he gets stiffed on the tip.

"It's people like him that are dragging this country down," he says. "They'd rather wait for a handout than put in an honest day's work."

"Oh sweetie," Nicole's mother says. "Don't start."

"I mean it," he says. "In my day we had to work for what we had. Now people would rather complain than get anything done. I work hard for my money. My taxes shouldn't go to holding them up."

No one answers him, and Nicole's mother keeps staring at him.

He changes the subject to a fishing trip he hopes to go on, but I tune out of the conversation. I know his words weren't aimed at me specifically, but I'm still pissed. This asshole is too busy leisurely traveling the country in search of shitty antiques to say anything about an honest day's work.

I haven't talked for awhile when I feel Nicole put her hand on mine and squeeze a bit. I look at her. Her look is equal parts apology and pity. Not wanting to make things even more awkward, I rejoin the conversation with a smile, saying just enough so that her parents won't think that I'm surly.

A few more minutes go by and it feels like forever. Finally the waiter returns. "I'm so sorry," he says. "They lost your order in the kitchen. I spoke with the manager, and dessert is on the house. My apologies." He sets the tiramisu on the table and goes to walk past me to put down the ice cream. As he does I turn toward him, sticking out my foot at the same time. He trips, and I close my eyes as I'm covered in a banana split and two hot coffees.

The maître d' is really going to regret making me wear a jacket now.

The waiter hits the floor without stopping his fall, banging his head on the chair of a nearby table. He lets out a yell of pain and surprise but stops himself short of cursing. The coffee stings. Most of it is on the jacket and my shirt, but some of it splattered on my neck and hands too, and it burns.

"Ow. Damn," I say, giving my hands a shake.

"Oh my gosh, are you okay?" Nicole says.

"I'm fine," I say. "It's okay."

The waiter scrambles up quickly and starts stammering an apology.

"This service is unacceptable," says Nicole's father. "Young man, you go get your manager right now."

The waiter nods without another word and rushes off. I hope he doesn't get in too much trouble for this.

"Okay," I say, mopping at my shirt ineffectively with a napkin, wiping off a big streak of whip cream. "I need to change out of this stuff, I think. I'm going to hit the gift shop for a change of clothes and then go to the bathroom."

"Don't you let them charge you for anything in that gift shop," Nicole's mother says. "This is their fault."

"I'll come with you," Nicole volunteers.

That I did not expect. Shit.

"You think your friend needs help changing out of his clothes?" Nicole's father asks grimly.

"I'll be okay," I tell them.

I leave the table and head immediately toward the gift shop.

273

I've never been in it before, but it's selling the same bullshit every other store in the park sells. I walk in and quickly grab a backpack and a t-shirt, both sporting the Wonderments logo. I bring them up to the counter to pay for them. The girl behind the counter has pale skin and freckles, a sharp chin, and bleach blonde hair in a pixie cut. I guess she'd be cute if I wasn't in such a hurry.

"Wild night, huh?" she says, looking at my stained clothes.

"I guess you could say that," I tell her. I hand her some cash for the stuff and try not to fidget as she slowly counts out the change. As soon as she hands it to me I bolt out the door. I don't have much time.

I jog past the restrooms down the hall to the elevators and punch the button to head up to Nicole's parent's room. The elevator seems to take forever, but no one is around to see me pacing nervously back and forth. When I get to their room I look up and down the hall. There's no one else here, and I wonder if the hotel has security cameras in the hallways. I step inside the room.

I go to the safe immediately. My hands are trembling as I punch in the code: 1-2-0-6-2-5. It opens. I grab the backpack and stuff the jewelry box and the drawstring bag into the backpack. I shut the safe, hear it lock, and stand up. I strip off my shirt and stuff it in the backpack as well. I pull on the Wonderments t-shirt and fold the jacket over my arm. I leave the room key on the bed. With any luck, Nicole will think she just left it in the room by accident.

I rush back downstairs and try to calm myself as much as possible before I walk into the dining area. I feel even more out of place now, the Wonderments t-shirt glowing slightly as I walk through a room full of people in formalwear. I get back to the table and see the coffee and banana split have been replaced. Nicole has barely touched it. She looks at me apologetically when I come over to the table.

"Well, this has been embarrassing," I say. I flash them a smile I hope they think is sincere. "My pants are still wrecked, though, and there's nothing in the gift shop to help. I think I'm going to get going."

I make a show of grabbing my wallet as though I intend to pay for dinner. "That won't be necessary," Nicole's dad says. "We talked to the manager. They aren't charging us for the mess this dinner turned into."

Right. I expected her father to pay for the dinner for all of us, and I'm sure he would have, since he's that kind of guy. But as long as the meal is on the house, he can get out of paying without wounding his pride by letting someone else pick up the bill. I feel a pang of guilt at screwing the waiter out of his tip, but I'm guessing Nicole's dad is a shitty tipper, anyway. I shake hands with him firmly, then give Nicole's mother a more delicate handshake.

Nicole stands up. A handshake seems wrong but I don't want to hug her in front of her dad, or risk getting a stain on her dress. I just give her a smile and say, "Don't worry about it. I'll call you later."

I turn and head for the front door. When I get to the lobby I drape the damp and stained jacket over the maître d', and say, "Have a good night." I hear him scoff and mutter something, but I don't look back.

50

Outside, the world seems dim. It's not dark out yet, the summer sun giving everything a red hue. I hear people talking in the distance and even, faintly, the crashing of the waves from the beach. I can hear everything distinctly, but it feels like the volume on the world has been turned down.

I make it to the edge of the parking lot before I hear a single set of running footsteps. A cold chill goes down my spine. For a split second, I wonder how I could have been discovered so quickly. I turn around. It's just Nicole.

"Hey," she says, out of breath from trying to catch up with me.

"Hey. You didn't have to –"

She holds up her hand to stop me from talking, and takes a few seconds to catch her breath.

"I know," she says. "You're not mad. You've been a total sweetheart about this whole thing. My dad is an overbearing ass and the whole night was awkward and you somehow managed to get burned by coffee and covered in whipped cream, and you're such a gentleman about the whole thing."

The backpack in my hand feels heavy.

"I don't know," she says. "You're not the kind of guy I normally go for. I've had such a great time being around you, and you've told me about your dreams, and I really feel like I know you."

"I've liked spending time with you too," I agree.

"You've never tried to get in my pants even once," she says. "I don't know if you're playing hard to get or what."

"I —"

She holds up a hand to stop me. "Let me finish," she says. "I can tell that you've liked me for awhile, or at least it feels that way. You admitted as much. I'm sorry about everything that happened recently – our fight, and me sleeping with your roommate. I didn't want any of it to happen. I was just pissed I guess. That's not a good excuse."

All of that seems so far away now, like it happened to someone else.

"I know we didn't talk about being exclusive or romantic or anything, but that still has to suck for you, and I really am sorry. I like you, and I want to start over. I'm asking you to start over with me, please. You're a great guy and I don't want to mess this up. I feel like it's all my fault."

"Sure," I say. "I'm not mad at you anymore. Really. And the dinner was no big deal."

She leans in, putting a hand on my shoulder. She kisses me, not on the mouth, but not on the cheek either, sort of halfway in between, on the corner of my mouth. It's a long, gentle kiss. I feel hot all over, and when it ends, my skin tingles where she kissed me.

"You've been amazing. Maybe you're the guy I've been looking for. I like you. You don't have to be shy. Usually I let the guys chase me, but not this time. I'm putting myself out there."

"I've kind of had a crush on you all summer," I say.

"Well, you promised to call me, so call me," she says. "I'm going to hang out with my parents for a little while but they won't stay up too late. Call me tomorrow, or call me tonight, and when you call, we'll meet up. Just don't stand me up, okay?"

"I won't," I say.

She reaches in and hugs me, a hard, squeezing hug, which I return with my one free hand, letting the backpack dangle in the other.

"Good night," she says, and turns and walks back to The

Velvet Room.

* * *

The entire ride back to the dorms I imagine the train conductor, sitting at the front of the novelty train with his ridiculous conductor's uniform, getting a call on his radio and being told I'm on board and to be careful. I imagine one of the Wonderments security Jeeps catching up to us and hauling me off. It just feels *wrong* somehow to just be sitting, riding along, everyone else unaware of what is going on around them. I feel like I, personally, should be moving. I resist the urge to get off the train and try to run home, reminding myself that this is much faster, even if it doesn't feel that way.

When I finally arrive the park is starting to wind down. The shops and rides are still open but people are starting to mill toward the exits, trying to beat the rush and avoid getting stuck in traffic. It's a bit like the tides – in the mornings you can feel the crowds rushing into the park like water, eager to start their days and get the most out of their vacations. Now, at dusk, the tide of people is just starting to shift the other way. It's that specific time of day, close to dusk when, for the first time, more people are leaving the park than entering it. I blend in with the flow of people easily as I walk back to the dorm. I knew my time here wasn't going to last forever, but I'm still going to miss it when I'm gone.

Cory isn't there. I breathe a sigh of relief. I'm not sure what exactly is in the bag, but I'm certain that it will be enough to cover my trip to São Paulo, and it's way more than I would have made the rest of the summer no matter what I tried. I've never directly stolen anything valuable before. I expected it to feel different somehow, but other than the nerves and the sense of danger, it feels pretty much the same.

I pull the stained shirt out of the bag and drop it in the trash. I stuff the bag full of a few random handfuls of clothes, my passport, and the little money I'd re-accumulated since the rest was stolen. Most of this shit doesn't matter. I wonder if maintenance will come in to clean it out as soon as they realize that I'm gone, or if my stuff will sit here until the end of the summer, no one bothering with it the same way no one bothers with any of the other maintenance in this shithole.

I consider leaving my phone behind as well and decide against it. I take a few deep breaths. Even if they do discover the theft right away, which is unlikely, it's going to take them a little while to realize it was me, and then longer to get someone over here to try and catch me. I use my phone to find the location of the closest Greyhound station and get bus directions there. I consider picking a destination, but I don't bother. I'll just go on whatever bus happens to leave next and get off somewhere that has an international airport. I can pawn the jewelry there, I guess, and then spend some time getting ready for my trip.

I look around the room once to see if I've missed anything. I consider doing something to Cory's stuff just as a final "fuck you" before I leave, but I don't. I feel more apathy toward him than anything else at this point. I'm just getting ready to leave when the phone rings in my hand. It vibrates and startles me, and I drop it. It hits the floor and the battery pops out and skitters away from the rest of the phone.

"Damn it."

I collect the pieces and put the phone back together and turn it on. One thing I'm definitely doing is getting a phone that isn't so shitty.

I have one new voice message. I press the button to listen to it.

It's Nicole. Her voice is cold. "I'm outside. Get the fuck out here." Her voice cracks. "I'm alone."

51

For the first time all summer, I notice all the fire exits between my room and the front door. Each one has a red sign with white letters next to it that says, "Do not open except in case of emergency. Alarm will sound. Security will be notified." This seems like it qualifies as an emergency, but somehow I think I'd have a hard time explaining why to security.

Nicole is standing right outside the door, pacing back and forth a little bit, her arms crossed. I notice my mouth is dry and my hands are shaking. I recognize the feeling well: it's the same one as the first time I shoplifted something as a kid. The same as the first time I tried to rip someone off to their face, and they fell for it. The first time a girl broke up with me.

"All my parents' jewelry is gone. I went back upstairs later to get my necklace, and the safe was empty."

"Wow, really?" I do my best to look concerned.

"I know it was you," she says. "How could you do that to me? You took advantage of me to rob me, and then I stood there like a fool and told you how much I liked you and you just let me."

"I like you too," I tell her.

Her eyes narrow. "I'm not sure if you know this, but you shouldn't steal shit from people you like."

I wonder if it's possible for me to just keep denying it until she believes me. Even if I convince her now, she'll know as soon as I'm gone, anyway.

"Just give me what you took, and I'll put it back in the safe. No one has to know."

I look around to see if anyone can overhear us, but there aren't many people around, and no one is paying attention to us. "Why, so you and I can forget this happened and have a fairy tale summer romance?"

She looks disgusted. "You're an asshole. You can forget every good thing I ever said about you. You should give the stuff back, because that's what a decent fucking human being would do. That's why."

"You didn't tell your parents?" I ask.

"No," she says. "Not yet. I wanted to give you a chance to make things right, I guess."

"I can't give the jewelry back to you," I tell her.

She closes her eyes and takes a deep breath. "I don't know anything about you at all, do I? Were you honest about who you were at all this summer?"

"Some stuff."

"Like what?" she asks.

"It'd take too long to explain."

"I can't believe I took you to my parents," she says. "I am so fucking stupid. Any of the other guys I met all summer would have been a better choice than you. You're worse than all of them."

For the first time in the conversation I have the urge to defend myself. I can't be upset at her calling me a liar and a thief – after all, she's right. But lumping me in with all the shallow, directionless, flat out stupid guys she usually hangs around with really bothers me.

"I'm nothing like them," I say.

"Well, right now, I can't see the difference."

"I know." I can't explain it to her. "Are you going to tell your parents?"

I sit down on a bench nearby. I leave room for her, but she doesn't sit down. Instead, she stands over me, glaring down, lip curled slightly, like if she were less polite, she'd spit on me.

"No, because you're going to give it all back to me. Right now."

"I'm not," I tell her.

"Why not? You can't just take shit that isn't yours."

"Look, at the end of the summer, you get to go back to your parents, or go back to college, or do whatever it is you want to do with your life. Your parents have plenty of money. You get to go and be whatever you want to be. I have nothing. All I have is this."

She laughs at me. "So you stealing from my parents is my fault somehow? Or their fault, because they have more money than you?"

"They won't even miss it," I say. "Their insurance probably covers it, and even if it doesn't, who gives a fuck? The money is actually valuable to me. They barely even notice it. Who keeps that much stuff in a hotel safe, anyway?"

"They're going to find out it's you."

She must really like me. She's trying to convince me to find a way out, to put things back the way they were. If she were less attached, she'd be threatening to call the cops by now.

"I won't be here," I say.

"Where do you think you're going to go?"

"I have some friends in New York. I guess I'll go there and lay low for awhile." That's a complete lie. I've never been to New York. I don't know anyone there. It just sounds romantic, and that's why she'll believe me.

She stares at me in silence. I'm wondering what I'll do if she does call the police. Her parents certainly will, when they find out what happened. I was hoping to be gone by then. I still am.

"Give me back my necklace," she says. "The rest of it is just junk they bought. That necklace means a lot to me."

I want to give her the necklace back. I know it's important to her. "I'll give you the necklace back if you don't turn me in," I say.

"They're going to find out soon anyway," she says.

"I just need enough time to leave. Just take the necklace. If you turn me in I'll make sure no one ever finds that jewelry."

"Fine."

I stand up. I walk inside assuming she's going to wait for me outside, but she follows me in. We walk upstairs, passing two tan guys in bath towels on the way. They're joking and laughing. One of them says something about getting laid. Just another inane, forgettable day for them while we walk past, unnoticed.

We get to my room. I open the door and step inside. She starts to protest, but I shut the door in her face and lock it. I go to my suitcase and dig through it to find the jewelry box. I set it on the dresser and open it – Nicole's star necklace is right on top. For just a moment, I have the urge to open my bedroom window, throw it out, and tell her it's gone forever. Just to see what happens next.

I hide the jewelry box in my suitcase again, then shove the suitcase under the bed for good measure. I unlock the door and open it again to find Nicole looking impatient and checking her phone. Even now, she can't resist.

I hand her the star necklace, which she takes from me gently. From the look on her face I'm betting she wishes she could snatch it out of my hands more aggressively, but her desire to be careful with it wins out. I realize for the first time that the money wasn't the only thing I lost thanks to Cory's party, and I laugh a little. It catches Nicole by surprise.

"What's so funny?" she asks. She thinks I'm mocking her, I guess.

"Not too long ago someone stole an envelope of money from me. It's a big part of why I need this jewelry," I tell her.

Nicole stares at me in disbelief. "Don't try to justify yourself to me," she says. "Seriously, don't."

"I'm not," I say. "My chess piece was in there. When they stole the money, they stole that, too. I didn't even think about it until just now."

"You'll have to forgive me for not being sympathetic," she says.

"I'll miss you," I tell her. It's true, but it comes out like a lie anyway.

"I won't miss you," she says. She turns away from me and walks down the hallway without looking back. She turns the corner to head down the stairs, and she's gone.

52

"One ticket to Nashville, please."

I don't know much about Nashville. I've never considered going there before. All I know is they're famous for country music, my phone tells me they have an airport with flights to São Paulo, and no one at Wonderments would think that's where I'm headed. With any luck a steady stream of losers trying to make it as country stars means they also have thriving pawn shops and cash for gold stores I can use to get rid of this jewelry.

The girl behind the counter says, "Okay, we have a bus leaving for Nashville in thirty minutes." That would be the other reason I chose it. "The trip will be eleven hours and forty minutes. All times are approximate. Have you traveled with Greyhound before?"

I look at the girl behind the counter, her voice small and distant as she goes over the details. She reminds me of Nicole. She has the long, dark hair and pale skin, although she doesn't bother with any sort of makeup. She has a small scar on her chin. As soon as I notice the imperfection, I realize she doesn't look like Nicole at all. She's too skinny, with a look of slight of disdain in her face for anyone who has to travel by bus. Her eyes seem dull. She doesn't smile easily. I look for a name tag. She's not wearing one.

"Yes," I say. "That's fine."

"Actually..." she clicks away on the keyboard for a few seconds. "There's another bus that leaves in a few hours that will shave some time off the trip, if you wanted to take that one instead."

"No thanks," I tell her.

I sit down on a bench and look at the itinerary while I wait for the bus to show up. A Greyhound bus trip easily takes three times as long as any other means of transportation and is guaranteed to be miserable, but I like it. It's one of the few ways you can still travel and, as long as you don't try to cross the border or anything, not have to give your real name or any other information.

I wait, and time seems to pass slowly. I stare at my phone thinking I should call someone, but I don't really have anyone to call. My parents would want to know. I'll tell them after I settle in in Nashville. They'll ask why I gave up a good job. I'll lie and tell them I found a better one. My mother will assume I'm making a bad decision and say as much, but ultimately they'll be fine with it.

I think about calling Nicole. I know I won't. There's nothing to say to her. There are no words to make things right. It's finished. I go through the contacts and delete all the numbers I accumulated while I was here. Dave, Grace, Margaret. The Wonderments Human Resources number. The pizza place that delivers to the park, which I discovered early in the summer but never used. I save Nicole's number for last, then delete that too.

I'm not sure why, but Greyhound stations always look so dull. They aren't dirty, exactly, but no matter which Greyhound station you're in, it feels like there must be a corporate policy against decorating with colors that would make people happy. I realize I could be on the bus for a long time, so I get up to take a piss. The bathroom is splashed with the same dull colors as the rest of the terminal. I stop at a vending machine to get a bottle of water, then go back to the bench to wait.

The bus pulls up. I get in line with about half a dozen other people and we board the bus, showing our tickets to a bored-looking bus driver. He barely looks at them. It would be easy to give him a fake ticket, if it was worth making one. I had hoped that the bus would be mostly empty since there weren't too many people in the bus station, but the bus is already mostly packed full of people, coming from wherever, going to somewhere else.

I look for anywhere I can sit that won't have someone sitting next to me, but the bus is too full, so I sit down in an aisle seat next to a teenage girl who is asleep with her head against the window. Her hair is greasy and she has a smattering of perpetual adolescent acne. I wonder how long she's been on this bus, and the last time that she showered. I imagine she's come a long way.

I close my eyes and try to sleep. The hydraulics hiss, then the bus lurches forward. I know I will never be back here again.

ACKNOWLEDGEMENTS

Writing a novel can be lonely work, but it is rarely, if ever, accomplished alone. I would like to thank, first and foremost, my wife Stéphanie, who encouraged me without wavering. She is my first and most dedicated reader, also lending significant feedback and formidable editing prowess to this project.

It's fair to say this novel would not be what it is without her.

I would like to thank Rebecca Weaver, the talented artist who provided cover art for this book. More of her stuff can be found at www.rebeccaweaver.com. You should check it out the next time you want to commission some artwork.

This project would also not be what it is without the advice of Sunshine Somerville (author of the science fiction novel The Kota and its sequels), who helped me navigate the perils of self-publishing.

I would also like to thank Lorin Yelle, Mark Ruster, Grace Oxley, Karen Lean, and Stephanie Doell for taking the time to read my rough drafts and share their thoughts.

Finally, I would like to thank everyone who has purchased this book, written a review online, visited my website, or otherwise contributed support to this project in any way. I wish I could thank all of you personally. Without your support this book – and future works – would not be possible.

Thank you all. You have my deepest gratitude.

ABOUT THE AUTHOR

Isaac Jourden loves theme parks, hates retail, and dreams about the criminal intersection thereof.

Isaac is a 32-year-old American living in Canada with his wife Stéphanie, son Simon, and cats Darth Kitty and Cooler.

His interests include poker, board and card games of all kinds, a fledgling collection of Ultima computer games, Korean pop music, and watching Doctor Who. His next novel is a modern fantasy, but unfortunately does not contain time travel, Daleks, or bow ties.